I0782090

THE PRIESTESS STONES

Clive Ousley

Acknowledgements

I would like to say a huge thank you first to Dr Jan Lewis and Paul Cheetham for their professional guidance and correcting my errors in best practice archaeology, then briefing me on modern high-tech tools such as LiDAR. We have had really interesting discussions exchanging ideas on exactly how such an important discovery as a stone circle could remain hidden in a much explored and scrutinised British landscape. It was amazing luck meeting them through a friend at a local gig.

After my last draft, thanks to my long-suffering wife, Margaret, who is always there to read things through and offer advice. Then to beta-readers, Liz Phillips, Mick Ball, Mark Arnold and again Jan for invaluable advice on the flow of the story, spotting typos and small slipups.

Also, thank you to Rob Barnes who set a writing task during a meeting of a writing group I belonged to about eight years ago. His brief was to write a short story containing the words: Butterfly, Stones, Dance, and Sunset, from the resulting story, grew inspiration for this novel. Next, Suzanne Ashworth and Jackie Williamson in the same writing group, who gave valuable advice on details, especially poetry, in the very early stages of writing this novel.

Last but not least Paul, who fed me with Neolithic and Bronze Age information every time we met up with him, some of which I used as background in the novel.

Somewhere hidden in one of England's densest forests, a tumbled-down stone circle awaits resurrection from under a carpet of woodland vegetation.

Three storylines weave around each other: an archaeological search, a metal detectorist's discovery, and an 18th-century mystery.

Contents

CHAPTER ONE

The Welsh dresser with its time-worn arched top had been in Dave Dorsett's family for the last three generations. Its dark varnish was tarnished with deep scratches, faint hot-drink rings, and bare-wood chips knocked from the sides. Even the chunky door hinges looked well-used as generations of people opening the doors had worn them down. Every dark shelf edge was now bare wood untouched by any restorer, giving the piece an authentic provenance of centuries of wear and tear.

The dresser looked so bereft, Dave decided it was time to give it a shabby-chic facelift to suit the tastes of the third decade of the 21st century. It would be a project for the coming winter. Already occasional October sun had been joined by cold winds and an above-average rainfall for the time of year.

His grandfather had reputedly bought the piece at an unwanted item sale in the stables of Springborough Manor near Monmouth in the days when the well-to-do Richardson family had owned the sprawling residence with its 32-acre grounds. The family had decided to refurbish the dining hall and auctioned this dresser, along with other miscellaneous furniture. Dave thought that if they had known of the treasure hidden in the dresser, Sir Reginald Richardson would have insisted on repaying the 11 shillings Grandfather Rupert Dorsett had paid him.

The back of Dave and Liz's garage was full of junk. Yesterday it had taken them all afternoon to clear space around the dresser. Now rescued from the dark corner, the arched cupboard had over the years also become smothered in cobwebs and splashes of paint. After an hour of brushing and cleaning with a damp cloth by Dave, Liz insisted he treat the multitude of woodworm holes dotting the back bottom panel; she said the piece could never gain its rightful place inside their home unless he did.

It was when he was crouching down to look at the back panels and wiping off the excess chemical that his damp cloth tilted a hidden latch. An almost inaudible pop, followed by a louder click, made him wonder whether he'd rubbed the antiquated panel too hard and broken some rotting timber. To his surprise, the loose wood did not show any damage, but something had just sprung open. For a moment, Dave wondered whether he ought to nail it back but curiosity took over. He tried a gentle pull on the panel edge, but the hidden hinges stuck fast, showing only a tantalising slot with a dark cavity beyond. I'll make sure there's no woodworm in there, he thought, and tried to get his fingers into the space. The corroded hinge edges bowed and looked as if they would tear away from the wood. Dave crouched on his hands and knees and tried to get close enough to work out if the slot would reveal anything other than undamaged internal wood. He had heard of old furniture having hidden compartments, false bottoms, and other concealed places to foil any would-be burglars. An expert would usually find these secret spaces when called in to value the piece. All these years had passed, and none of his family had known that the dresser contained a secret compartment.

'Liz, I've found something. Come and see what I've discovered,' he shouted to his wife of 38 years.

'What now?' Liz replied from the front bedroom.

'Come into the garage and look at this. Who would have known this compartment existed?'

'What was where?' She questioned, with a rare note of anticipation in her words, as she walked down the stairs. Some of his excitement had transferred to her. That pleased him, as she had her own problems to deal with, and she thought of little else. Liz was the vice-chair of a well-known local women's social group, and a committee member was causing her unnecessary trouble by spreading lies behind her back.

They bent over the sprung compartment. He pulled on the panel, but it was still clogged solid with years of polish and dirt. 'Damn, don't want to break it.' He bent further forward to examine the rear edge where the recessed hinges must be.

'Forget your old training. Force it open.' Liz was also on her knees behind him. She reached forward to help.

'No. Don't touch it.' His once professional patience returned to overcome his natural curiosity. He rummaged around on the old workbench and minutes later, carefully sprayed the recessed hinges with penetrating oil.

'That'll do it. Give it a try now,' Liz hissed urgently.

'No, correct procedure at all times,' he announced. Then walked away to make a pot of tea and let the oil do its work.

Liz mumbled as she strode into the kitchen. Then, after a cuppa, his old archaeological training took over again, and they returned with a pencil-beam LED torch to shine into the crack. He had his 15 megapixel camera ready and snapped a shot with the flash activated. Inspecting the camera screen, he saw a shadowy obstruction - something was in the narrow cavity. It looked like a large letter or perhaps only a length of wallpaper folded to look like an envelope.

He showed the screen to Liz.

'Get it out, Dave. We'll learn nothing about it in there.'

'No, I'm still examining the picture.'

'Remove it now, David. Stuff procedure, we left archaeological best practice behind long ago.'

Dave ignored her and made sure he shuffled over to be between her and the back of the dresser. Any kind of professional procedure needs to be carried through with slow precision and thorough documentation. He estimated that someone could have placed the package in there before the 19th century. Until that time, there was no such thing as safety-deposit boxes or any services to store valuable items in banks, so most people of wealth stored their treasures in cleverly concealed compartments in furniture or under floorboards.

Three minutes later, he retested the hinges. They loosened without even a creak. Carefully, he opened the door wide, noting the clever latch mechanism that he had accidentally sprung. With shaking hands and his head filled with curiosity, he withdrew a musty-smelling envelope made of thick handmade paper and covered with centuries of grime and mildew stains. Turning it over in his hands, he noticed it had been sealed with wax at the point where the folds met.

'Hurry up,' hissed Liz from behind him.

Taking no notice, he photographed the letters LMR that had formed indentations into the once hot wax, then used a scalpel to cut under the seal. Liz snatched at the envelope with excitement and with curiosity blazing in her eyes. He managed to keep it away from her and moved the find to the dresser top. Dave tapped the bulky envelope on its bottom edge, and it opened with a cloud of dust. He blew the coating away with a puffer brush and fully opened the envelope. The whole procedure brought memories of his old career flooding back. It had done something to Liz, too. She now had her laptop open on the flat dresser top to assist him and had tapped in a file titled, 17th century Welsh Dresser, subtitled Hidden Contents. She always had been the best assistant anyone could have wished for, bar her barely concealed impatience over meticulously recorded detail. He smiled. Computers were a long way from his old tatty notebooks, filled with context information and details of finds from digs he had been involved in all those years ago.

But he and Liz knew from the work being carried out by their daughter, Amber, how archaeological projects worked these days. He knew she would approve of his technique, even though perhaps the envelope only contained a collection of love letters from a clandestine affair. He reigned in his wandering thoughts and imagination and delicately worked the envelope flap from its seal.

'Open it for goodness' sake.'

He ignored her and slowly lifted the thick paper. Inside was a document that was folded twice. It was quite a large sheet, he estimated about 18 inches by 11 inches, a size he knew was known hundreds of years ago by the name Demy. Dave could see it was in good condition and rubbed a corner between his fingers. Memories of a course in traditional bookbinding leapt from 20 years ago into his mind. One minor skill the students learnt was how to bind and glue old materials used in the days before modern paper production.

'Mould formed wove-paper with faint laid marks,' he muttered, remembering the course tutor handing round a sample. The sheet also appeared to have been hand-burnished with an agate stone to give a fine texture to the surface. These clues indicated it had to be 18th century paper. His hands began shaking; he had before him a very old document. Slowly, he removed it from its centuries-old hiding place and with uncharacteristic haste unfolded it. In the centre of the yellowed sheet was a beautiful line drawing of a stone circle. He scanned the illustration with a historian's eye. The circle looked ancient, probably Neolithic or early Bronze Age, or perhaps equally obviously a figment of an artist's imagination. Then, with his reading glasses on, he carefully scrutinised the faded sepia lines and a lot of archaic text surrounding the illustration. 'Hand-written Latin, possibly 18th century', he noted without realising he was muttering.

Liz's long silver-streaked hair ruined his view as she peered at the detail. 'Is it? Are you sure?' she said, not taking her eyes from the thick paper.

'No, I'm not an expert. I just picked up a little knowledge trawling archives many years ago.'

He was familiar with the major, and most of the lesser-known, stone circles in Great Britain, some in Brittany and a few in the rest of France too. He also knew some of the megalithic chamber tombs, stone avenues and large standing stones in Great Britain and Europe. This stone circle was depicted nowhere that he knew, but then the document was hundreds of years old, so maybe all that time ago devout Christian locals had dismantled the stones, eradicating evidence of the old religion from their locality.

Dave continued to stare at the document, and after Liz had wiped away the last of the dust with a soft-haired brush, reached for a magnifying glass. They both stooped over the paper and stared, and stared, in silence.

Liz sighed and straightened.

'Intriguing - but it's only an artist's dream. Bet he was a pagan, perhaps an 18th century druid showing his devotion to a fading religion by creating this,' she said and stood upright. Her decision meant she could return to whatever she was doing upstairs.

He grunted and continued his examination. The old, yellowed, and dog-eared illustration showed an unknown circle with the suggestion of an embankment and what could be a ditch within. At either end of the circle were two large vertical stones topped with a horizontal lintel stone known as a trilithon. His professional instinct also screamed 'artist's imagination'– it could not exist in reality. But there was something about it. The centre flat stone, for instance, under the magnifying glass he could see the shape of a butterfly with open wings. It looked ready to receive a sacrificial victim, perhaps a lamb, a pig, or even, he thought in horror, a human life. Then he remembered the altar stones theory had gone out the window years ago. The outer ring looked as huge as the sarsen stones of Stonehenge; it would have been an equally prodigious feat to haul and erect these. Another stone looked like Stonehenge's Heel stone, whilst small vertical slabs formed what looked like a four-sided cove near the embankment.

The stone circle was almost definitely a figment of the artist's imagination, but perhaps the text would tell him something factual. Dave focused on trying to decipher the handwritten Latin that started after an ornate letter T. It took only moments to realise he was not up to reading or understanding much. He picked out a few words, 'sol' meaning sun, followed by 'stitium', meaning still or stopped. Dave recognised a few other words, but not a single sentence leapt out. He struggled on and picked out two solitary words, meaning guardian and temple.

'It's no good,' he sighed to himself in frustration. 'I need an expert.' But he knew no one these days. Having left his old profession behind 27 years ago, he had no contacts left to ask. His thoughts flowed to his daughter, Amber. She would know an expert for sure. Her job in the Banbridge Archaeological Trust, when not out on funded digs, was procuring finance for the next project and occasionally, as now, cataloguing finds. Last week, she had helped assemble and record many pottery sherds from a refuse pit situated in a newly discovered Roman farm complex in Suffolk.

As a child, tales of digs and finds fascinated the now 25-year-old Amber Easterton. Dave had fond memories of telling her of his key success as a bedtime story. It was this single enormous achievement that had briefly turned the public spotlight on him and Liz. They had met, as post-grad students, on a dig near Bristol, excavating six skeletons that looked as if they had died violently. One skeleton had chipped bones from sword thrusts, and they found another with an arrowhead in its ribcage.

He had been ecstatic to obtain a post on the Bristol dig, as in his spare time, he was researching a local rumour that had circulated for generations. It concerned a horse-drawn plough that had unearthed a collection of spearheads in the early 20th century. The local museum had a shield boss donated sixty years ago from a local field, which was rumoured to have been dug up with the missing spear heads. Of course, no one knew exactly where they were found, and the donation included no more information. The university carrying out the dig was happy to include him even after he explained his private research project, as long as it didn't interfere with the priorities of the university dig.

At the official site, he had been scraping back layers of soil in a predefined grid area for weeks and the entire team had unearthed nothing significant. Whilst working he had a growing hunch, backed up by his research in the Cambridge University library and recently in the public library in Bristol where he had spent many evenings examining all available publications on Anglo-Saxon defence against marauding Vikings. Then he had matched this new knowledge to the landscape around where he was now digging. As he scraped the trowel through rich soil, he had paused now and again to study the surrounding countryside, its contours, and where he would have fought a primitive and vicious battle. His gaze gradually fixed on a small hillock which rose on a rise half way up another hill. Tall weeds covered the cliffs that surrounded the rise and made it only accessible from below.

He obtained permission from the landowner to search there and dig a couple of exploratory trenches, following all due diligence and with proper standards observed. He mentioned his project to Liz one evening in a local pub after a hard but fruitless day working under a sky that threatened downpours at any time.

'You need another pair of hands, Dave. That's me. I'm going to be your assistant.'

So the next weekend, he and Liz started their first trench together in the area between the nearby cliff and the high-rising ground. His assumptions became solid fact; they were the ones to find the legendary battle site and the Saxon warriors' fierce opposition to a Viking horde. He had been the one to discover the spearheads, the high-status *seax* fighting knife, the bones and then the spot in the valley below the high ground where someone of importance had been buried with engraved body armour and the ritually broken, jewel-encrusted sword.

Someone in the local paper had christened it Volgrom's Last Stand, and the title somehow stuck without any supported research to back it up. Consequently, this title became included in textbooks on this period's British archaeology.

It had bought him and Liz fleeting fame, and it had also brought them together. They married two years later and then Amber arrived to fill the gap left by his diminishing archaeological career.

Years after the event, the repeated bedside tales, lovingly crafted for Amber, had somehow become exaggerated to include the life of the Viking King Svein Volgrom and his exploits. As his daughter grew older, she never lost the romance in his stories, and they became the inspiration for her choice of degree, History of Early Medieval England, and her thesis, Vikings, in the 10th and 11th centuries. Now aged 28, she'd had a tough time in recent years with her separation from her husband Tim Easterton, and often said it was the love of her parents and her job at Banbridge Archaeological Trust that kept her sane. As Dave accepted one dull administrative post after another, it had been enough for him to pass on his investigative interests to his daughter and her archaeological training. His longing to find another historically important site had never quite died, and now, with this old wove-paper, the spark had reignited. Intuitively, he knew the stone circle existed - but it could only be hidden and tumbledown in, or possibly under, dense woodland - somewhere.

Neolithic and Bronze Age circles and megaliths were a little outside Amber's speciality, but he knew that as a teenager she had a fascination for visiting the most well-known stone circles in the UK. He phoned Amber that evening.

'I'll have a look at the parchment on Sunday, Dad, after we get back from lunch.'

It was family tradition that once a month, they got together for a meal at the Kings Arms. She echoed Liz's opinion. 'Sounds weird, though. Surely the drawing's just a romantic dream, someone who longed for the return of an old religion, perhaps.'

'But what if it isn't someone's dream, and he knew the ring's location, and then created the drawing whilst looking at the stones? Or maybe he visited the site on ceremonial occasions and drew it afterwards.'

'You're on a flight of fancy, Dad.'

'Alright, alright, maybe I am.'

'Has Mum seen it?'

'Of course she has. Have a look on Sunday, Amber. Maybe you can translate some of the Latin, and we'll get a clearer idea of the artist's intent.'

'Will do, Dad, it'll be a distraction from Mum complaining about her aches and pains. I am intrigued though, it's a chance to see what an artist or scholar was thinking, albeit perhaps a bored one, letting his imagination fill his day. Love you, see you Sunday.'

The line went dead and Dave sat and held the phone whilst pondering. He'd come up with the scenarios without thinking too hard, but what if somewhere there was a weather-worn circle covered in moss and ivy with mature trees growing through the ring, creating a thick canopy overhead? Some stones would be out of true, the two trilithon lintels would definitely have fallen, some other stones knocked over, a few missing, but its circular layout should still be recognisable, as would a shallow depression for the ditch with its associated rise for the embankment. He hoped a full translation of the text would reveal the location. Could be anywhere here in England, Wales, or even Northern Europe, he continued to ponder...

'Dave, get down here. Dinner's ready. You haven't helped prepare it. You're lucky you have me to do the work around here.'

'Sorry, Love, I'll be right down.' He slid the thick wove-paper into a drawer, ensuring it was flat and placed a sheet of card on top to protect it. He reminded himself of the upset the committee member was causing Liz. It was all so unnecessary. He thought Liz would eventually have to confront the woman to clear whatever grievance she harboured.

The next day was Friday, so he worked a short day. Now that he had turned 55, retirement beckoned, and he had taken up the option of going part-time. He had decided to leave running the warehouse to the youngsters. These days, his job primarily involved troubleshooting, chasing overdue incoming stock, returning faulty items, and other mundane but necessary tasks. It also gave him time to wander the internet, so he started searching for recently discovered stone circles. As he suspected, there was one found recently in Scotland, but a nearby farmer then owned up to building it years before. A few accounts on the Megalithic Portal website described small moorland circles that had not previously been listed. He did find drone photos of the remains of a stone circle in a field adjoining the 5000-year-old passage tomb of Newgrange in Ireland. It was the fourth to be found in that location, but there was, of course, no article anywhere reporting a large circle being found with any intact or even in situ stones.

So that left him with three options. One: it was a figment of the wove-paper artist's imagination, two, it had once existed, but all traces were removed centuries ago, or three, it existed in some densely forested location where no one had bothered to struggle through nettles and brambles for over a hundred years. Maybe it existed in northern France or in Devon woodland, or in a remote spot in a glen in the Scottish Highlands. He caught his imagination there and went back to ordering products for tomorrow's inward delivery.

Soon, it was time to leave the warehouse offices. He drove home so deep in thought that he could not remember the journey because he'd worked out how to progress the research. Some of the repeated words on the top right of the document had become clearer as his subconscious drew on his almost forgotten lessons at Cambridge. The notation had to be directions like, turn left at the carved oak and then right alongside the stand of hawthorns.

Another line of investigation had also occurred to him. What did the letters LMR stand for on the wax seal? The last letter R must stand for Richardson, the family that once owned the dresser. He needed to Google them to find out if LM were the forename initials for any of Sir Reginald's ancestors. Dave knew a little of the family's history and believed their ownership of the manor went back three generations before Reginald. He could go to the house and ask if he could see any surviving letters or documentation related to whoever LM Richardson was.

After the evening meal, he helped Liz tidy the kitchen and then made an excuse to go upstairs to the spare bedroom that passed as a study.

Examining the stone circle wove-paper again, he began typing words into the Google translator in the hope that its opinion would make sense. It didn't. By 11 o'clock that evening, he had given up trying to translate anything accurately and had no confidence in what he had worked out. It was possibly a set of instructions about the location of the stone circle. Obviously, he was missing something in his rudimentary translation, so he gave up and joined Liz in bed.

She was asleep, and soon so was he. In his dreams, he continued to work at the problem; he kept following his translated instructions, but no matter how far he walked, he never reached the stones, other than to glimpse them occasionally through a camouflage of ancient oak and sycamore.

Dave and Liz always eagerly anticipated Amber joining them for the Sunday meal, and this time, they felt a sense of excitement beyond their usual routine. He knew that his daughter would add some new interpretation to his theories about the circle on the wove-paper. Over the last couple of days, he had come to realise Liz wanted Amber to confirm the entire project was based on the fanciful creation of a bored scholar or monk, so she could persuade Dave to return to their everyday routine.

It was a sunny morning; Liz was in the driveway weeding and pruning when Amber's car crunched the gravel and halted alongside her wheelbarrow. Dave was upstairs in their small study and was ensuring all his notes were legible and articulate. He had the laptop open on the Stones' file, and all his useful accessories were to hand.

With one last look at the document lying flat on the desk, he paused to give Liz and Amber a chance to greet each other before walking downstairs.

As Dave exited the front door, mother and daughter were deep in conversation. Liz spotted him and drew Amber away to the far corner of the front lawn. He hung back as Amber held her mother's hand briefly before striding toward him. Dave hoped she had been offering reassurances to Liz, probably that she would quickly resolve the documents' provenance. But maybe Liz was discussing her problem with the committee member with Amber.

'Hi Dad, lovely day again, fantastic early autumn this turned out to be,' Amber began cheerfully. She reached him and they hugged. Dave was unsure whether to leave mentioning the wove-paper until Amber had completed her usual tour of the rear garden. It was her way of unwinding after driving the 60 traffic congested miles from where she lived near Witney, in Oxfordshire. Amber saved him from the uncertainty.

'Come on, take me to the document. I've been looking forward to examining it. It must have been so important to its creator for him to secrete it away. I'm guessing the author had something controversial to hide, or he would have pinned it to a wall or had it framed to display in one of the manor's rooms.'

'Yes, my thoughts entirely,' Dave felt that instant rapport with his daughter and her logic, and felt a pang of sorrow that her mother no longer shared their interest in historical and archaeological curiosities and the associated research. Amber must have been reading his mind.

'Mum will be okay; she just doesn't want all the stress of dealing with the press and jealous colleagues to return. She remembers how it drove you to distraction all those years ago.'

'I know. I've not discussed the document in depth with her for those reasons. Has she mentioned the trouble in the social group she helps organise?'

'Yes, she's confided in me. I've offered to come along to the next meeting for support, but she said she can deal with it.'

'Okay, she knows she has my backing too.'

'Come on, lead the way.' Amber visibly switched away from the problem and focused her curiosity on her father's find. 'Let's have a look.'

Out of the sun, the north-facing room was cool and dark. Standing behind Amber, he clicked on a pre-adjusted table lamp as if he were spotlighting a treasure in a museum display cabinet. With a hand stroking his neatly trimmed beard, he watched Amber as she stooped over the document with hands clasped to her knees. She uttered exclamations like 'oh' and 'wow' over it.

With great care, she turned the document over, then grabbed Dave's magnifying glass, followed by more excited muttering. Dave stood behind her and waited patiently for an opinion. Finally, she made more sense. 'I just love it, Dad. I mean, the author, and artist, went to so much trouble, but some of the text is scrawled and blotted as if he was constantly looking over his shoulder, and perhaps quickly hiding the document when someone came into the room. Look at the top left corner of the back, there's a faint shadow of the text at the bottom right of the document. It looked as if he had to roll it up quickly before the ink had dried to stop someone from discovering what he was doing.'

'Or maybe he was so engrossed he forgot the time and was called away, as a monk would if following the Breviary.'

'Or maybe he merely preferred to store his work-in-progress rolled up.'

'Yes, that's a possibility. But if the author was not a monk or scholar, who could he have been? In those days, the author could have been someone who was rich and educated enough to write Latin and have a formal education. Have you done any work on the history of Springborough Manor to see if you can identify the author or artist who hid this?'

'I've only searched under family and estate papers for the Manor. I registered with the local Gloucestershire archives, which gave me access to all the local title deeds, maps, and electoral registers. There was some information on the Richardson family, but none had Christian names with the letters L and M. That's as far as I've got.'

'Of course. This document will provide weeks of work interpreting its author's motivations and hidden meanings. I can't read much either. I'm not an expert on Renaissance

Latin, but near the top left, it may say that this sacred place hides from something ... maybe prying eyes.'

'Right, that's good - and more than I figured out. It was probably nowhere near a road or track even then. See here, it said Litha and Yule, pagan names for the summer and winter solstices. Note that these names are not Christian. I can only think that refers to two dates when special ceremonies were performed at the stones.'

She looked again at the handmade wove-paper and continued, 'Look, here as well, in Latin – *sol* and *stitium,* which are summer and *hiems,* meaning winter I think.'

'So you think, because these ceremonies are mentioned, that the stones were not a figment of the artist's imagination?'

'They were real once. I mean, this circle cannot possibly exist now.'

'That was my first thoughts. But how about if it's a fairy circle like the one at Doll Tor in the Peak District? It would be so small that a few square metres of brambles or ferns could hide it these days.'

'If that's the case, tree roots or even cattle or deer would have disturbed the stones over time, and no in situ stones would exist now. Also, don't forget that Doll Tor had its missing stones reinstated back in the 1980s.' She paused for a moment as the illustration drew her back. She muttered, then grabbed a magnifying glass. In an excited voice, she gasped, 'The artist has given some indication of the circle's size. Look here, beside the nearest trilithon;

there are two small marks I thought were originally splashes of ink.'

She pointed, and Dave took the magnifying glass from her. 'Butterflies, almost a repeated motif of the butterfly-shaped stone.'

'Yes, but deliberate marks. If he drew them to scale, then the entrance stones would be about four metres tall.'

'Yes, agreed, someone must have drawn them as a reference point for sizing the stones - very clever.'

'It's possibly a hint to a summer ceremony as well - butterflies don't live through the winter.'

They both paused to contemplate the document and the points she had discovered.

Finally, Dave asked about an obvious but fanciful new line of enquiry. 'The dresser came from the Springborough mansion, and that's only 12 miles from here; therefore, can we conclude the stones were somewhere local too?'

'Why should it be near here or the manor, Dad? The owners could have been friends of the artist, who could have been a guest there. So he hid it somewhere no one else from his usual locality could have guessed.' She glanced fondly at her father with a smile, 'Is that wishful thinking, so you don't have to travel far?'

'No, not at all. I thought, maybe, it was in this area merely because the document was hidden in the Springborough Manor dresser.'

'I think we can only confirm that if we can discover who the person is who hid it. Don't forget that it may not have been the artist and author. Someone else could have handed down this document generations later. Then, for whatever reason, it became sensitive and sought after by persons unknown.'

'Possibly, but the paper is in such good condition. I doubt it had been on display anywhere. I would have expected to see dirt from greasy fingers, soot from open fires and damp stains from unheated rooms on it, and if it was in a sunny spot, UV may have faded it much more than it has. Nowadays, an artist would have framed it to display to admirers, it's such a mesmerising image.' He paused the train of thought, stoked his beard, and continued. 'I think I'll concentrate on researching the Richardson ancestry and history of Springborough Manor to see if I can pinpoint its artist and author.' Dave paused again to allow his racing thoughts to refocus. 'Another thing, I've tried to use leading search-engines translating apps for the Latin, but ...'

'They're not accurate, Dad. I mean, not accurate for an exact period of Latin.'

'So I discovered. I thought modern translation apps on computers were reliable.'

'Not for Latin. You try putting English into Latin on, say, one app, then put that Latin back into English on another app, or vice versa, and see what gobbledegook comes out.'

'I see. Do you know of anyone who can accurately translate the text then?'

'I think so. I have a friend of a friend who once tried to get off with me at a uni disco. A bit of a creep, but I think I can swear him to secrecy with a little encouragement.'

'You mean promise him another dance at a disco or a night of passion?' he laughed, breaking the intensity of the debate.

'Certainly not, Dad. I have my reputation to think of, and he has some controversial theories to nurse. He's a minor celebrity now because of them.'

'Oh God, I came across a few of them many years ago. They tried to link Volgrom's Last Stand with fantasies of buried treasure and even a link to King Arthur.'

'Yes, I remember reading the scrapbook Mum kept. Volgrom became King Arthur in some obsessed eccentric's mind, who then ended up with a cult following. But Nathan's theories are a little more down-to-earth but equally controversial. Let's not go into them for now, but he has a degree in Classical Latin and has an ongoing interest in translating old documents. I believe he's fluent in Middle Ages, Renaissance, and post-Renaissance Latin. I'm sure he can give us an accurate translation.'

'I'm not giving him the map. And we can't photograph the whole thing for him to peruse, or we might have competition in tracking the circle's location down. And if he's a celebrity, he's sure to want to boost his reputation and visibility by announcing a sensational find.'

'That's true.' She paused, and Dave noticed her eyes fix on the wall as she thought. 'I've thought of a solution to misinform him. I'll use Photoshop to divide the pic's text into segments. I'll give him sections of the text in the wrong order and only one segment at a time. Say, the third segment first, and then wait for his translation before he gets another section. Leave it with me, Dad.'

'You think that's enough to subdue his curiosity?'

'It's the best I can do. I'll spin a yarn about a beautifully illustrated journal from 1850 that has short passages of Latin dotted through it. I'll say to him, we want to publish it along the lines of an 80s book called The Journal of an Edwardian Gentleman, but I want to check the accuracy and content of the Latin first.'

'I like that. I suspect you've been plotting as you drove here.'

'Of course. I know Nathan and his lust for publicity. Deflecting his curiosity is a necessity.'

'Did I bring you up to be so shifty?' he laughed.

'It runs in the family.'

Already, he felt his project moving forward. Amber was such a devious schemer, as well as an efficient and talented researcher.

'Come on; let's not keep your mother waiting. We'll take my car to the Red Lion. I'll email you photos of the document this evening.'

CHAPTER TWO

After a glorious lunch at the pub and a walk along the banks of the River Wye, Amber left to return to Oxford. Dave settled down in the study to photograph the document. Nowadays, he used the digital equivalent of the old Nikon SLR that his university department had used to photograph finds. It was so much simpler now. He remembered how fiddly it had been to load the 35mm film and then send it away to be processed, along with the tedium of ordering enlarged prints of selected frames. He set the DSLR camera up on a tripod and set it to take RAW picture files, adjusting the aperture settings, then carefully taping the manuscript to the wall with a desk lamp aimed to shine an even light on the manuscript. With it all set up, he took a series of pictures using different exposures. Choosing the best two, he emailed them to Amber, dismantled the tripod, and took special care to remove the tape from the wall and manuscript edges. With the circle illustration safely back in the drawer, he returned his attention to further research on the Richardson ancestry and the history of Springborough Manor.

It took three evenings to gather information about the manor online. He explored a number of sites and tried many searches until finally he unearthed a gem of a PDF file. Someone called Jane Baxter had researched a number of lesser-known stately homes in the southwest of

England and the Welsh Marches in the late 1990s. After her death, Rachel, her daughter, uploaded a large file to an ancestry site. The sixth stately home on the list was Springborough Manor. He found the research to be professional and thorough; his investigative curiosity quickly became filled with facts. Jane began by noting that her first real discovery had been a 1593 collection of bills and estimates that showed that the manor built by Gerald Rourtier in the years following 1538 was already in need of expensive repairs. Jane then noted the change in ownership and described the Richardson family tree. Reading forward two hundred years, Dave suddenly found the truth about Sir Reginald Richardson. He had not sold the furniture to refurbish the dining hall, but was selling anything he could to repay gambling debts and recoup some of the money. This consisted of furniture and other items, including rare books from the library and three paintings by well-known artists. Then, five years later, nearly bankrupt, Sir Reginald sold the manor to the Christie family, who Dave realised still owned the manor today.

'Interesting background,' he mumbled to himself, 'But of no use to me.' None of Sir Reginald's ancestors or the previous owners had the initials L or M. It seemed like a dead end, and there were no details of any individuals. He had hoped there would be an eccentric artist, or perhaps an antiquarian, he could focus on. He pondered the possibility that a servant or another relative with knowledge of the hidden compartment had concealed the document. Now, after so many years, there was no way for him to pursue this line of inquiry.

It was a shame; he had hoped he could follow a name trail to locate the author and then move onward to researching more documentation about him. From there, he was after evidence that would lead to something substantial about the location of the stone circle. But still in the back of his mind was that lingering doubt – the circle drawing, although meticulous, could still just be a figment of a talented artist and author's imagination.

He was about to give up late on the third evening when a sudden thought pierced his drowsiness. He reread a paragraph aloud. 'Edward Rourtier inherited Springborough upon his father Gerald's death and carried out some significant work, including a west-facing wing. Sixty-four years later, his grandson Simon and his wife Beatrice had no real affection for the residence after their daughter Linda died after falling from a window. Consequently, in 1714, Charles Richardson of Nottingham purchased the manor.'

He'd missed the significance of the young child who had died. Her surname was Rourtier—so that provided the initial R. Her first name was Linda and if her middle name began with the letter M, then that must be her initials on the wax seal. However, working that out added another list of unanswered questions. Why would a child have her initials stamped in the wax that sealed the wove-paper? Was it sealed by someone else before or after her death?

It was hard to resist phoning Amber right away. Somehow, Dave got through the next day without pestering her either. Then, when he knew she would be home from the archaeological trust, he phoned.

'I've made progress, Amber,' he announced, and wanted to blurt out his discovery of a name that fitted the initials.

'That's great, Dad. I'm settled now for the evening, so I can make notes and see what we can brainstorm on this. I've Photoshopped one of your RAW files, and I'm trying to contact someone who has Nathan's number. It's going to cost me time with him, but hopefully the ordeal will be worth it.'

'Thanks for your help on this, Love.' He waited as he heard her tapping on a computer keyboard. Then, quickly, he quoted paragraphs from Jane Baxter's account and told her further details about Jane's stately home research.

'Hold on, logging in. Damn laptop's slow tonight.'

Finally, he could not stop himself. 'Amber, listen, there was a child called Linda in the early 18th century who fell from a window at the manor. She has the correct first name initial, but must have been too young to have created and concealed such a document before her death.'

Amber paused and said, 'Hold on while I get the Baxter research up. Ahh, I've got it... searching for the manor... okay, here it is.'

Somehow, he managed to wait 30 seconds. 'She's too young to be of interest to us. It must be someone else.'

Amber sounded disappointed. He realised she had also hoped for a breakthrough.

He continued, 'Who else could the initials be on the seal though? Maybe someone used her name as a kind of cover-up?'

'Yes, it does seem possible.' She paused, and Dave could hear his daughter's soft breath over the phone. Then her breathing sped up and ended in a gasp. 'I've got it!' she exclaimed. 'Jane's history of Springborough Manor does not state the age of this Linda, who died. Could she have been older than you presumed? I mean, Linda could have been an adult; she would at that age have had the skills to produce your document.'

He thought it over whilst the sound of fingers tapping keys came from the earpiece. 'Yes, it fits. So did she just fall after leaning out too far with a youngster's exuberance, or was she older and leaning out the window for another reason?'

'Could someone have pushed her?'

'That opens up whole new avenues of investigation,' he mused. 'I wonder why someone would have pushed her?'

'That's one scenario, Dad. The truth could be very different, but more mundane. Perhaps she'd had one too many glasses of wine.'

'I'm hoping it's more than that, though.'

'So do I. Your ancestry research may provide more unexpected twists, Dad. Linda is beginning to sound intriguing.'

Dave went to bed at 1 am with his mind still buzzing with questions over the new line of inquiry. He plodded through his day at the trade equipment warehouse with his mind filled with imagined Renaissance and Enlightenment period intrigue. The next day he came to the conclusion that his job had become just an annoying interruption to his re-emerged investigative interests. He decided to take his 16 days annual leave owed to him, three-days at a time, starting next week. Liz never wanted a holiday, even a short break away, so over the years he'd never taken all his leave allowance. He wrote on the department's holiday chart and was relieved to see that the first three batches of days did not clash with anyone else.

He'd discovered that Springborough Manor was only open to the public on rare occasions. He needed to explore the nearby countryside and villages as well. A search of the graveyard around the small chapel in the grounds of the manor was also required. He assumed that the graveyard was the burial place for all the Rourtiers and Richardsons. Perhaps he could find the girl's grave. First, he needed to investigate Linda M Rourtier online and see if anyone had posted more information on her.

That evening, after dinner, he trawled the ancestry sites, hoping to find posts from a Rourtier who believed they had common ancestry with Springborough's previous dynasty. Two nights later, he hit a rich online source of information and found Emily Sandaker. She thought herself a direct descendant - Rourtier had been her mother's maiden name.

He messaged her.

Dear Emily,

I am a historian researching the life of Linda M Rourtier, who died following a tragic accident at Springborough Manor around the year 1710. I am hoping you may know something about her and, if so, I wondered whether you would be prepared to share this information.

Kind regards

David Fletcher

The next day, he got home from a supermarket trip to find a message in his inbox.

Hi David

So nice to hear you have an interest in my ancestor. I can see why you chose to research her — she's fascinating. Two different accounts mention she died around 1711 from a fall. But I have unearthed other histories that show she lived a lot longer.

These say she was a little wild and not of her time. Reputed to be an outspoken atheist, she was apparently going to be tried as a witch, but her father's influence had the charge dropped. Although young and attractive, the local gentry and potential suitors shunned her. I found a letter from a local priest that said, 'God-fearing folk fear she would turn their heads toward the devil with her unkempt appearance and prolific preaching. Even her dress and other attire were unbecoming of a daughter of the gracious Rourtiers.'

I also found an undated letter from her parents imploring local folk to search every yard of the river and every foot of woodland for her, as she had drowned after breaking free from a ducking stool.

However, three years later, I discovered an entry in a coroner's journal stating that as her remains had never been found, her monies would go to her next of kin. Other correspondence elsewhere mentions that her father searched for news of her until his death in 1749.

So, which version is accurate—death by a fall or by drowning, or did she survive a witch's punishment and disappear to a new life? There appears to be a lot of deliberate misinformation going on. I've not explored her any further, that's all I can tell you.

An eccentric guy, Trevor Banyon, may know more. He doesn't do email and computers, so his phone number is...

If I can be of further help, let me know.

Emily

PS. By the way, her middle initial, M, stands for Mary.

After forwarding the response to Amber, he reread the email three times, absorbing the information and adding it to what he already knew. He tapped a reply straight away.

Thanks so much, Emily.

I will keep you informed of my progress. Should you come across any additional information, could you please email me or my daughter Amber, who is my research partner in this project.

Her email is....

Thanks again

David

He settled into the office chair and wondered what Linda had done to be accused of being a witch. Dave knew enough about 17th and 18th century witchcraft to know that any woman showing unusual character traits or merely being single and childless qualified to be accused.

He Googled 'accusations of witchcraft in the 18th century' and found a case that looked as if it might fit Linda well. At the trial of one Rachel Clinton, her accusers justified the case against her by saying she had, 'the character of a bitter, meddlesome, demanding woman, who railed, scolded and threatened'.

So had Linda died from a fall? Had she run away to escape the fury of devout parishioners or even witch hunters, or had she drowned? The punishment of the cucking or ducking stool was an often-used penalty for the crime of witchcraft in the 17th and 18th centuries. This barbaric sentence involved repeatedly dunking the victim underwater when tied to a chair attached to a long pole and a wooden beam structure. This resulted in the accused routinely dying of drowning or shock.

Dave found the variety of different outcomes to Linda's demise intriguing, and was determined to find further information. Emily's research implied that Linda was in fear for her life and maybe this was the reason she had hidden the wove-paper. The document's beautiful illustration would have been taken as proof that she did not follow Christian teaching. He stopped pacing suddenly. Did the document itself cause her to disappear or go into hiding, so that the circle's location could not be forced from her? He had not expected his research to go off in such an unusual direction. The whole thing threatened to turn into an Enlightenment-period detective story. It could not be an issue concerning location though, because such a huge structure, like a circle of stones, would be hard to conceal even back then. So, what event could have caused Linda to disappear? After all this time, the truth was going to be hard to discover, but he had to try to find answers.

He resumed pacing his study, oblivious to the creaking floorboards as he merged the information into what he had already surmised.

The document was key to resolving this mystery; he was sure.

Liz came part way-up the stairs and shouted. 'Are you moving furniture up there?'

'No, sorry, Love, I'm only walking and thinking.'

'Well, do it somewhere else. I'm going to nail that floorboard down tomorrow. I've asked you before, but as usual, you just add it to a list of jobs. Come down to the kitchen. I've made you a coffee.'

He put his musings to the back of his mind and joined Liz.

Two days of mundane work passed with evenings that were filled with absorbing but frustrating research. On Thursday evening, he went downstairs at 9.45 and realised he'd not spoken to Liz since they'd eaten together at 6 o'clock.

Liz pushed a steaming mug toward him as he sat at the table opposite her. 'I've been video chatting with Amber on Facebook. She's going to ring you shortly to see what progress you've made. I asked her to hurry up and prove that the document is a fantasy, then we can get back to our normal lives.'

He agreed and wondered how she would take his plans to explore the locality around the manor. Facebook and video messaging were not something he did. It was another facet of modern life he had not got used to. They chatted about something inconsequential until the phone rang. He was relieved, especially when he heard Amber's voice in the earpiece.

'Hi Dad, are you upstairs or with Mum?'

He knew that his daughter had something to discuss that she knew would upset Liz.

'I'm out of earshot now,' Dave whispered as he stepped into his study.

'Right, listen up. I've been in touch with Jess, who gave me Nathan's mobile. I phoned, and he agreed to help. In fact, he sounded intrigued with my explanation, so I sent him the bit of Latin text from the middle left of the document. Then yesterday he wouldn't give me his translation by email or verbally – it's going to cost me a meeting in a pub 20 miles away and halfway between our homes. I've had to elaborate on the story a bit because he said the text implies a route that connects somewhere to a treasure of great worth. It's probably the route of a public footpath leading past a farm these days. Apparently, the directions are vague and may refer to a place elsewhere in the document. He said the passage also implies a threat of death, which apparently is quite normal for documents that imply there's something valuable hidden. Nathan also said, if he knew where the text referred to, we could try walking it together and see what we can discover at the destination. He asked if he could see the rest of the document, so I made up some rubbish about not having the original and not being solely in control of the text.'

Dave could tell from his daughter's words that the tension was building and knew something was coming that would worry him.

'Then he refused to give me all the details unless I told him more. Something was in that small section of Latin that intrigued him, and he's holding out. I'm worried we've played into his treasure hunting illusions.'

'Can you elaborate? Tell him the document's only day-to-day observations of a well-to-do country lady with a vivid imagination? Then you could make out what he's discovered only referred to her favourite fantasy.'

'Yes, I was thinking along those lines, but it will be hard to maintain plausibility after he translates the next segment. I now think it was a mistake to give him that snippet. We should have used an online translation company. There must be a few good ones out there. One section to each company and none would have been any the wiser.'

'Except, if one section contained a bombshell, coupled with directions, and they get ahead of us in a physical search,' Dave's voice rose in pitch as that particular problem hit him.

'Well, yes ... I suppose that's possible, but if we give Nathan the next snippet and he realises what the wove-paper is all about... or if he translates the next passage and it tells him where to pick up the trail? Nathan isn't stupid. He's a capable researcher and has the advantage of being able to interpret Latin accurately.'

'Yes, tricky. Hold fire with giving him a second section then. Tell him the project is on hold.'

'Okay. Let's suppose that the circle once existed, and someone has confirmed its whereabouts. We are going to have to field-walk wherever it is to see if we can find clues as to what was there. I'm talking out of context stuff like...'

'... let's worry about that when we've got a complete translation.' The conversation paused as they both thought about what little they had discovered.

'I think we need more help, Dad – someone totally trustworthy.'

Another person giving a new perspective could be more than useful, Dave realised. It would have to be someone Amber already knew well; a dedicated historian could be very handy. 'Who have you in mind?' he asked with trepidation.

'I work with a lovely guy called Ben, who's a brilliant Field Archaeologist, his hobby is researching obscure historical items, and he's also a martial arts fanatic.'

'You mean tell him the truth, let him in on the whole manuscript? Is he reliable? And do you really think we're likely to need some muscle in a physical fight?'

'Hold on. No, I'm sure Nathan wouldn't use any strong-arm or illegal tactics to get his hands on the wove-paper. But Ben Tarrant could be a useful third opinion, and he may see detail in the document or work out a line of research that we haven't thought of – he has an agile and analytical mind. I can vouch for his reliability and have got to know him well over the last two years. If he's interested in what we're doing, he may know of different archives and resources and perhaps find us a lead, or even a new perspective.'

'Like, talk us out of our fantasy with faultless logic,' he joked, then wondered whether it was true – were they deluding themselves with wishful thinking. 'Maybe we are caught up in an illusion, fuelled by a mysterious woman called Linda.' He paused and came to a decision, 'Okay, let's see what Ben has to say.'

'Linda will cast her spell on him too - I'm sure.'

***

As Amber entered the finds repository, she was bathed in bright fluorescent lighting, which penetrated every recess and left no deep shelf or corner in shadow. She glanced at a glass cabinet containing replica models of valuable or curious finds, then at the cluttered long tables that were covered in bagged and labelled finds from the recent rescue excavation at Tarston near Hereford. She knew that Craig Dalgarth, head of the archaeological trust, was leading this project, and Ben had been second-in-command. The room smelled of soil and damp plaster; it was the familiar and lovely smell that lingered around all new finds. A display, mainly of pottery, lay before her. She resisted picking up some again and scanned the neatly laid out collection, all tagged with their context number. The major finds were not there. The gold brooch, with its silver pin hidden in a clod of earth, the coins, especially the two Roman dupondio coins, would already have gone away for conservation and then post-excavation analysis, she realised. Unable to resist a quick survey of the remaining pieces, she noted that Ben had separated the sherds of pottery into Roman Samian ware or Iron Age, or prehistoric for referencing and cataloguing. She smiled at his accuracy. The Roman pottery had the internal grooves created on the potter's wheel, but the older sherds did not. He had a camera on a tripod to photograph them, a ring binder on the side bench displaying soil-smeared context sheets, and a laptop with one of the department's custom spreadsheets open.

Ben was at a corner table on a swivel chair, making notes on a second laptop. He finished tapping in a long entry and looked up, 'Hi Amber, come to revisit the pieces you found?'

Amber cast her eye over various finds and spotted a group of three fragments of the lip of a pot she remembered teasing from the soil with her trowel. She picked up the largest shard and felt the thrill again of being the first person in over 2000 years to handle it.

'S profile bowl with rolled rims and carinated shoulders,' Ben said intensely as he glanced up again from typing notes.

'They're so beautiful,' she said. 'But that's not what I came in here to see you about.'

'Oh, what then?' he looked up and stopped what he was doing.

'I came to see you.'

He stopped typing and stood up.

She had Ben's interest. That pleased her; he was so fit, the best-looking man in the department, but had never made a move on her, not even to ask if he could buy her a drink. She gathered her thoughts and prepared for arguments. 'I've begun a private project that could lead to something quite extraordinary. Its basis is an Enlightenment period document that if it turns out to be genuine, then leads to the location of an unknown structure, and then my dad and I could become household names.'

'Wow, it's unlike you to say something so dramatic.'

'The document's captivated my father, and has drawn me in too. Let me explain,' she spluttered, hoping he would not dismiss her presentation in an instant.

'You're not exaggerating, are you?' He said with a surprised look.

'No, there is the potential for a mindboggling find, but conversely, the document could be a complete fantasy. We'd like you to join us, to help us authenticate it and find this structure's location - if any evidence of it still exists.' He looked less than convinced, so she ploughed on. 'The whole project is hypothetical at the moment, I admit, and revolves around this detailed early Enlightenment period wove-paper document. My father has also found some intriguing clues to a character who may have written and then hidden the document 400 years ago. I'm organising the first translation of one Latin passage, which hopefully will give clues to where it is.'

'Who's doing the translating?'

'Nathan Daniels.'

'Oh God.'

'I know. I know.' She raised her hands as if in defence. 'He's got his theories to publicise, but he's also an expert on Latin as well.'

'I hope he doesn't twist the translation to promote his theories about the vast amount of treasure buried near some archaeological sites, or his daft hypotheses about a civilisation that he thinks existed before the Sumerians and ancient Egypt.'

'I've trusted him to give an accurate translation of a first snippet of 100 words of Latin.' Then she tried to squash a thought about the circle in the document. What if it predated Stonehenge by hundreds of years? Would Nathan use it to support his theories just to get more publicity? It was possible. They may have made a mistake involving him.

'Did you know he's recently captured some shady billionaire backer that wants him to head a project to prove authorities around the world are part of an archaeological cover-up?'

'I didn't know he had found significant funding. You're referring to his ideas about the apocalyptic event that hits the world every ten thousand years. A lot of books have already expounded these theories, some of them best-sellers. It's all been a kind of absorbing hobby to him until now.'

'Maybe, but now that's all he ever promotes. Have you read any of his books?'

'Only one,' she had to admit. 'It had some controversial ideas which came close to plagiarism and libel, but I enjoyed the free thinking. It's good to keep up with all populist theories; they tend to have some effect on our sponsors and funding.'

'True, but his books contain too many vague generalisations that pretend to be clear concepts, and facts that he coerced into something completely different, or changed subtly to show a particular argument. To sum up, they're written to make money.'

'Okay, I know he's accused of twisting facts, discovering vague clues with little reference data and then forming them into populist sensations, but Nathan Daniels is the best guy for our job. He has a good grasp of Middle Ages, Renaissance and Post-Renaissance Latin. You can see it in his research.' Ben's scathing views of the guy began to sow further doubts about her decision to give the text to Nathan. 'I'm worried now that I'm onto something that will add fuel to one of his projects.'

'Probably not, but before you make any more suspect decisions, let's have a look at the document. Then I'll decide whether to get involved.'

'Of course, I have a raw format file on a flash-drive with me.'

Ten minutes later, Ben was still sitting, engrossed, in front of the laptop, and was zooming in and out of various sections of the file.

'I'm going to get a coffee,' she announced. 'Don't let anyone else see it while I'm gone.'

'Okay, I've got it. It's top secret,' he said without taking his eyes from the screen.

Amber left him for half an hour, then returned to the Finds Repository. Ben was still sitting where she'd left him, but now with an electronic notebook open and a digital pen in hand. He had made lots of notes, she thought that was a promising sign.

'How are you getting on?'

'Interesting. The drawing has fantastic detail. A class two henge with two trilithons, both are entrance arches, that would be unique in the UK. The carved tapering of the top of the stones makes it look authentic – and the lintels over the orthostats – wow. Every groove, lump and angle is carefully drawn, although the vertical stones of the trilithons are slimmer than Stonehenge, the other stones are unworked too. Having said that, it would have been an incredible work of imagination to invent these stones from nothing. I can see why you're captivated, but it involves an impossibility – I mean, this circle may have existed once, but now ... no way.'

'Yes, I agree. My dad and I have been discussing all the obvious scenarios, including that. Also, there are no other circles in the UK with trilithons other than Stonehenge, so that would make it of national importance if its remains could be located.'

Ben didn't answer. She glanced at him and could see he was deep in thought as he stared at the drawing. After a loaded minute she decided on another angle, 'So what about the Latin text?'

'I can translate a word here and there – that's all. Not my field of expertise.'

'That's fine, but Dad thinks, and I'm beginning to agree with him, that...' She went on to explain about the Linda mystery, the few translated words Nathan had given her, and tried to describe their vision of a tract of remote woodland with ivy, brambles and naturally camouflaged, fallen stones that blended with multiple shades of green within dark pockets of gloom.

Ben rubbed his stubble as he thought. His eyes kept going back to the laptop screen.

'There are usually signs of a surrounding ditch or an embankment or both, making the whole area stand out even these days. Recumbent stones can usually be identified.'

'Of course, but over the years, many generations of farmers may have removed stones, then ploughed and flattened the surroundings of the circle,' Amber argued.

'Aerial photography would have spotted the changes in soil colour. Multispectral drone surveying will show very accurate terrain, including tree cover. Then there's LiDAR surveys which can see through tree cover.'

'Yes, I know about all those, especially LiDAR. Light detection and ranging of course. But I don't think that people have analysed and even spotted every interesting landscape detail in the UK using it. The same goes for multispectral drone surveying.'

They paused as each mulled over the possibilities.

LiDAR, as they both knew, directed a laser at the ground from an aircraft and measured the time it takes the laser to return to the equipment. This is used to create a 3D map of the terrain and nowadays is a useful tool for archaeologists.

Amber spoke first. 'The ditch and an embankment must be within deep woodland, and the stones tumbled down as well. Maybe a terrain of natural rocks would camouflage the stones themselves.'

They both subsided again into a tense silence.

Finally, he sighed, 'an archaeological mystery or a complete fantasy. Which one?'

She could see evidence of a battle going on in his head.

'If I get involved, I don't do anything by half measures. I like the idea of this; if it's an artistic dream, then I'll risk that. It is probable that, if they exist, the stones are buried under soil or vegetation. Someone may have partially removed or broken them up. If we find they once existed, like a filled-in circle of sockets, a shallow ditch, evidence of an embankment, even, who knows how many years we'll have excavating the site properly and piecing its story together.'

'Yes, think of the papers we can write for every respected journal, definitely collaboration for a book or two, and funding will be no problem.'

Ben looked intently at her. 'Umm, I'm not sure about all of that, but I am tempted to join you, Amber.'

'If we find any evidence at all, then backers will be falling over each other to become involved in an archaeological sensation. But that's not all.' She briefed him on Dave's approach to finding out where the document had originated and the author and artist of it.

'Okay, okay, I'm in.'

'That's cool. Welcome to the team, Ben.' Without thinking, she leaned over and hugged him.

'Hey, go easy, Amber, you'll be buying me dinner next.'

'Certainly – when we find evidence of the stones, I will.'

'I'll start trawling obscure online sources tonight and then both of us and Dave can pore over what we uncover – if anything.'

She spent the rest of the day on admin and trying to persuade a company to fund a proposed dig near their headquarters. All the while, she could not get images of Ben and imagined conversations with Nathan out of her mind. In the end, she gave up work and took the afternoon off, saying she had a headache. The walk along the paved parkland paths, with their overhanging willow and hazel trees, restored her equilibrium, and she went home to start researching alternative Renaissance and Enlightenment period Latin translators.

CHAPTER THREE

Their first meeting was at her parents' house two days later.

Amber spent an hour making sure she looked her best, dressing in a bright top and slim-fit jeans with the finishing touch – a subtle misting of an expensive perfume. She arrived early and left Dave to fuss around in the dining room, placing files, notepaper, and pens, and clicking on his laptop. She chatted with Liz for ten minutes until her mother made herself busy in the kitchen. It was obvious she had no intention of joining the meeting.

'Is everything alright with your annoying committee member?'

'At the moment, she still glares at me at every meeting, though. Then later, always when others are within earshot, she says the oddest things to me with an utterly expressionless face. I'm ignoring her.'

'Best thing, Mum. There's always one at any large gathering.' Amber wandered off and sat at the dining room table to wait for Ben to arrive and for Dave to stop fussing.

Amber felt her excitement rise to levels she had only experienced when first meeting Tim – she felt lightheaded and free of other burdens for the first time in two years. It was such a relief to come to terms with the bad overtones caused by memories of her ex-partner. The bastard had taken off, leaving her with the mortgage and unpaid loans she had taken out for him to service his debts. She should never have fallen for his advances laced with constant subtle drip-feed about creditors chasing him and having all his available funds paying extra interest payments. This unique project had filled her subsequent dreary personal life. She felt a sense of new beginnings and looked forward to the possibility of her life expanding again. The doorbell rang, and she dived for the door.

He was there, grinning and casually leaning against the porch wall as if he'd been there for an hour waiting for her to answer. 'Come in, Ben,' she smiled back.

'At last. I thought I'd gone to the wrong house.'

'No, you didn't think that,' she laughed and ushered Ben through.

After introductions, the three made themselves comfy with mugs of tea or coffee. 'Now, down to business,' Dave announced. 'Thanks, Ben, for joining us in this archaeological gamble.'

'No probs, Dave. It's gonna be exciting whatever we discover about Linda or the stones.'

Dave nodded. 'As our new accomplice, would you like to kick off proceedings?'

'Alright. Would you both like another way of swapping and storing info?'

Both Dave and Amber immediately agreed.

'Okay. I've opened a new account on Datacloud. I'll give you both the password. It'll be an easy way to share documents and info.'

Amber realised Ben was on her wavelength – she'd done the same, and on Datacloud too. They could all add to Ben's folder at will. She decided to say nothing about her account.

'I'm afraid I've printed out the progress from my research.' Dave said awkwardly, 'I'm not as up to speed with modern methods as I should be.'

'No problem with that, mate,' said Ben.

Amber laughed inwardly at Ben's invented Australian accent, or was he originally from down under? There was a lot about Ben she didn't know.

'Apologies. If I can work it out, I'll add my progress to the appropriate online folder next time. With photos to illustrate my ideas and investigations.' They discussed adding a digital map of the search area to Datacloud, and marking it with location information indicating their progress, with shaded areas showing ground covered. Amber noticed they'd lost her father with the technicalities, but he was gamely taking it all in to reference later. After a few minutes, Ben handed over to Dave.

'For now, I've a hard-copy of my ongoing research into Linda Rourtier.' Dave looked at Amber, then at Ben. 'Perhaps I ought to brief you first.' They both nodded, and he continued. 'You will see there are only two pages, which may be a short report, but they contain a bombshell.' Dave looked at them both again, and Amber recognised a look of triumph and excitement in his eyes. 'I had made no progress until I found a note when accessing a magnificent old register of births, deaths, and marriages in the Gloucester record offices. The years 1720 to 1730 were missing from the ledgers, and after consulting an old card index, I located the said pages in the local museum. I had to call in a favour from Christine, the archivist, to take the leather-bound and fragile volume from a display case in the museum. No wonder no one spotted this note before. Any casual investigator would have been put off by the red tape needed to overcome, remove then view the volume. The month of August 1729 has an interesting note after the entry for Linda's demise. I have typed the text onto a separate sheet. I'll read it to you.' He passed them both printed sheets.

'It states, *the magistrates followed the correct procedure described in Malleus Maleficarum and judged punishment by cucking stool appropriate. The honoured gentlemen decided punishment should proceed with utmost speed to stop the evil presence of this one Devil worshipper from taking hold in the local citizens' minds. On the day of punishment, it was observed that this witch caused a spell that allowed the rope fastenings to become unbound. The witch floated and was immediately taken by a strong current. All feared to extract her lest they be cursed, so she was swept away. After a laborious search, her body stayed not found and hath therefore been claimed by Satan.* Dave looked up. 'This was an extraordinary event; hence, the note. As her remains were never recovered, there is no record of burial after this entry.'

'So she didn't die from a fall at all.' Ben looked at them both in surprise. 'That must have been someone trying to have the written record show a respectable death, not that of a drowned witch.'

Dave muttered, 'The family is probably trying to ensure the fall is officially recorded.'

'Of course, yes, a strict Christian outlook on life was approved of in those days,' Ben added.

Amber thought over the implications of the note. 'So she floated; therefore, she was a witch. The innocent were the ones who drowned,' she stated, drawing on her knowledge of witchcraft. 'So they followed the procedures described in *Malleus Maleficarum,* the book also known as Hammer of Witches. It was a late 15th century document on how to search for, identify and then interrogate witches, an absorbing but horrific guide.'

'Yes indeed, this was a book used by both Catholic and Protestant governments in most of Europe.' Dave placed his hands flat on the table. 'So, did she drown, or did she swim to a secluded bank and climb out? I'm guessing that it was the latter. It suited her to be recorded as drowned so that she could take on a new name and life to stop the witch hunters from hounding her.

'A friend loosened her constraints beforehand to allow her to escape,' Amber mused.

'Your explanation, Dave, verifies another I've unearthed in a private collection,' Ben added. 'It's the account of one Reverend Alistair Bentley, who was a witness to the punishment.' He consulted the laptop screen, which was now open on a file from Datacloud. 'Bentley said, *good men dragged the accused to the stool despite copious protestations from her father, Simon Rourtier. Once lowered to the river, she was seen to cause the iron band about her waist to break open and then, once immersed, to escape from her bonds despite a strong binding between her right thumb and left big toe. Her skirts should have weighed her down, but still she floated and became swept along in the river. All that watched were afeared to rescue her lest Satan became affronted by having her denied to him."*

'Fascinating, Ben. Would Trevor Banon be the owner of the private collection by any chance?'

'Ah, yes, he is Dave. I see you have similar sources to me.'

'Not a lot of contacts these days, most apart from Christine, have died or moved on. Emily recommended Banon to me, my sole other contact so far. I believe he's an eccentric guy who doesn't do email and computers?'

'Correct, but Trevor also read me a little more on Linda over the phone. I recorded and transcribed what he said. I've got it here. *Linda is the enigma and mystery in the* Rourtier's *family tree that shunned polite society. Apparently, Reverend Bentley of the local clergy frowned on her as she had denounced Christianity in favour of a pagan cult. Letters from Bentley even hint that she was the high priestess. According to him, she turned young people's minds away from all that was godly and led them down the road to Satan by beguiling them with witchcraft.* Trevor then said he had little other information about her other than photos of two portraits that were reputed to be of her. Apparently, there is quite a story behind one of those. He said he would be happy to share these photos.

The original paintings are in storage at the National Gallery. He's posting hard copies to me.'

'Another avenue to follow up, Ben. I'd love to see what she looked like.' Amber recalled all she knew of Middle Ages witchcraft while Ben was speaking. 'Linda doesn't fit any model of a witch I've heard of. I mean, most witches were poor and lived off the land. People thought they had powers to curse, but they were probably only skilled herbalists with the ability to cure as well as, supposedly, implement curses. Linda came from the landed gentry so the accusation did not fit the usual criteria.'

'That's where your document comes in. I'm betting it holds some interesting answers to those questions,' said Ben. 'It fits that she was the author of the wove-paper document.'

'But how exactly had Linda managed to become accused?' Amber pondered aloud. 'Was it because she had merely forsaken Christianity for paganism? Had that been enough for pious people to level the accusation?'

'Maybe, especially if she had preached her pagan religion in an outspoken manner,' added Dave. 'If you broke virtually any rule in the Bible, you had entered into a pact with the devil, so that would have been justification enough.'

'So, we have a woman who didn't fit the standard of behaviour for the time. She was a pagan and possibly a priestess of a cult, and stands out as our author-stroke-artist,' Ben summarised.

'I'm looking forward to finding her mark in the document.' Amber said, wondering whether there would be a noticeable feminine slant to the translated wording. So was the cult only Linda projecting her longing for something long gone, even in her time? Did she just have visions of her temple – the stone circle, in the same way that Christians saw angels or experienced miracles? Maybe it was a detailed sketch that she used as a guide to get prices from local stonemasons to build the circle. She stopped herself there, going down that avenue immediately refuted any idea of the circle's antiquity.

'We'll see if it's her soon,' Dave said. 'Once we have Nathan Daniel's translation. 'I'm somewhat alarmed about him holding back his translated account, though.'

Amber felt her cheeks redden and felt a wrench in her stomach; she should never have involved the guy. She dared not look at Ben's face in case she saw disapproval written there. 'I'm sorry,' she began, and gathered her resolve again. 'I propose we give the other passages to a proper translation service to compare the style and content of the translations. We could see if Nathan's rendition fits in stylistically and see if the passages on either side precede and follow seamlessly with his...'

'... and maybe to work out if there's something important, he's keeping from us,' Dave finished. 'No, let's trust him for now. Don't give him any more of the text, and I vote we go elsewhere for the rest of the document.'

'I'll go with that. Let's not get too concerned with his small passage yet,' Ben concluded. 'Have you a company in mind to send the other passages to, Amber?'

'Actually, I've three.' Amber felt their approval; she'd been forgiven for her error. 'One is fairly local – Birmingham Translation Services, but I recommend Worldwide Latin and All That's Latin because they are both in the United States and a geographical distance from us; therefore, less likely to want to become involved. I recommend giving each company two short out-of-sequence passages.'

'Good, yes,' Dave approved.

'Yes, I agree for sure,' Ben said. 'I would also recommend Transglobal Latin from Canada as well. I've heard excellent reports of accurate work, but give each company only one passage each, because then no individual translator will draw conclusions from too much of the document. Then, when we see what that overall content is, we go from there.'

'Yes, okay,' said Amber, eager not to go against his ideas. Dave nodded approval, too.

'I'll email Worldwide tomorrow, with the photo-text and payment. We'll go for the express service and the translation will be back with us the next day.'

She noticed Ben smile and nod.

'So we all have leads to create, or to follow up on.' Dave stated, 'I've ordered an Ordnance Survey Explorer map of the area to figure out the densest woodland and have time off work organised. Then I'm going to walk public footpaths in these wooded areas near Springborough. I'll also have a look in the Springborough Manor's chapel graveyard for Linda's gravestone. I believe it's on a footpath around the manor and I don't need permission to enter.'

Not to be outdone, Amber chimed in. 'In the meantime, I'll be emailing the sample texts and then work on the resultant translations. Meeting Nathan will be a tricky task, and then verifying the info he gives will be a check on his honesty.' Amber felt elated; she was doing her share to progress the project. Inadvertently, an image of Nathan in his younger days from their shared Uni experience filled her mind. It was a college disco, a regular weekly event. Nathan had dyed his hair purple and had had it cut to form a fashionable mullet-style long-hair look. He was dancing on his own, rather awkwardly, completely out of his head on alcohol and possibly some illicit drug. She shuddered and snapped back to the meeting.

'Deep in thought Amber?' Dave questioned.

'No, an unwanted memory of Nathan just sprang up,' she said with a shiver running down her spine.

Ben nodded in understanding and brought the meeting back to the topic. 'More archive research for me, plus see what I can do once I've received Trevor Banon's photos. I'll then hope to narrow down the location of the circle remains. Although I think searching for the circle's location is just too big of an ask before we have a translation of all the Latin in the document. I mean, the area between Gloucester and Monmouth is huge, with massive tracts of woodland like the Forest of Dean and other smaller woods everywhere.'

'We could narrow it down considerably,' Dave said. 'Most circles and some other megalithic tombs, like the Pentre Ifan cromlech in Pembrokeshire and Castlerigg circle in the Lake District, are built on high ground with fantastic views all round. So we could discount all low-lying woodlands on that basis.'

Amber considered her favourite stone circles and ancient monuments and added, 'Yes, Arbor Low, Sunkenkirk, the Men-an-tol stone, and many others are certainly in fantastic locations.'

'But that's not an exclusive criterion,' Ben argued. 'The Rollright Stones in Oxfordshire, for instance, in an area of flat fields, spring to mind. Exploring the whole Welsh-English border area on foot and in detail would take years. We're not even talking about walking public footpaths here; we would be trekking off track over private land to get to potential small woods on hills that may conceal remains behind thickets of bracken and brambles. We all know that trespassing is a definite no. We would have to get so many landowners' permission to search; it's unfeasible.'

'We can eliminate all modern conifer plantations, though,' Dave added. 'Sadly, we have to assume tree planting, then cutting down, replanting, etcetera, and the associated heavy lorries and tractors will have churned the ground many times over, and stones would at best be buried; certainly, any semblance of what we are looking for would have been long destroyed.'

'Yes, a ditch and embankment would certainly have been levelled and planted over by forestry employees,' Ben added with a sad note.

After a short pause while they weighed the implications, Amber said, 'Agree with that, sadly. Yes, you're right, Ben. The remains of our circle could be anywhere within 30 to 70 square miles and hidden in any patch of ancient woodland. However, on a brighter note, I recently read of excavations at Arthur's Stone, a Neolithic burial chamber near the Golden Valley in Herefordshire, where there's now evidence of a possible stone circle 20m in diameter. Also, the Queens stone at Symonds Yat may once have been part of a bigger ancient site, and that's fairly near to our search area.'

'So there's evidence of, or speculation about, undocumented structures on known sites that gives us some hope we can also find evidence of ours,' Ben paused deep in thought. 'I'll look into other known sites near the area we're interested in and see if there's any conjecture about any of them once being part of something bigger. Then, if anything's been published, I can see if they detail soil changes to show whether the position of their stones matches the configuration of our illustration's stones.'

'Yes, worth looking into,' Amber said.

'Agreed,' Dave added.

'So let's also see what our translations tell us, then proceed from there, – okay?'

'Yes, of course. We need to cut the search area down as much as we can.'

'Thumbs-up from me,' Ben smiled.

Then, at lightning speed, she mentally reviewed the modern British countryside. 'Hold on, guys. We need to discuss this further. Nowadays, almost everywhere, even areas of common land are owned by someone, whether it's a farmer, the National Trust, Forestry Commission or other private landowners. Some would have groundsmen, estate managers, gamekeepers, or wardens to manage their land. There is no way that at least someone would not be aware of a collection of fallen stones on their land or on frequently walked or grazed common land. There's one other possible conclusion to come to. If a recognisable circle exists, someone is keeping it secret, possibly not wanting the publicity, or an archaeological investigation and the subsequent crowds trailing onto their property.'

'Of course, I should have added all that to my argument, especially if the stones are out of local knowledge because of long-term owned private land.' Ben added with a look of respect showing on his face.

'Recognisable is the key word here.' Dave took over. 'It's possible a collection of fallen stones would not be recognised, especially in dense woodland where they're all fallen, half buried by a millennium of rotted plant matter and hidden by undergrowth.'

Amber visualised the situation. Her father was correct. 'People would ignore a collection of natural-looking rocks if they'd known they were there all their lives.'

'The stones may also have been removed for building materials. There could only be a couple left in situ,' Ben added.

'Before we begin searching, the next step is Nathan's translation, and then we'll get our first real clues. I'm meeting him tomorrow night,' Amber said, and felt a shiver of trepidation.

***

The car park alongside The Angel, an 18th century pub, was nearly full with an assortment of vehicles from brand new electric Teslas to beat-up builder's vans. Amber took one of the last spaces in the far corner. A welcoming yellow glow spread toward her from wall lights near the pub windows. Smoke drifted upward from a large chimney. The building's timber frame consisted of a profusion of dark oak beams contrasting with white render in the panels between. It was a popular local meeting place, going by the buzz of conversation as Amber entered the large hardwood door. Inside was much the same dark timber and white walls. Wood partitions with plaster infills in the old-world interior created shadowy alcoves where the light from small wall lights failed to reach.

Amber had arrived deliberately late; she didn't want to sit around on her own, waiting for Nathan. Smells and the sight of cooked food being eaten filled her senses. With a glance around, she noted diners dotted around tables throughout, whilst locals were grouped, standing or sitting on stools around the bars of both the lounge and public bar.

She again remembered Nathan as a young guy from uni – slightly overweight from lack of exercise, with black bags under his eyes framed by thick green spectacles. Beneath this, she recalled a little goatee beard and wild dyed locks that framed his face. He had looked like a typical student, up late into the night gaming and on other evenings attending every heavy-metal rock gig in the area. He had also been so boring as he expounded his embryonic viewpoints on populist archaeological mysteries.

She scanned the public bar, suspecting that would be where he would sit. After a careful study of the obvious places she expected to see him, Amber drew a blank and then spotted an overweight 29 year-old with a thick beard and short, neat, hair sitting in a secluded corner sipping a pint of dark bitter. He wore a single-breasted Chesterfield overcoat of the style businessmen wore. Red-framed spectacles sat on the end of his nose as he stabbed at his phone. If it wasn't for the style of his glasses, she would never have recognised him. Even his creased trousers looked respectable.

With a hammering heart, she bought a mineral water with ice and a slice of lemon, and then approached him. He didn't look up from his phone.

'Nathan?'

Reluctantly, he separated his eyes from the device. 'Hello, Amber, I thought you weren't coming.'

As he spoke, his eyes wandered over her from head to toe. She felt her skin crawl.

'You haven't changed at all.' He tried a smile, revealing a mouth of yellowed teeth.

'But you have Nathan. What's happened to the head-banging concert goer image?'

'It passed, just youthful exuberance, of course. I found far more important and prestigious avenues to fill my time once I'd obtained my first-class honours degree. Now I have television companies knocking on my door offering high fees for my participation or advice.'

'I'm sure they do, Nathan. I've read a lot about your theories.'

'They are not just theories, Amber. There is a global cover-up reaching from the depths of universities to the workings of global governments.'

'If you say so.'

'There are major finds still out there, Amber. I have written evidence of hoards that were hurriedly buried after skirmishes with Viking raiders or secreted away from looting medieval brigands.'

'Really, how did you find the written evidence? Surely there are very few accounts surviving from Viking times. The only text I know was of a Viking funeral written by an outsider. As I remember, he was an envoy of the Caliph of Bagdad.'

'Pah,' Nathan snorted. 'There's more, and I've found them.'

'Okay, I'm not going to argue that. But I'm sure there are exciting finds still to be found, but probably not by your methods. If discovered, the location needs to be left undisturbed so an archaeological investigation can retrieve valuable artefacts with the context intact.'

'Of course,' he leered as his eyes continued to explore her.

She folded her arms over her jacket and made a conscious effort not to glare back. 'How did you get on?' she asked.

'With what?'

She felt irritation begin to transfer to her face. With an effort, she controlled the annoyance. 'My requested translation, of course.'

'I suppose we had better begin business then,' Nathan announced and tore his eyes from their exploration and reached into an inside pocket of his coat, and then produced a buff envelope. 'This is my accurate text based on my considerable experience in Renaissance period Latin,' he announced with more than a hint of pomposity. He flapped it at her as if to taunt her with its contents and then replaced it in his coat pocket. 'What does this text really refer to, Amber?'

What had he discovered? She felt suddenly icy cool, and in an instant ran through what he may have deduced. Location, he's discovered it. The words seared painfully bright in her mind. It had been a mistake to involve him.

'It's only the fantasy of an educated Victorian lady, as I said before,' she replied quickly. 'Do you want me to pay you for your translation of that simple passage, Nathan?'

'I don't want payment in money, Amber.'

She looked at him coldly, and revulsion seeped into her expression. He made her feel small and a mere object to be used.

He leered again and showed his yellowed teeth in a semblance of a smile. 'No, I don't want you either, although that would be a bonus. I want to see the whole of the document and I'll pay you for the privilege.'

'It would be of no interest to you. There's no treasure to be found here.'

'But I think there is, Amber. I have a backer who's willing to contribute handsomely to your Victorian lady's fantasy.' He sneered the last few words, suggesting he had seen through her cover story.

She stared at him and felt her resolve harden. There was no way she was divulging anything else. It looked like they would have to rely on an alternate interpretation from one of the other three Latin translation companies. 'If you won't give me the translation, Nathan, then we'll go elsewhere. It's a shame if a beautiful document like this can't reach the light of day. It'll be a coffee table bestseller for sure.'

Nathan leant toward her, and she moved her chair back away from the table.

'My backer has a private collection of antiquities. One large group is from a single find here in the UK. I have been researching another potential treasure, which is, in some ways, linked to what you have. I believe this translation is a clue to the treasure's location.'

'It's not a physical horde of gold or associated valuable objects like you seem to think, Nathan. Its value lies in the beauty of an inspired and technically perfect drawing and its surrounding fantasy.'

'Explain more.'

'No, let me see your translation, and then I can explain more succinctly.'

'Maybe I won't.'

'Please,' she emphasised, being polite but forceful, and held out her hand. As she did so, her mind raced. His backer may be so unscrupulous that he would loot an unknown site of importance and keep the finds to himself. Anyone finding more than a few coins or gold items had to leave them in situ for professionals to extract. The coroner had to be informed of any find that could be treasure as well. It would appear the appropriate authorities had not been informed of his backer's collection. She was aware of all the large finds in recent years and they had all been from people who were metal-detector enthusiasts. She remembered that more than 800 objects had been unearthed in 2021 in a field near Melsonby in North Yorkshire and had only recently been disclosed to the press. When this horde, and others elsewhere, were reported and officially investigated, the location of the site was always kept secret, even after details of coin or artefact hordes were reported in news headlines. This was to stop unscrupulous nighthawk detectorists from plundering the sites and keeping their finds.

'Will you tell more if I show you?'

'I'll try to provide another interpretation or meaning behind your translation, and how it relates to the drawing.'

He pondered for a moment, then produced the envelope again and started rotating it in his hands as if to taunt her. 'Very well.' He thrust the buff-coloured package at her.

Nathan's eyes refused to meet hers as she thanked him and took the envelope. Carefully, she tore the corner and inserted a finger to tear it open; she withdrew two sheets of computer-typed text.

Dear Amber,

I have spent some time getting to the exact meaning of this piece. I believe it was written by a scholar, or someone else highly educated for the time. This is a person who is literate with some schooling in Latin, but although poetic, it is not succinct, and in places, the syntax is unusual. However, I can confirm this is actually a genuine early Enlightenment period Latin and not written by a later Victorian hand, as you assume. The following is the best meaning of the text.

Regards, Nathan

Amber flipped the loose paper over and read the translation.

Woden's temple be dedicated to him, king over all the Gods who have decreed that a great treasure resides there. These riches will be beyond the imaginings of mere men and all will benefit from these wonders as they heal all who attend. The entirety of this cleansing is worth more to the soul than the treasury of the King of England, more than the wealth of all royalty in the known world, even that of the holy Catholic Church. A place with the Gods can be yours, dear believer, if you follow the sacred route and then allow your mind to go beyond this earthly realm to meet these mighty Lords. I cannot speak here at length of the treasures you will experience, but be assured, the great Woden will endow you with some of his wealth and you will be satiated with riches beyond any you can imagine. Prepare to tread as lightly as the flutter of a butterfly in summer and dance thy feet in a fashion akin to their flight. The ecstasy of this dance will lead to a place where riches are abundant. But beware, if you wrong our shrine or faith, you will be dispatched to a place of deprivation, hunger, and bedlam.

She looked up, aware of his eyes staring intently, judging her response. She had been careful to hide her reaction again, not wanting to give him even a clue. The translation fitted all their speculation but actually contributed nothing, not even any directions that made any sense. The stones themselves must be the treasure referred to, but that didn't make them treasure-trove or anything that could be worth a private collector removing anything from the location. Nathan was misconstruing the circle for the location of an ancient treasure. He had also seen straight through her Victorian-stroke-Edwardian cover story.

'I see how you think I'm deceiving you, Nathan, but it's absurd to think of this as a physical horde of treasure. The document has no visual reference to such things at all. It's more of a spiritual nature. Your translation doesn't give any lucid directions to find anything either. You're reading far too much into this.'

'Am I? If you say so, then I guess I am. But I think the rest of the document will contain more facts. You're holding out on me.'

'I am not,' she retorted indignantly. 'You have read too much into a fantasy. And that is all it is.' As she said the words, Amber realised that was the most likely interpretation of the translation, anyway.

'When would you like me to work on the next passage?' he barked.

NEVER, the word screamed in her head, but aloud she said, 'I'm surprised it's not a high-status lady who wrote this piece. But apart from that, it proves the document is a somewhat mystical flight of fantasy. I'm going to consult my father, who is hoping to write and publish an accompanying book based on this document. Based on your translation, I don't know if it's worth carrying on with the project.' At that moment, she knew her statement was for real. This one paragraph showed the whole thing was a fiction. Part of Amber hoped her reaction would be enough to put off Nathan.

'Then perhaps I can offer you a good price for the original document. You were always in need of money.'

How does this man manage to irritate me every time he opens his mouth? She seethed. 'No, it's not for sale to you or anybody. Thanks for the work you've done, Nathan. But that's it – finished.'

He nodded and frowned, then came to a decision. 'Very well, I respect your decision.' He paused as he looked at the table in thought. 'Let me buy you a drink and we'll talk about our days in Oxford. They were the best of days, don't you think?'

CHAPTER FOUR

Back in her flat, Amber tried to stop herself from shuddering. What a sleazy guy. She hoped never to meet him again. With the TV on to distract her from the evening's disappointments, she made a coffee and sat snacking on crisps. It was something she always seemed to do when wound up about something. The sharp tang of the food eased her anxiety and got her thinking again as she reached for Nathan's translation. It was an unlikely hope, but maybe a second read in the comfort of her home would provide a snippet of worthwhile information. She read it again twice, and then shook her head in frustration, as she found no more information to reinterpret. It was only a single section of the Latin, though. What about if the rest of the document had the more interesting and useful information, including directions? Once she read the rest of the translated text in order, maybe it would all slot together and make perfect sense.

With another mug of coffee to keep her awake, Amber started the laptop and brought up the bookmarks, then took her credit card from her purse. 'Time to test another translator,' she muttered and clicked on the bookmark labelled Worldwide Latin. There was a button with the option to pay for the premium fast service. She clicked it, and in moments she'd paid and emailed the first paragraphs from the top left of the document. The resultant email confirmation said she would receive the translation within 48 hours. Next, she went to Transglobal Latin. The site was professional, so she clicked on the payment page. This site didn't do express translations; the reason given was that they were thorough and committed to accuracy. Express delivery left too much chance for rushed work, and the possibility of errors. Fair enough, she thought, and clicked payment, then uploaded the fourth passage. A receipt came back telling her the translation would be with her in seven working days.

'Let's see about passages two and five,' she muttered, then stopped herself from going to the site of All That's Latin. It would be best to report to Dad and Ben when she had the next translation. They should read Nathan's translation before she emailed any more of the text. She emailed them both the same message.

I have Nathan's translation. It looks above-board. I have also used Worldwide Latin's express translation service for the first paragraph and Transglobal Latin for passage four, which will take a week. Can we meet on Thursday night? Your place, Ben, is about midway between Dad's and mine. Is that Okay? Amber x

She went to bed, then checked her phone for their replies. Dad had not spotted his message yet, but Ben had replied, *That's cool. I also have some intriguing info for you. My place will be fine, the directions are...*

A small thrill coursed up her spine. All she knew about Ben's place was from casual work conversation. He had once said, 'My damned mortgage is hard to manage on a single wage and it's only the middle place of a small terrace of five in Charlton Kings too…' So now she knew he lived in Orchard Close on the southern fringe of Cheltenham.

The Satnav guided her round a complex route of roundabouts and traffic lights, then advised, 'Arriving at your destination.' She noted the road sign, Orchard Close, and looked for number 14. There, she parked behind Ben's Ford in the concreted-over front garden, noting that her father was yet to arrive. Good, she thought. Her scheming should have allowed for at least half an hour alone with Ben before Dave arrived. However, as it happened, this was reduced to 10 minutes due to a road accident causing a tailback. A sudden gust of wind blew her hair as she exited the car. I should have worn it tied back, she admonished herself and pressed the doorbell.

'Hi, Amber,' Ben greeted her as she finished tidying her hair in the reflection of the door glass. She dared to squeeze his arm as he ushered her into the small living room behind the stairs. It was tastefully furnished with a three-seater leather sofa and a matching armchair in front of a small flat-screen TV framed by two new-looking hi-fi speakers. An extensive vinyl and CD collection sat in an old, much-used cabinet in the only other available space. Patio doors showed the neat rear garden in the darkening evening.

A large-format book sat open on the sofa, which she noticed was called Megalithic Temples of Britain, so she leafed through it. It listed every known circle, tomb, dolman, long barrow, avenue, and large solitary megalith listed in Britain. Photos, a detailed description, and a clear location accompanied each entry. Ben's been familiarising himself with our subject, Amber thought as she heard the sounds of coffee and snacks being prepared in the kitchen. She opened her laptop and left the photo of the document on the screen. She dumped her folder containing the translation printouts next to it.

'Can I help?' she called, mainly to hurry Ben along, but also in the hope of being near him.

'Nearly done. Just seen Dave pull up across the road.'

'Good timing,' she shouted, but thought the opposite.

A minute later, her father was with them in the living room. Coffee and homemade flapjacks were on the table. She added Ben's culinary skills to what she knew of him.

After a few minutes of polite chat, Dave kicked the meeting off.

'The most important part of our research is the document itself, so Amber, you brief us first.'

Feeling her spine creep, Amber relived the evening with a rundown of her conversation with Nathan. Then, to dispel the memory, she opened her folder, which contained hard copies, including printouts of the translation that were in her inbox when she arrived home from work earlier. 'I think we ought to read both pieces first and then see what the two together suggest. Passage four will be with me next week. First, here's Nathan's translation of the third section of Latin.'

Both men read and reread Nathan's rendition, then she handed them the new piece that she'd read for the first time two hours ago. 'This is the top left and first piece written on the document. Worldwide Latin offers Latin translation into a style of English which reflects the usage of earlier forms of English or a modern translation – I went for the latter, so there is no ambiguity in parts of the translation.' Whilst they were reading, she reread it to herself.

You may at first think this sacred text is the ramblings of a simple mind, but there is within it the strictest of directions concerning a righteous pilgrimage to a holy temple - this being the union between heaven and earth. The mighty Gods have adjudged me worthy of seeing many wondrous things there, so now I have cast aside my worldly existence and dedicated my life to that of a guardian of this holiest of places. My labour is now to honour the Gods by forwarding worshippers to the treasures this temple can gift. Woden, the King of Gods and his lesser divinities have used this holy place to bring forth wondrous visions, this be where the dead can be seen to walk and the still-to-be-born to speak. I have conversed with my masters and mistresses and this is their account of how and why they created such a grand place.

She glanced at the two men as they read avidly. Ben soon exclaimed, 'Wow, amazing,' then carried on in silence. Dave just read with intense concentration, which froze his face of any expression.

After ten minutes, she put her copy down and said, 'Your thoughts, please, guys?'

Dave replied instantly, 'Two things struck me straight away. First: I wonder if it's written by a female – and if so, that has to be Linda. Second...'

'Hold on ... I have some information to add later, which may lead us to surmise that Linda is the author,' said Ben. Carry on, Dave...'

'Second: I was about to say that if she disappeared instead of drowning or falling, then did she somehow stay incognito as a resident guardian of this temple for the rest of her life, and without being discovered?'

'Seems unlikely, even back then,' Amber added. 'A lot of people barely ever visited the nearest city. Each rural community knew their localities extremely well. I think members of her cult sheltered her. Imagine dense ancient woodland containing a hidden place of worship – our circle. The surrounding area would be sparsely populated countryside with rural farms and communities only accessible on foot or horseback, with no roads, only muddy tracks. Then, if there are believers living on nearby farms, she could walk a few miles without neighbours or farmhands giving her away to the authorities. It is possible that they provided her with a cottage to live in, probably near the temple. Factor all that in, and you have a perfect formula for concealment. But she must have had a lonely life preaching to the converted and not being able to travel to lecture other communities.'

'Unless others brought new believers over to her, after having them swear an oath to absolute secrecy,' offered Ben.

'Conjecture, my friends,' Dave said. 'Let's see what else we can glean from the two passages.'

'Treasures?' Amber said as a question. 'What can they possibly be if not of a spiritual nature?'

The silence seemed filled with background noise, the hum of a freezer, traffic passing on the road, and a slight buffeting of wind on the windows.

'Hard to know,' admitted Dave.

'Maybe the rest of the document will give us more clues,' Ben finally said. 'I think Nathan believes there is physical treasure buried there, though. It's what his publicity machine constantly promotes, and he sees it as a chance for major publicity.'

'I hope we've heard the last of him,' Amber added, with a note of trepidation in her voice. 'Back to the first paragraph translation,' Amber suggested to take her mind off thinking about Nathan again, 'the phrase, "bring forth wondrous visions," might be indicative of drug-induced euphoria, possibly from magic mushrooms. The priestess pretends to see visions, leading her followers to believe they must also partake in what must have been herd mentality.'

'Very possible, but still mere conjecture,' Dave cut off the surmise.

'Agreed. Let's get the rest of the document translated to see if it throws more light on the ceremonies. You have three more translation services, Amber. So how are you planning the release of the rest of the sections?'

'The second went to All That's Latin. Three was Nathan's. Four is Transglobal Latin's. The last passage will go to Birmingham Translation Services here in the UK. I'm confident they will handle it as confidential, but in case they don't, I hope that its brevity will make it unworthy of being leaked to the press or to others, like you know who...'

'Yes, unfortunately, we do know who,' muttered Dave grimly, then his words sounded brighter. 'Let's go on to my search. I have eliminated about ten miles around Springborough. Using an Ordnance Survey map of the area, I worked out overlapping circular walks where I covered all footpaths and all the easily accessible woodland. We were correct in our assumptions. It's hard going, forcing a way through bramble patches and stepping around tangled, fallen, dead branches mingled with new sapling growth. Most of the footpaths are overgrown that way, some wooden signs have fallen, and others have been removed by persons unknown. To sum up, nothing positive, I'm afraid. So, onto your info, Ben, I'm looking forward to this.'

'You've unearthed something spectacular?' She asked in the hope of an upbeat revelation.

'Well, I can't lead you to the location of our stones, so don't get too excited. I've trawled the internet and specialised sources on local archaeology to see if there's anything published, or just for any educated speculation on the Bronze Age and Neolithic sites in our search area. Unfortunately, there's nothing else specific, and nothing new has been mapped or published that I can try and fit the configuration of our stones into. So that idea has drawn a big zero I'm afraid.'

Amber felt her feelings and expectations sink. She looked at Dave, who also had a grim expression. Ben surprisingly still looked upbeat.

'However, I've not drawn a complete zero elsewhere,' he smiled reassuringly. 'I have some more verification that Linda was what we would, these days, call a pagan, but still a much-loved daughter of a noble family. I received the portrait photos from Trevor Banon yesterday. He states the first came from an art collector of female portraiture who knew of his interest in local ancestry. It's a miniature, to fit in a locket, and without detail in the background. They were popular at the time, showing head and shoulders only. Look at the picture and memorise the woman depicted. Trevor reckons it's a study taken from the main picture he sent. This other is a full-sized work kept in the British Museum storeroom. Here's my scan of this picture - a superb portrait ...' He touched the laptop screen, and then turned it so they could both see the screen. 'It's the same woman, don't you think?'

'Yes, without a doubt.'

'Now look at the signature.'

'William Hogarth,' she gasped, 'one of the most famous and accomplished portrait artists of the period.'

'Trevor Banon thinks Hogarth painted this early in his career, possibly about the time he attended the academy of Sir James Thornhill in Covent Garden to learn to paint in oils.'

Amber stared at an imposing woman pictured standing with a hand on a wrought-iron gate. She was in her mid-twenties with unruly, curly ginger hair escaping from a lace bonnet. Linda was dressed in a simple, high-necked, light green blouse, with a light grey shawl draped over one shoulder, which led down over a longer dress of darker green. The only ornamentation was a simple red rose pinned to the shoulder. The red from the rose highlighted her hair nearest the rose, and a hint of it appeared in her cheeks. Immediately, Amber saw a meaning. She muttered, 'In the language of flowers, a tea rose means, I'll remember always. Any significance here... I wonder.'

'Interesting. Perhaps it's a reference to her beliefs. But let's look closely at the background of the picture.' He tapped the screen again, spread his fingers, and zoomed into the top right. At the point where the background brush strokes showed less detail, a distinctive shape filled the screen.

'A stone circle,' gasped Dave.

'But not any circle – it's our monument. This looks undeniably like the one in our document. It has two pairs of trilithons with lintels, and the other stones look the right height and shape in relation to each other,' Ben added with a note of triumph.

'And there's a sunrise or sunset through the trilithons, showing it's aligned as Stonehenge and other circles.' With her thoughts racing, Amber stared. 'Surely the artist is not depicting Linda posing in a real-life background. I mean, if this is outside Springborough Manor, then the circle would be in full view from a boundary wall.'

'With my walking the area, we can take it for granted that there is no evidence of a circle within ten miles of the manor. There are footpaths everywhere, so I comprehensively surveyed the land. Where I could not get to, I examined the area from high ground with binoculars. It would be beyond our means to get permission to hire a team with ground radar to survey for socket holes in the grounds. We would need to convince the owners of the manor to stump up the funding and put up with the publicity. A big no would be their quite obvious response.'

'Perhaps the cult faded away when Linda died and the structure was torn down,' Ben offered.

'Or it's elsewhere,' Amber added.

'We can hope,' said Dave. 'But I believe the artist was showing us what mattered to his subject, not a physical location behind where she posed. He was adding something more than the image of a beautiful woman. If you look to the left, there are the red roses again, this time a whole shrub. I'm guessing Linda had a passion for the flower; perhaps she loved gardens and gardening.'

'I doubt she was a gardener as we understand the term these days,' Ben said. 'It would have been unbecoming of an upper-class lady to physically garden. They were expected to sit outside and draw and paint their surroundings. Botanical illustrating was an acknowledged pursuit which high-status men said upper-class women were particularly suited too and adept at. They would not have got their hands dirty digging or weeding.'

'Look at her skin, though.' Amber was taking in every detail of the picture. 'That is not the pale, delicate, skin of a lady who spent her life out of the sun. She has the tan of someone who loves being outside. I wonder if she had long fingernails? That was considered proof that a woman had a high-status position in life and did not have to earn money. Her well-to-do peers would have considered her a commoner if her fingernails weren't manicured because she did physical work.'

Ben looked at the picture as he spoke. 'But she would have had input into her portrait and asked for her skin tone to look naturally tanned and not to be lightened. Maybe she had some of the attitudes that you describe, Amber, being brought up in a noble family. Also, it looks to me that she specified the background and the specific elements she wanted included.'

'Hogarth seems to have depicted her passions – roses, her temple, and being outdoors,' Amber said with conviction. She stared at the portrait, and something about it struck a note with her. The woman was looking at the artist as if she were gazing out from the painting at her. She zoomed the screen onto Linda's face and noted the intelligent, focused look, brown eyes, and smooth skin. 'A striking woman, she projects conviction, a passion,' she said with a feeling of awe.

'She does indeed,' Dave agreed.

'It's an incredibly well-realised painting for a young Hogarth,' Ben admitted. 'He must have been in awe of her, and it inspired him. The circle's inclusion says it all for us.'

'We can go no further for now, though,' admitted Dave. 'Let's wait for the translations, then meet again. Tomorrow I'm walking in the area again, so I'll be off now, early night for me.' He paused, 'Oh, I nearly forgot. I walked the churchyard and found five Richardsons and a very time-worn tomb with three Routier names on it. One was her father, and I think her mother, but that was illegible. But there was no Linda on the other inscription. I expected it really.'

'Why, because her death was out of the ruling class and clergy's expectations for a lady from noble birth?' asked Amber.

'Yes and no. She could have an unmarked grave there somewhere. It may have been her preference.'

'Or she could be in the tomb with the other three Routiers,' Ben suggested.

'We'll never know. Anyway, it's a dead end I'm afraid. He hesitated and laughed, 'No pun intended there.'

'Time to go, Dad,' Amber smiled at his joke.

'Alright, I'm away. Let's meet once the next text is with us.'

They agreed and said their goodbyes.

Dave left, and Amber lingered, coat in hand. The two chatted in the hallway until it became obvious that was all

Ben intended to do. 'Time to go – work tomorrow,' she announced, keeping disappointment from her voice.

As Amber drove home, she mulled over her and Ben's conversation. All the time, her thoughts went back to him and his lack of interest in her. Maybe he was gay–, but she'd never heard of him having any relationships with either gender. Then she parked with little thought as tiredness took over. She forced him from her mind as she left her car. Her phone said 12:43 as she let herself into her home. *I must question him more about his life outside the job*, she consoled herself, then went upstairs to her bedroom.

Her eyes opened wide, and Ben was instantly forgotten as her stomach lurched. Something was wrong. The framed poster on the wall was lopsided. She looked down in shock – the three drawers of the small cabinet in the hall were wide open; the contents were strewn around the floor. 'Oh no. Oh my God,' she exclaimed as the phone in her pocket started ringing.

Amber ignored it and went through to the living room. One quick sweeping glance at the chaos strewn around was enough. She sat on the stairs and dialled 999. The officer on the other end logged her call, then asked her to stay on the line and make sure there were no intruders still inside. She ran upstairs and checked both bedrooms, then the bathroom. 'No, no one, except for more damage and mess, and my belongings are strewn everywhere,' she sobbed. He gave Amber a crime reference number and said someone would be in touch, and the phone went dead. She held it to her ear, listening to the buzz, then brought herself back. 'Oh my God,' she repeated and put the catch on the front door lock, then checked the rear French doors and all the windows. Someone had wrenched away the downstairs toilet window, letting in a blast of cold air. She realised someone had used it to break in and exit, and wedged it closed as best she could. After closing the toilet door, she pushed a chair against it, and burst into tears. At some point, she went to bed and slept fitfully, unaware that her phone rang three more times amongst her pile of discarded clothes.

The sun filtered through her thick curtains as she woke. Scene after scene scorched her consciousness: a smashed digital picture frame, drawers emptied over the wood floors, and broken china. Amber buried her head in her pillow for a couple of minutes, then sat bolt upright as she recalled what Ben had told her about Nathan. "... Do you know he's recently captured some shady billionaire backer?" Would that backer be criminal enough to burgle her, looking for copies of the manuscript? She had had her laptop with her last night, and it was the only place she stored photos of the document, so they had found nothing here. A sense of relief flooded over her.

In a moment, the whole scenario and potential crime leapt into sharp focus, not only her place, how about Mum and Dad's home?

She threw clothes around until she found her phone in the jeans pocket and stared at the screen, trying to decide whether to send Nathan a blistering accusation.

Amber's finger hovered over the recently entered contact, then she scrolled to her father's number and tapped it.

'Hi. This is an honour, Amber – an early call.'

It was soothing to hear that voice, the one she'd come to with problems all her life. 'Dad, I've been burgled,' she blurted, and felt like a child as she tried to keep tears at bay.

'What- ... When? How?' He sounded devastated and bemused.

'It happened while we were at Ben's. I got home to a house that looked as if it had exploded inside.'

'I'll drive over straight away. Don't go to work, you must be in shock.'

'I think it must have something to do with Nathan – he's paid someone to look for our manuscript.'

There was a pause, and then Dave's voice sounded grim in the receiver. 'Yes, he may well be involved. Have you phoned the police?'

'Yes, I have a crime number. They said they'd be in touch.'

'Phone again and ask to speak to the officer in charge. Tell him about our suspicions, but don't go into any detail about the document.'

'Okay, Dad.'

'Have you accounted for all the digital photos I emailed you?'

'Yes, they were on my laptop and that was with me last night. I hadn't got round to backing up on any flash drive, only on DataCloud.'

'Good. I'll be over in a couple of hours.'

She broke the connection and surveyed her ruined home, then went into the kitchen and put the kettle on. She phoned in sick to the department, relaying her bad news to Craig Dalgarth, who always started work early. Sipping a cup of tea, she texted Ben.

Later, Dave arrived with her mum, and after hugs and considerable consolation, they asked about Nathan and her report to the police.

'He's so creepy and there's something not quite normal about him.'

'In what way?' asked Liz.

'He's so intense, never looks you in the eye. Shifty, is the word I'd use to describe him. He refused to say who his backers are, only said they were interested in his research into various promising treasure locations.' She felt that same crawling sensation rise in her spine that she had experienced when in the pub with him. 'I told the detective constable of my suspicions. He really sounded harassed and said they had a huge workload and would not be coming round to survey the scene here, but took Nathan's number and said someone would go to speak with him.'

'We must get sharper with security on this project. You informed Ben?'

'Yes, he's coming over too. I gave him my address.' Normally, the thought of getting Ben over would have sent a thrill coursing through her, but now she was glad of the extra support.

As they were tidying, Amber went through scenarios. The main precaution to take care of was her father's manuscript and his digital images of it. She broached the subject as she tested a cracked digital picture frame.

'I've put the manuscript back in the hidden compartment and added two flash-drives. The external drive and laptop are in the car.'

'And I made sure all windows and doors were locked,' added Liz.

'Does Nathan know I'm involved or have the original manuscript?' Dave asked.

'I only said you were hoping to write and publish a book based on the document. It was only a drawing, and it was absurd to think of the document as a physical horde of treasure. I kept dampening his interest, remembering to say it had no visual reference to treasure at all. I snapped at him and finished with, "The translation doesn't even give any lucid directions to anything either," and told him he was reading far too much into his translation.'

'That should have put him off. But unfortunately, the thought of bright gold and glittering jewels is a powerful incentive to such a man.'

The doorbell interrupted the conversation, and Amber rushed to the door.

'So sorry to hear this has happened,' Ben began.

'It's okay, nothing stolen, a few replaceable items damaged. I'll put in an insurance claim.' She showed him into the kitchen, which thankfully now looked almost tidy as Liz continued to busy herself clearing the mess.

'I'll get some tools from the car and fix the hinges on the toilet window.' Ben strode out, and she couldn't stop herself from watching until he got to his car.

Indoors, Dave was hauling her upended bookcase upright and then began replacing the books. Amber was grateful for the extra help and spent the next hour tidying and cleaning.

Later, after checking Dave's security regarding the manuscript and digital files, Ben looked relieved. 'So I think our quest has taken on more urgency. We know someone else has the scent of treasure – although the actual treasure is of a vastly different nature than they think. I propose we try to get the other translations urgently. 'Let's get passage two emailed to All That's Latin.' Ben said. 'That will still leave section five to send.'

'Okay, I'll give five to Birmingham Translation Services ASAP. I know they run an express service, as do All That's Latin.'

'Good. We need to step up a gear,' Dave agreed.

'I'd rather we went out of gear and put the handbrake on,' Liz added. 'This is getting dangerous.'

'No, we're going to be fine, Mum. The whole burglary thing may have been a coincidence.' As she spoke, Amber opened her laptop and waited for it to produce the home screen. 'I can't believe Nathan would come round here and break in. He has his sensation-seeking reputation to think of if spotted or caught. He's too large to get through the toilet window anyway,' she attempted a smile.

'That may be so, but what of his backers?' Liz said in a suspicious tone.

Ben answered, 'I dug into this online. All I know of them is, they made their money in the oil industry, and there have been rumours for years of billionaire collectors buying up looted ancient artefacts. There was a hedge-fund manager from Manhattan arrested last year for accumulating looted artefacts. The whole ghastly industry is rife, and it looks to me that our friend Nathan may have his fingers in that honey jar.'

As they spoke, Amber tapped and clicked on the laptop and brought up Birmingham Translation Services. In moments, she'd clicked on their express service and entered her credit card number. She uploaded passage five, and then repeated the order to All That's Latin with passage two, and logged out. 'Done,' she announced, interrupting Ben and Dave's debate on illegal archaeological site robbing.

Having silently left while Amber was tapping on her laptop, Liz was now in the kitchen, and Amber could hear her clearing up. She felt so sorry for her mother, who only wanted normality to return. She had her own problems to deal with; the women's social group meant an awful lot to her.

Amber felt a pang of anxiety as she wondered what resources Nathan's mysterious backer had and what lengths he would go to. She hoped her mother felt safe and sufficiently distanced from the problem.

'Let's meet at my place tomorrow evening if Amber gets the translations through,' Ben said, interrupting her thoughts. 'Hopefully, there's more substantial information in them rather than all the mystical clap-trap in the first passage.'

'Okay, fingers crossed, and I'll forward you both passages the minute I receive them,' Amber said and wondered how much work she would get done tomorrow, as every email alert would send her hand reaching for her phone.

CHAPTER FIVE

Sweeping his detector in a steady left-to-right scan, Matt Bradley continued along the area of public footpath near the picturesque town of Symonds Yat in the Forest of Dean. This daily search was ideal therapy to escape the confinement of his home; the back-and-forth motion was both hypnotic and soothing. When he started each day's outing, he always had expectations of finds, but when he finished without finding anything, it didn't seem to matter. Today's slow walk, scanning the ground, was just what he needed to overcome his health issues. The sound of birdsong all around and the babble of the river on his right-hand side were all the therapy he needed.

This routine had been ongoing for six months without any change to his fortunes; he was still on a very tight budget and had almost given up on finding anything of value. Matt preferred the internal speaker on the detector rather than wearing headphones so that he could hear nature's accompaniment. Being new to the hobby, he had wanted to buy a detector that didn't need any manual setting up, and this machine matched his needs. He continued sweeping with the detector set to detect all metal, it seemed to give the best results. Metal detecting had become more than a hobby, almost an obsession, he admitted to himself. But he needed this distraction from his life, or perhaps from the life he once had.

He let his thoughts wander along his life's journey, as he often did, and now the upset of all the disasters seemed easier to cope with. He used to earn good money as an experienced mechanic in a main car dealership, with showrooms and a workshop, just outside Ross-on-Wye. Then fate dealt him the first unlucky blow. He was bent under the bonnet of a beautiful six-year-old Ford when it happened. He'd had warning twinges in his back for over a month, and he should have heeded them and shouldn't have twisted into awkward positions to get to any confined space. As a dedicated mechanic wanting to complete another perfect job, he had decided to check the tightening of the last bolt to a replacement housing. He stretched down to the bolt, which was just out of comfortable reach with the spanner, when his back clicked, followed by a searing pain in his spine. He had forced himself to tighten the bolt and then tried to get upright. His shriek of pain had alerted the other guys working on cars nearby. With his arms levering himself up, he managed to stand almost erect, but the pain increased in waves. He remembered thinking, I've pushed my back once too often this time.

A workmate helped him into the canteen for an early lunch break. During the next hour, he found he could not sit comfortably, and getting back to work was impossible; it just made the agony worse. The pain became so intense that he had to stop removing a suspension arm, and stood bent-double and panting. Chris, the workshop foreman, came over as he stood, face contorted and grasping the top of his drawered tool cabinet.

'You okay, Matt?'

'No boss. I've fucked up my back. Agony, can't stand. Only bent into the engine bay to check a fucking bolt.'

'Get home, mate, and get the doc to look at it.'

He had staggered outside and somehow had managed to get into his car. A month dragged past, in which the doctor told him to take it easy and lift nothing heavier than a teapot. The pain eased and then stopped; his back felt fine again so he ignored another week's sickness benefit and went back to work. A week later, it happened again as he bent to pick up a new shock absorber he was about to fit, this time with double the pain and complete incapacity.

A year of sickness benefit, pain, MRI scans, X-rays, and drug treatment followed. The consultant had diagnosed him with spinal-cord compression from a prolapsed disc. His prognosis wasn't good; he may recover from the immediate pain in a month, but it would be months more until he was free of most of the discomfort. But ongoing, he was liable to reinjure his back again and again in his job at the dealership. The consultant had said, 'You are young at 43 to have a spine weakness like this, unfortunately. Do not lift anything heavy again, do not twist, and avoid bending over to lift anything. I'd try for a desk job if I were you.'

He'd obeyed the professional diagnosis. Further tests to find the cause of his condition were so far inconclusive, and he was soon to be checked for a series of rare conditions. Company HR had been very sympathetic, although they were based in group headquarters in Hertfordshire and didn't know him personally. He was unsuitable, given his lack of required skills and qualifications for a desk job, so he was offered a job in sales. Dealing directly with customers was not his thing; they irritated him, and he didn't have the people skills needed. After failing a month's trial in the showroom, he was given redundancy on medical grounds and a good pay-off for his 26 years of loyal service.

Matt emerged from the series of unhappy memories and carried on sweeping along the riverbank footpath under the majestic outcroppings rising on either side of the river. He compared his new life out in the fresh air to his old one. He had been used to the sound of air-guns, power tools, and revving engines, the smell of oil and exhaust fumes, and the hard, mucky, physical labour. Now out here with the sound of birds, only the occasional passerby, and the hope of finding a lost coin or two, it was as if he had been born again. He knew he could go on with this life, living of his severance money, disability benefits, and his wife's life-insurance payout, paying the bills.

His detector felt like a friend, it had helped him adjust to a new life. He'd spent £300 on the lightweight detector with all the high-tech features. A small pin-pointer detector for close scanning each hole, a digging tool, and a carrying case had added another £150 to the cost, but it had been worth it. He'd learnt so much in the last six months and found an assortment of interesting items, but nothing of value. This futuristic machine compared all the low, medium, and high frequency signals at once, which used to be only available on top-end machines. This feature gave every chance of detecting any metal at up to 30 centimetres in depth, and all in one sweep. No extra tuning or switching needed, just a clear indication of what maybe under the detector loop. He was pleased with his machine ever since he had first swept his garden and found a 50 pence coin.

A neighbour saw him detecting along the nearby footpath while walking her dog, and asked him to look for her long-lost eternity ring, which had disappeared somewhere in her garden. Reg and Amy had been delighted when he found it and insisted on giving him £50 in cash.

These initial successes helped to banish the terrible upset of his physical weakness. He remembered the day, 16 years ago, when he'd been cheered by the other workshop guys for lifting and carrying a large new gearbox from the parts department to the car that was under repair. 'Who needs a forklift?' he had boasted. Matt wondered whether this kind of macho feat had weakened his back and not his calcium-low diet, as the consultant had assumed.

It wasn't as if he had a wife or any children to worry about either. Dianne had been gone for eight years now. It had been a terrible accident. Two policemen had rung his doorbell that evening to tell him what had happened, and were very sympathetic. It had been a head-on accident, and she was likely killed outright, without suffering. They took him to the hospital to identify her body, but he had no memory of them taking him home. He tried to keep her locked away in the back of his mind, but every now and again she resurfaced with a memory or a line she had said. He remembered her saying, You always smell of oil and exhaust fumes, a wonderful aftershave, my dear. She had reached up and kissed him on his grime-streaked face. He grinned to himself, she often said he looked dishevelled and never had his hair cut, but apparently, she loved him for all of it. Then he remembered the complex legal proceedings, as she hadn't left a will. It had been a frustrating time, piling all this hassle onto someone who was grieving. Eventually, he inherited her half of the small bungalow, and the mortgage had been paid off, and then he had the social security benefit payout issue. He was also left with Diamond, the Red Setter; she was some consolation until she passed with stomach cancer. Matt stopped thinking about the problems at that point and concentrated on the detector-coil in front of his feet. The disasters had all been resolved three years ago, and now he found he was happy enough on his own - or at least he kept telling himself he was.

He had got used to the trauma of losing his job, with no chance of reemployment in his trade, and now with this new-found hobby, he was contented. One day, he was going to find something valuable, and he wondered whether it would change his life.

Six weeks ago, he had decided to try and get permission to detect on a farmer's land somewhere near his home in a village in the Forest of Dean. He thought the direction of Symonds Yat looked more promising as it was familiar already, and was such a unique and attractive area, always popular with tourists. From past conversations in his local pub, he knew of a farmer, Edgar Woodrow, from that way, who was agreeable and probably wouldn't reject his request out of hand. He owned the woodland and fields six miles to the east of Old Rainsbrock, where Matt lived, and only a mile from Symonds Yat. Matt had repaired his Land Rover's front suspension once for cash-in-hand, so the guy owed him a favour. They'd joked about the unfortunate accident and how robust the vehicle was. Matt remembered saying, 'Other makes of cars would have been a right-off crashing into that ditch, but these Landy's are so well made they last forever.'

He dropped by the farm on his way home that day from his monthly appointment with the physio, but the farmhouse was locked and there was no sign of the farmer, his wife, or Rod, his farmhand. They're busy in distant fields, Matt decided.

Two days later, Edgar the farmer finally answered his calls. Matt checked, and Edgar confirmed the land was his, he owned it, and that he could detect on it. He also said a metal detecting club had been over the fields and into the woodland about 15 years ago and had found nothing other than a rusty scythe, two Edwardian horseshoes, the brass percussion caplock from an old shotgun, a Victorian farthing, and seven other unusual but worthless modern items. The farmer's interest rose slightly when Matt explained that his modern state-of-the-art detector may find more items.

'Okay, me old Butt, but make sure you show me your finds,' he said using the local colloquialism, then added, 'and I want 50 percent if you find anything valuable.'

That had been nine days ago, and every afternoon since, Matt had ticked off another segment of the mental grid he'd set up in his mind whilst walking the first two of the fields. This afternoon, Matt had already swept the detector for an hour along a field edge. It was the last section of this field's grid before moving on to the next field. He had thought it looked promising, somewhere people would have walked because of its views through the woods leading down to the river. It overlooked the footpath he'd been detecting along for six weeks, so he knew the nearby area well.

As usual, he wore an old, light, rucksack that contained some snacks and a small bottle of water, along with a thin waterproof jacket. He had to keep the rucksack light so as not to risk his back and always took it off before digging the ground after a potential find was indicated. His rubbish bag in one pocket felt heavy with junk, the other bag for finds was in another pocket, and was almost empty apart from one item. This was a bronze horse stirrup that looked either time-worn by rubbing against a horse's flank for years or maybe just nicely cast.

It started to rain, and the wind had increased enough to make him feel cold and damp below his camouflage jacket. His denim jungle-style hat started to sag and drip water, so he decided the tree cover, even with its golden November foliage, would shield him from the worst of the elements. By now, he was over at the end of the last field owned by Edgar, so he turned into the trees the farmer owned. If he started to detect here, he could head back through the limited cover toward his car, detecting as he did so. He hadn't used his detector in thick woodland before and discovered this was a new and different experience. The ground was uneven with small saplings and low-level shrubs constantly getting in the way. Last year's leaf compost was slippery as well, so he took a slow course on slightly more level ground so that the slope wouldn't put strain on his back.

He soon had an unpromising signal from the detector. He'd learnt to recognise the subtle tones the machine emitted and thought it was junk, probably silver paper. Not wanting to pass up on any possibility, he took the small lightweight trowel from its belt fastening and scooped a hole through the dark compost. Sure enough, it came up with a scrunched ball of silver paper of the kind used to wrap chocolate bars in thirty years ago. He added it to his scrap bag to take home and get rid of responsibly. He'd read that it was the right thing to do and didn't want to re-detect the same junk on another day anyway.

He smoothed the woodland floor back over and carried on his course along a flatter path in between large beech, lime, and alder trees. The detector was silent, occasionally emitting a slight bleep that he couldn't get it to repeat when resweeping the area. He felt that an almost hypnotic state of mind took over again. Matt recognised it as that newly acquired wonderful zone where nothing in the world mattered apart from watching the waving of the detector loop as he moved it around larger rock obstructions or small shrubs.

Then, after an hour, the hum changed to a definite blip. He refocused as he thought the alarm buzz had carried on for a whole second, where the detector had continued to travel a foot further. He backtracked, no, it was only a single blip, but a sharp one. The detector's internal speaker seemed sensitive to any slight audio signal, and he was beginning to learn its very subtle differences in tone. It seemed to screech at him in a higher pitch than he'd previously registered. Then he remembered the similarity in sound to his test burials in the garden, where he temporarily covered up his old wedding ring and his mother's silver brooch. He checked the screen on his detector; it was set to all-metal still, but he knew the tone that junk made now, and this was not that tone. He stopped and stood still, waved the detector over the area again. A crystal clear but faint signal reached his ears. He looked at the depth indicator. All four segments were lit; it was at the maximum depth, about 30cm. Quite deep then, he thought, and laid the detector down and started scooping leaf mould and rich soil away. Soon, he had gone down eight inches, and still his little pinpointer device clearly said something was there.

Then his hand-trowel hit something that was dull and tarnished, almost black. He looked closely, it was metal and had an interesting shape. Carefully, he used the trowel point to tease it up, but it was fastened to something that showed a sudden glint as he scraped compost away. He held his breath and hardly dared believe what he had seen. He dug a bigger hole around the object. More of the item went deeper down, and he instantly knew this was one hole worth being patient over to keep the object intact. On his knees now, he wished for some really fine tools, like a smaller trowel or dental picks to help. I'll buy those later, he vowed. Carefully, he took more compacted soil away, and a small leaf shape, stained dull black, appeared. It was connected to a chain that glinted yellow and bright.

Careful not to tug on the connection to what he hoped was a gold chain, he rubbed the leaf between his fingers, and it took on a brighter appearance. He thought it could be silver.

A large drop of rain fell on the object, allowing the finely textured and wrought detail to show up. It was an unusual leaf shape, but definitely artistically carved and very beautiful. The thought fascinated him, and he felt a pivotal moment in his life had finally arrived. This is what he had waited for since beginning the hobby. His heart pounded, and he started to perspire, despite the steady rainfall sounding on the autumn tree foliage around him.

The gold glint transformed to a bright tangle of woven strands that went deeper.

He carried on, but with extreme care.

He lay down on the wet leaf-matter to get a better angle on what he was doing.

Another gold glint. This one was another slightly larger leaf shape.

He rubbed at it with a finger. A single gold oak leaf, he was certain. Utterly beautiful, the craftsmanship was exquisite.

The hole had become almost two feet wide and went down 11 inches now. He realised he had only detected the top two leaves, and possibly only part of the woven gold chain. He dared to wonder whether there could be more down deeper.

It could be a necklace.

He inched out more soil, and two more silver leaves showed, glued together with soil. Around them, the gold chain with compacted soil formed a temporary binding.

Soon, soil formed a large heap before he realised that was it, the whole item was there in daylight for the first time for… he didn't dare think of how many years. He counted four more silver leaf shapes in the earthen clod.

With the trowel under the clump of metal and soil, he gingerly removed the whole thing. He took out his finds bag, removed the bronze horse stirrup, and put it in another jacket pocket. The dirty clump of treasure was harder to push into the bag. He didn't want it to come apart. He could see both ends of the gold chain. One had a hook on it as if it fitted into a small loop. The other end of the chain had no clasp and looked broken. He guessed it was a necklace and maybe had come apart as someone had ridden their horse too fast through the trees and been raked by a branch, or had run at speed and fallen to the ground.

With excited thoughts tumbling through his head, he packed up the detector and the other tools and headed back to his car. It was now raining hard, and he was soaked and covered in soil. Matt didn't care; it was a small price to pay for what he'd found.

A mud-splattered tractor stopped alongside him as he closed the car boot, and Edgar's farmhand, Rod, leaned from the cab's open window. 'Found anything, mate?'

'No, just junk so far,' he lied. If he was going to tell anyone, he had to be sure of what he'd found first.

The drive back home seemed to take forever as he tried to keep his excitement down. One thing was for sure; this really was a great way to fill his huge amount of free time.

CHAPTER SIX

As Amber predicted, the next day dragged. Not just because she was examining her phone every five minutes, but the burglary ordeal was still fresh in her mind. Would Nathan refuse to give up? She paused regularly as she worried whether the burglars were back, turning her house upside down again while she was at work. Giving up compiled costs for a potential dig, she researched burglar alarm set-ups and tried to work out which exterior security cameras were best. Then, when her phone pinged, she looked at it and froze. The incoming email was not one of the translation services but from Nathan. She had deliberately not given him her email, but somehow, he had discovered it. The message was titled; Curiosity killed the cat and the investigator.

Why had he typed such a strange heading? She hovered a finger over the closed email, worried about what threat it contained. The word 'killed' and all its possibilities alarmed her. Was Nathan being deliberately intimidating, or was he so curious that he obsessively needed to know the rest of the translation? Finally, she stabbed the phone almost against her will, and the email's contents appeared.

Dear Amber.

Following our conversation the other night, I would like to increase my offer for your document. In fact, I'd like you to name your price. A friend and I are overwhelmed with curiosity, and we must know what other information it contains.

I feel I must level with you and justify my interest in your document – it matches the description of an intriguing passage described in an 18th century journal I have in my possession. I would be prepared to share an entry or two if you would include me in your investigation.

Wishing you all the best
Nathan

She drew a sharp intake of breath. Who was this friend? Was it his backer, the burglar, or another even shadier operative? As for how he had found her email, she knew that she and her archaeological colleagues were connected on social media, so that he could find someone with just a few clicks. Making up some creative fiction to obtain her contact email would be simple for him.

Should she reply or ignore it? After a few minutes, she forwarded the message to Ben and Dave and asked their opinions. Then she attempted to update a spreadsheet of finds loaned to museums. After an hour of mistakes and typos, she gave up and got a coffee from the machine in the corridor. As she got back, her phone pinged again. This time, it was Birmingham Translation Services with the translation of their paragraph. Without any hesitation, she opened the attachment and read.

Now prepare yourself to meet the unborn and your ancestors. These charmed stones will not allow the Gods to speak with their subjects, but will show the devout believer a place wherein wonders can be observed. We will share an invocation to the glory of the Gods and will break bread together, then I will bestow on you some small directions to the treasure, but I cannot advise you further, for your journey will be your own.

She didn't need to examine the text too closely to realise they were dealing with a fantasy. Nothing in this paragraph was substantial. It was metaphysical and was almost the last chance of taking their manuscript seriously. She couldn't stop her thoughts plummeting to black depths and had to admit that she had allowed a fantasy of a lost stone circle to build false hopes in her.

Further gloomy thinking was dispelled as Ben messaged back: *'I was tempted to ignore Nathan, but I am now curious about his journal. Let's see how Dave suggests handling this.'*

Dave, being her father, was easy for her to predict. He would not even look at emails or any other electronic messages until the evening. Her impatience grew. After an hour, she took her lunch break and walked the familiar track around the nearby park. The afternoon dragged, and at the first opportunity, she left her office for the day. Her phone pinged again as she arrived home. For a change, it was her dad answering quicker than was his normal habit.

Dear Amber and Ben

Interesting, I wonder what his journal is. It clearly doesn't state the circle's location, or he would have no need for us and our manuscript. Amber, how about if we ask him for more information, perhaps an extract or two, so we can test its authenticity?
Regards
Dave

Okay, you must be eager, Dad. I'm not as curious as you are, though, Amber thought as she walked to her front door. I'd better help him, don't want to show my disappointment. She decided to carry out Dave's suggestion whilst preparing supper. Routine cooking left her thinking about Nathan's journal and who could have written it. She went through prime candidates. Only one name came into sharp focus – Linda. If she could prepare a beautiful manuscript with its surrounding Latin text, she could also have kept a journal. Perhaps she felt the rituals, hymns, and devotions needed to be handed down to the next priest or priestess, or maybe she'd created a record of various duties and important ceremonies. Amber put the thoughts to one side whilst she ate. Her phone beeped its usual email alert, and as she activated the dishwasher, she opened another reply from Ben.

Hey, Amber and Dave
See what you can get from Nathan, giving none of our research away. I'm really loathe to include him in our search, though.
Ben

Trying to devise a response to Nathan, she made a cup of coffee and picked up her phone as it pinged again. It was a reply and an attachment from All That's Latin. Not wanting to read on her phone's small screen, she fired up her laptop and abandoned thoughts of a restful evening watching a TV drama.

It felt like an eternity, but she logged into her email account and brought up the attachment.

The congregation of Gods represents the forest, the mountains, the fields, the sea, all the creatures, and the very air itself. It was a necessary assembly, for they had been forced to discuss the earthly domain and how its people were becoming scornful of their rulers' power. After a time of debate, the great sun God Almorth appeared to prevail over Deidre, Goddess of the moon, and over the Gods of the forest, the rivers, and the deities that govern all that is alive. For three seasons the debate raged, many passionate and wrong arguments were brought forth, and all but one were discarded. It came to pass that the Gods decided to instruct mortals to build a great temple of worship. It was to be a place of wonder as well as adoration, and the Holy Immortals would reward those who attended with demonstrations of their magick. It was decreed that this power would take an unusual form, for the temple must remain an enigma visible (visitable? Translator's query) only to the chosen. The ancients did as they were instructed, and over two lifetimes, the people of the forest created a great temple to rival any in the land. Then the God of the night, Smalran, sent down the light of three stars to bless the holy place. Morrigan - the Goddess of shapeshifting, endowed the stones with her own peculiar magick, and this house of the Gods then became one with the forest. From that time forth, our shrine was blessed with this divine power. This is the true account of the creation of our sacred temple, as told to me by the mother-priestess before me and to her by the mother before her.

This time, the disappointment was crushing. The whole manuscript was a fantasy. She knew enough about pagan religion to know that Morrigan and Deidre from earlier sections of the manuscript were ancient pagan Goddesses in Ireland, and Woden was a Bronze Age God. It appeared as if someone had been to the Globe theatre in London and seen Shakespeare's A Midsummer Night's Dream there, then realised they liked fables about mythical deities. The latest section's translation had again not provided many more facts, and these were spread very thinly. She knew Linda had been what these days would be called a pagan, and had been persecuted because of her beliefs. They knew the Hogarth painting depicted Linda's same stone circle – but that was about all. It had been good reasoning to hope that the wove-paper document would yield more concrete information, but so far it had failed dismally – and there was only one more passage to come. She regretted having sent the fourth passage to TransGlobal with their snail-pace service. If it wasn't for that, the sorry investigation could be concluded now.

The whole of this saga had taken up too much of her time, and she wanted to let it go. For a long minute, she stared at the translation and sighed, but then she had to acknowledge that the same earlier curiosity still nagged her. There was some kind of reality hidden behind the metaphysical prose that would not quite reveal itself. Amber sighed again, There were still three days to go before she could expect to receive passage four, the last text, and draw a final conclusion. There seemed to be no point in waiting before sharing the latest translations with Ben and her father, so she forwarded them and then distracted herself by opening the post. In minutes, she had put the translations aside as she read a letter from the police stating her crime number, followed by what routine inquiries they were conducting.

The next day, Amber found concentration at work easier, but felt she was subconsciously trying to form the investigation's next steps. She refused to think about Nathan and his request. Even images of Ben faded as she began a task requested by her department head for preliminary planning for a dig to be started next spring in Cambridgeshire. The rest of the week passed in a haze of work and everyday life. All she heard from Dave was a quick email saying how much he was enjoying walking further afield from Springborough Manor. She heard nothing from Ben, so she assumed he had no new progress to report and was also becoming disillusioned. It was tempting to drop over to the Finds Depository to discuss the project with him, but knew he was hosting some important clients there.

Slowly, she formed a response to Nathan. Any subsequent vague reply from him would not be good enough, though. With a crystal-clear, simple decision, she decided that no matter what it cost, she needed to read the whole of Nathan's procured journal. It could allow their manuscript to slot into a related and wider story from the same timeframe.

That evening, after preparing a spag-bol she started her laptop and logged into email. The message to Nathan needed to be precise, not so easy to do as a quick text on her phone, but first she needed to see if she could persuade Dave and Ben to include Nathan in the project. If the circle was a fantasy, then it would not matter if he was involved, but if the location where the stones once stood could be found, then Nathan would surely grab all the publicity. His access would need to be limited, only swearing him to secrecy would not be enough. The actual location would have to be kept hidden from him – he could not be in any search party either. She continued to think through the problem as she hesitated, fingers poised over her laptop keys.

She hoped the last section from Transglobal would show how to get to the stones. It had to, because if the manuscript was anything more than a fantasy, then logically this last section should contain real-life directions. She emailed Dave and Ben and asked for their thoughts.

Hi Guys

I haven't messaged Nathan yet, as I need to formulate a precise response to him. But my curiosity is almost overwhelming – I really would like to know what Nathan's journal contains. It could hold clues to our circle's location or other useful information. Even if it only details the life of someone close to Linda, it could reveal fascinating info about her.

I propose we only give him the sections of our manuscript that we have had translated — and only send them out to him in return for his whole journal. We can keep the still-to-arrive section from Transglobal to ourselves if it proves significant. I'm convinced that the passage will contain directions.

Opinions please ASAP.

Amber

She knew they would both consider the implications of including Nathan carefully and didn't expect immediate replies. Ben's response came through first, an hour later.

Hi Amber

You suggest a difficult and slightly unethical course. His journal possibly doesn't contain hardly any concrete facts, probably why he's offering sections to us. After much thought, I think we can play him at his own game. I agree with trading our info for the whole journal.

Go for it!

Ben

Dave didn't reply until 10 o'clock. Amber wondered whether he'd waited for the old carriage clock to chime before pressing send.

Dear Amber

This is a potentially risky course to take. We will have to be very careful if our last segment contains directions. I am sure Nathan is harmless, but his shady backer may not be. What if the break-in was by criminals employed by this backer? We could get into deep water if they eventually discover our last section and that we've deceived them.

I give my reluctant approval because I have to admit the life of Linda is gripping me as well, and I'm passionate about knowing what happened to her. I feel certain Nathan's journal must be hers.
All the best
Dad

A shiver of anticipation ran through Amber. Fantasy or not, their document, written by Linda, should be fleshed out more if Nathan accepted their terms. If Dave could get enough information on Linda, he could expand it into a 70,000-word documentary quest and perhaps get his name known for historical research. It had the potential to even become a bestseller, even if the stones didn't exist. If Nathan could build a name and career over this kind of thing, she was sure her father could regain some prestige from this project.

Over a cup of coffee, she tapped a draft email to Nathan. By the time she had edited it again and again, and it was ready to send, it was nearly midnight, but she was pleased with the result. Amber read it through one more time.

Hi Nathan

We do not want to sell you our manuscript, however, the story it contains cries out for further investigation – even if it turns out to be the fantasy of a bored intellectual, as I suspect.

I confess we went elsewhere to get the rest of our manuscript translated. If we trade our translated document, I first need to know if your journal is written in Latin or in period English. This would obviously affect whether the trade is viable, as we will need to read the original journal ourselves – not just see copies of your translations.

We may be prepared to let you read our complete manuscript translation in return for a thorough examination of the whole of the journal in your possession.

Kind regards

Amber

Amber realised they may receive a digital copy of Nathan's original journal and may need to get their own translations done, which may involve scanning or photographing a lot of pages. With her finger hovering over the send button, Amber sighed, It wasn't much of a trade. Nathan would insist on seeing their original manuscript, which they could not allow. She got up and started pacing as she thought and thought. There must be a way of manipulating their translations without actually making anything up or lying to Nathan.

Then some Photoshop techniques came to mind. What if she digitally cut out the Latin section from Transglobal, the section they didn't want Nathan to read? Then she could copy the illustration; paste it to a new backing by telling the A.I. plugin to simulate the document's background, which would become the new base layer. She could enlarge the Latin they wanted to give him and refit it around the stone's image again, using the A.I. to filter out any old background colour. It was fiddly, but she thought it possible to do with the other layers comprising the text set to a transparent background. The whole thing could then be merged into one layer and saved as a low-resolution JPEG. The more she thought about it, the more she knew it would work, especially if Nathan negotiated to send digital copies of his journal. He could, of course, edit in the same way, but if the journal contained no useful information, would he bother to edit out anything? She thought it unlikely he would bother and smiled to herself with renewed conviction. The entire project felt as if it were some kind of fiction that would sound quite dramatic when her father wrote the accompanying book.

She clicked the send button, then went to bed.

The next day at work, she had her phone on the desk, and as she worked, examined each ping to see if it was Nathan. Her lunch break loomed, and still she'd heard nothing. Then, as she was about to cross the courtyard to the canteen, her phone alerted her. She stopped and looked at the screen, then sat on a nearby bench. It was Nathan.

Hello Amber

I'll trade you a glimpse of my journal for a reading of your manuscript. My tome is written in 18th century English and is fairly easy to follow. I'm sure I can find a different angle to your interpretations, and together you and I (and who else is in your team, please?) can identify what happened to Woden's temple and the cult's accompanying treasures.

I'm not really one for long physical treks, so when we identify a location for the temple, I'll send a friend to represent my interests.

We must have trust in our collaboration, so I've attached scans of the relevant journal pages and can précis the remaining pages for you later as they stop abruptly. It would appear the last pages of the journal have been removed. In this spirit of cooperation, I have attached two scanned diary pages. I look forward to seeing a copy of your document, complete with the illustration and all the text.

Kind Regards

Nathan

PS. Perhaps we can catch up over a meal soon. It would be a good way of brainstorming theories on Woden's temple. I suspect from the journal I hold that it could be a stone circle.

Catch up – no way! Amber thought as she stood bolt upright in anger. Deep in thought, she sat at a canteen table with a mug of coffee and a pack of sandwiches and analysed his reply. She noticed an attachment titled Journal and stared for a moment at the title, and decided to wait until that evening to open it and then share it with Dave and Ben. Next, she thought about Nathan's questions. He had demanded to know who else she was working with on the project. I'm not mentioning Ben, she decided in an instant. I've already mentioned my dad and the possibility of his writing up the search and Linda's involvement, so it'll ring true that we're keeping it as a family project. So as far as Nathan's concerned, it's only the two of us. Then anxiety knotted her stomach. Who was this "friend" that he would send to join any search? Would it be a thug employed by his backer or a genuine academic, she pondered? She was certain Nathan would send her doctored manuscript to this backer, too, if only to justify the funding he was giving Nathan. She had to bide her time before replying. The Photoshopping would take her a few hours this evening, and it had to be 100 percent believable, look sharp, but with faded type and as discoloured as the original.

Her break was over, so she clicked the phone off and, determined to put in a productive afternoon, she went back to trying to get funding for a proposed dig in Devon. She left work pleased with her day. She had been promised funding and was sorting out a start date with her colleagues, and had finished by sending an update to Craig, head of the trust.

That evening, she ate a shop-bought salad with cold chicken and thought about Nathan's reply. She read it again and picked up on the last line. Nathan had thought their document was concerning a stone circle because his journal had mentioned one. Did he have further information in the journal that identified the circle? Could it be theirs? She would have to get more details from him and perhaps some of the journal as well. She put the possibility to the back of her mind and started the photoshopping.

The work was intense and involved multiple online searches on how to do certain aspects. Then, come 9:30, it was done. The digital copy retained its ragged edge, damp spots, discoloured areas, and even blemishes behind the drawing and text. The Latin characters were larger and in places overlapped the stones, but it looked complete and felt natural, as if Linda had accidentally written over the edges of the drawing. Feeling pleased with her upgraded digital art skills, Amber combined the layers and saved the document as a JPEG. 'It's good, really good,' she congratulated herself aloud.

The next task was unpleasant – having to type a reply to Nathan. As she began drafting the email, Amber realised she'd been so engrossed in altering their stones copy, she had yet to read his journal attachment. Probably some rubbish he's concocted to try to promote his theories, she surmised, but decided to read the thing in case it would alter the slant of her email. Without any expectation of reading anything useful, she opened the journal attachment on the laptop.

In moments, her eyes bulged; she gasped and became engrossed in events from over 300 years ago.

CHAPTER SEVEN

Extracts from the journal of Reverend Edgar Dalmont

Thursday 11th June, 1729

Blacksmith Robert Goodchild had declared himself much troubled by inner demons and asked me to bless and cleanse his mortal soul and, secondly, to give my wise advice. I thereby became horrified to discover he is no longer a God-fearing man. This transformation had supposedly been brought about by attending a ceremony held by a heretic, an evil witch posing as a priestess of a long-deceased religion. The mere transcription of this tale reminds me there is only one true faith, and that it is my duty to uphold the Lord's teachings from His Holy Bible.

Throughout my time as a minister to this community, there have been rumours of a devilish clan, one that holds demonic rituals in the depths of the darkest night. The whispers are nothing that amounts to any substance but often include tales of rites, frenzied dancing, and bloodletting ceremonies within an ancient temple. It will astound you, dear reader, to know that this unholy place is in our Godly England and not some foreign land where heathens abound.

The tale Mr. Goodchild related is full of the workings of the devil, for the man has been beguiled by one of Satan's servants — he even said that, given the chance, he would take her as his wife. Although I pressed him to give me the location of the ceremony, his reply was disconcerting. 'I know not where they took me, for I was met at the end of Lower Lane, guided into a cart blindfolded, then after enduring hours of journeying, I was unloaded, and taken on a march that lasted for hours into the night.' His is the sorry story of an easily influenced man, bewitched by ungodly preaching and led astray by a few who must live around these parts.

I had long suspected this parish's folk were not wholly converted to the Lord. Now I know this to be so.

Friday 12th June, 1729

I am now looking for confirmation of Mr. Goodchild's tale. I have been eavesdropping on whispered conversations over jugs of ale in the King's Head. At other times, villagers like Cuthbert Johnson, the gravedigger, were indiscreet when I was nearby. I am blessed with sharp hearing, which compensates for my having but one eye. These hearsays kept making their way almost unbidden to my ears. Folks would be quietly discussing this disturbing topic, and as I drew near, I caught many disturbing snippets with my keen hearing before they abruptly changed the conversation.

Then, this Friday gone, I was approached by a certain cooper by the name of Wide John Barrett, who sought me in my cloistered garden. We sat on a stone bench, and I listened. I will now endeavour to relate what he told me in his shaking and disturbed whisper. He told of evil goings-on and sought my help to rid him of these unwanted torments. Wide John told my shocked self of a procession of lost souls. He had been out one night setting traps for deer; the legality of such an act need not bother this tale, when a procession of some length wound through the woodland nearby. In the light of their flaming torches, he observed a striking female, a fallen angel with wild red locks and flowing white skirts. He noticed the finery of her clothing, being a self-professed expert in such things, and became awed by her ethereal grace. She carried a flaming torch and was leading two dozen willing victims in the direction of the cursed woodland. As she neared his hiding place, Wide John then noticed a thick gold torc around her smooth and shapely neck, hanging below it, almost to her ample cleavage, was a gold oak and silver rowan leaf bedecked necklace. Gold bangles encircled her slim arms and ankles as well. He was quick to conclude that where this procession was going was the forbidden temple hidden in the depths of the wildwood. The one place some miles from here, that all God-fearing people believed to be a handed-down fable.

I added his tale to the knowledge I had already gained. It was the first solid evidence of this blasphemous and evil sect.

We prayed together, and I asked the Lord to spare his soul and forgive his eyes for what they had seen. From that day, I began to pray regularly to deliver the people of this and nearby parishes from evil.

Monday 27th June, 1729

At last, the Lord has answered my prayers. I am to be a missionary for the good Lord. He has instructed me to go forth into the cursed woodland to seek this satanic cult and bring them back to Christian ways. My mission is to reclaim them by reciting the teachings of his wondrous book. So, duty-bound, I spent the day preparing for the trek with stout boots, a waxed cape, and a satchel containing food, drink, and handwritten copies of important scriptures to hand to the heathens. My trusty steed, Henry, a true thoroughbred, will take me to the edge of the cursed area, from there, I will proceed on foot.

Wednesday 29th June, 1729

I am much fatigued today, for last night I journeyed to an evil church, one where diabolical wonders abound. I must note at this point that if you follow my lead, then you must neglect your daily labours and at least a night's slumber to get to this God-forsaken place. Here, the devil's temptation was hard to ignore as he heaped ungodly treasures on me every moment of my visit.

The latest rumour was of a ceremony that very night, and I hoped their singing would make the congregation easy to discover. I tethered Henry to a suitable bough after finding a well-trodden path; there followed a laboured journey into the evening twilight. I prepared myself to enter an ancient place of towering trees, which be the realm of this unchristian sect. A note to you, dear reader - you will trudge along tracks overhanging with gnarled trees on a journey through an ancient forest that drips with dew and snatches at you with its twigs and thorns. Then you must venture down a steep ravine in which a sparkling stream races into the earth as if it were the river Styx. All these most normal of God's wonders here create an otherworldly atmosphere to aid the devil and his mechanisms. As you journey into this strange place from the world you are familiar with, you will enter a domain where our Good Lord has no sway. Be assured, dear reader, it is a journey of a convoluted nature and impossible to complete if you believe the curse that has been cast over this area for generations to be true. I must further declare that if you intend to follow my journey, then you need courage and independence of thinking. I also bid you to leave behind your Holy Bible and crucifix, for they hold no sway in this place.

At last, my journey reached its infernal destination — an ancient circle of stones surrounded by a ditch and an embankment. I steeled myself further, for strong rumour stated this temple is overseen by invisible fiends from hell itself. From a place of hiding, I observed this evil church. A group of about forty people were clothed in white, some of whom wore deer antler headdresses, others wore the skulls of wolves, whilst the remainder had on woven ivy masks and held aloft flaming torches.

I crept out from behind a large oak and dared to hold aloft the good book. Within moments, I was held and then barely escaped a makeshift noose. My mortal life was only saved by the words of the witch-priestess herself. I remember her statement even now, as it seems to have bewitched me. She said in soft, almost musical words, 'I knew sooner or later you would visit, dear Reverend. You are welcome, for although you barely know it yet, you are of the sun, the moon, of the stag and the boar, and are a brother to all the good people who are here saved from the clutches of your foreign church.'

I write now in this journal that I believe she may be right, for I then dared to imbibe a strangely tasting brew, threw off my stole and cassock and the cares and responsibilities of my position, and joined in the ceremony with gay abandon. Now I know not what enticed me, but fear my craving to return there is unstoppable.

I observed this pagan temple to have an eastern entrance created by a pair of pillars taller than two men. The tops of these support an imposing lintel of equal size. In flickering torchlight, I saw this enormous structure repeated to the west of the temple. Between these constructions, a circle of 13 less ponderous stones rose, and inside this circle was another of smaller stones. As a neophyte of this temple, the priestess informed me that each one was named after an important deity, and the smaller stones alongside some were those of the God's first-born. She and her acolytes guided me along a bright chalkstone path to an altar carved as a giant butterfly and with evidence thereon of fresh bloodstained sacrifices hinting at devilish rituals. At this point, I feared not only for my life but for my mortal soul.

This beautiful priestess handed me a gold goblet from which I drank again. A bough of holly was then waved about my head. She then ordered me to cower at the point of a jewel-encrusted silver dagger to swear an oath of secrecy. Again, fearing for my life, I promised not to tell anyone about this place and its location. In return, she granted me not only continued life but also further participation in this satanic religion and its treasures.

I became awed by this massive temple and its beguiling priestess. She presented riches beyond anything my theological learning could prepare me for. The devil abounds here as he tempts Christian fellows with his wealth and with a diabolical ceremony that will leave even the rich and noble of the land sorely tempted to return for further indoctrination.

Thursday 30th June, 1729
I am not, I fear, glad to be gone from this evil place and will be praying and paying penance when I have completed this journal entry. For I know I must go back; it is an addiction I crave. But beyond this, my precious diary, I will tell no one, ever, for my word to the great Priestess is my bond.

Aware that her mouth was hanging open, Amber snapped her teeth together and reread the whole thing. 'Oh my God,' she muttered slowly as she let the whole account fill her mind. Maybe it was why she loved being an occasional historian. It was the way a project gradually built up your knowledge and then added a sudden blitz of revelation that made you connect directly to the past. The extracts from this diary gave focus to their whole project, but without giving away its location. However, something tugged on her subconscious. There was another important piece of the puzzle just waiting to be fitted in – but again, she could not quite make the connection.

With this bubbling in the back of her mind, she forwarded the message and attachment to Dave and Ben with a few comments, ending each with multiple exclamation marks. But still, that elusive something nagged her mind. She looked at her watch. 11:45 – time for bed.

Her dreams seemed to act like a time machine, and she found herself under one of the circle's lintelled trilithons alongside the Reverend and trying to calm him as he railed about blasphemy and God's wrath. Then she was accepting a libation from a radiantly beautiful woman who seemed to sparkle as if she were an animation. The Reverend began waving a large tome, which she realised was his journal. It was leather-bound, and he opened it to show it to Linda, the priestess. In her dream, Amber noticed the pages were mould-formed, wove paper with faint laid marks. He turned the pages to where the missing ones had been removed, but the dream showed Amber the journal was intact. Linda smiled, ripped a page out, and secured it to the front of the butterfly stone with small stones. It was the illustration and its Latin inscriptions.

Amber woke up with a start and sat bolt upright.

In a flash, she realised her dream had inserted the missing piece. She had seen the journal with its contents written on thick, wove paper. The missing pages had left a ragged edge near the spine. Their document, hand written on burnished wove paper, had a ragged edge. It was the same size as the journal in the dream.

It had been ripped out of the journal.

Her bedside clock showed it was 5:35. There was no chance of sleeping again – her mind was in overdrive. Dave and Ben needed to know of this revelation, and Nathan most certainly did not. But she needed to see his original journal, to be sure. The dream had shown the tome, but she didn't really know its size or even whether its pages were wove paper or something older like vellum. She surmised they would most likely be wove, but needed Nathan to, at least, let her eyeball the book. That meant another evening out with the man. He may well be a fellow academic, but his position in their profession was so unlike hers.

Over an early breakfast, she tapped out a message to Nathan on her laptop.

Hi Nathan

Thanks for the journal entries. I have, in return, attached a JPEG of our document. My father took it, and I think you'll agree he's still retained his old skill as a dig-team photographer.

There is, however, one small favour I would like to ask of you. If I agree to meet you for an evening meal, would you be kind enough to bring the original journal with you? I would like to look it over. It'll put the entries you forwarded me into context – and who knows, a fresh eye might spot a small, insignificant fact that will help us further your project and hopefully ours too.

Kind regards

Amber

Pleased with the wording, she attached the Photoshopped stones JPEG and pressed "send". Then she tapped another blank email and addressed it to Dave and Ben, setting the priority to "high".

Hi Dad and Ben

Having read the journal entries, I've come to a startling conclusion regarding our manuscript. We need to meet ASAP to discuss this. Also, because of my discovery, I've had to agree to Nathan's request for a night out – but on condition he brings the journal with him.

Can we meet tonight at yours, Dad?

Get back to me as soon as, guys, please.

Love

Amber

She looked at her watch. Just time before work to reread the journal entries, she then muttered to herself, 'Thank God it's Friday.'

As the day progressed, she had messages from both Dave and Ben; they agreed to a meeting at Dave's that evening.

Come on, what's the dramatic declaration then? Ben wanted to know in his return text.

She texted back, *I'm not letting on. Want to see your face when I tell you of my discovery. See you later.*

Dave broke his rule of never replying during the day with a long email trying to work out what she'd discovered, and trusting she was as good a historian as she was an archaeologist. He finished with, *tell me now, Amber, please. So I have time to test your theory against the information already gained.*

Okay, seeing as it's you, Dad. She replied, *but don't tell Ben. I want to see his face when I reveal my discovery.*

Our document has been torn from a journal. I'm going to confirm it's Nathan's by looking at his original item.

See you later.

***

It felt almost irritating to have to reply to personal messages in work hours, but Dave instantly forgave Amber. Family emails were an exception, he decided. As his workday came to an end, Dave gave up expecting his phone to ping with another message from Amber regarding Nathan's reply. He suspected the man was holding out. He put the phone into his work bag along with the empty sandwich box and, after locking his office door, strode through the warehouse reception. He decided to take the long way round to his car, which was parked at the far end of the car park. It was another of his keep-fit schemes, which had the added advantage of his car being away from most parked cars, thus avoiding the chance of scratches and dents from inattentive drivers. It was one of his better recent decisions, he decided with self-congratulation. Dave reached the main exit at reception with its pair of large glass doors. He looked forward to striding outside and filling his lungs with fresh air to clear the stresses of the day.

'David Fletcher, I thought you'd exit this way,' said a voice from behind him as he opened the full-glass left front door. Dave froze as he wondered whether a rep had arrived without an appointment. Instantly, he prepared to send the man packing with the words; Sorry, I don't see anyone without an appointment. I close my office at 5 o'clock. Please make an appointment tomorrow before 4:30. Thank you. It was his usual reply, but it froze on his lips as he saw the man lounging in one of the two comfy reception chairs. This overweight and dishevelled man was not a typical salesman. Then, with a stab of surprise and anxiety, he grasped who the voice belonged to and did not want to admit the man could have the audacity to be there waiting for him to leave.

Dave turned and faced the overlarge figure seated near the reception exit. 'I presume you are Nathan Daniels. What are you doing here?'

'Waiting for you, of course.'

With a scowl, Dave realised it was the same old psychological control – trying to put someone off guard. A way of making sure he was unprepared to defend any argument. He disliked these kinds of people. They always thought it would give them the upper hand. Then he suppressed a thought that asked whether this was how major problems started. With his mind racing, he stared at Nathan, his hand frozen on the open door.

The man stared back with a look of disdain, as if he were talking to someone beneath his intellect. 'I've come over to offer you a meeting over supper. I thought we could go to Cath's Coffee Club round the corner.'

'You're supposed to arrange a convenient day and time beforehand, Mr Daniels. This is not the right time. I'm busy tonight and need to get home first.'

'Let's go now then, just for a coffee. I've brought the journal; it's in my car. I take it Amber has kept you informed about our negotiations?

Dave nodded. He didn't trust himself to say anything as he wondered why Daniels had not followed up on his appointment with Amber.

'Good. Can I offer you a lift?'

Getting into this man's car was something he wanted to avoid at all costs. He didn't want to be indebted to the man, no matter how small the accepted favour was. 'No, I'll walk. My car's parked near the walkway to Cath's. Why do you want to see me so urgently, and why are you not dealing with Amber?'

'Because I've examined the JPEG Amber gave me and I've discovered something that I think you should view personally. Also, I believe you did the original research on this, your err… project.'

Despite his feelings to the contrary, Dave had to admire Daniel's gall and skill at finding him. Then sudden dread made his heart pound. Had the man seen through Amber's digital manipulation? He examined Nathan's face closely to see if he showed signs of anger or distrust. All he could see was alertness and possibly a hint of excitement behind the half-closed eyes and permanent sneer. 'Discovered what?' he hissed.

'I'll tell all over that cup of coffee you may like to buy me.'

'No way. You should pay; you press-ganged me into this meeting.'

'You'll be glad to buy once I've explained what I've worked out. You can't deny me access to your project after this big reveal.'

'Really.'

'I'm getting somewhere with this. I'm going to be of huge use to you and your daughter.'

***

Cath's Coffee Club was a tasteful coffee shop much frequented by local workers and lower management alike. Even now, at 5:30, it was busy. Dave entered through the chrome and white door; he spotted Nathan seated with a coffee and a large slab of cream cake. With his heart still pounding, he walked to the counter and bought a cappuccino, then took his time finding the money to pay. Although Nathan had chosen a corner table at the back of the room, he doubted he would cause a scene to draw attention. He noticed a few familiar faces and a fellow manager who would come to his aid in an aggressive argument.

He sat opposite Nathan and leaned forward to meet his silent stare. The man's trying another controlling tactic by not speaking or offering any polite niceties, Dave decided, and glared back, then took a sip of the scalding hot coffee. With his mouth now tender, he carefully swallowed and continued to prepare a defence of the Photoshop-altered document on Amber's behalf.

After another few seconds, Nathan replied, 'I thought it best I meet you straight away after examining Amber's document thoroughly. I've compared the handwriting style and its general grammatical arrangement to the text in the journal and made a startling discovery.'

Feeling simultaneously alarmed and relieved, Dave cursed to himself. It looked like he's worked out something new in our document. To play for time whilst thinking about how to handle the development, he asked, 'Have you brought the journal in here so I can verify what you've discovered?'

'I haven't told you what I've discovered yet.'

'Let's not play games, Nathan. You've brought the journal with you?'

'I have.' his eyes darted to the floor, and Dave noticed a bulging carry-case of the kind some artists used.

'Let me look through it first, then we can sort out how to progress the work.' He would have to give Nathan some kind of access to their project, but this was getting tricky to work out. Examining the book may give him time to get the approach right.

'Very well. Let's see if you can come to the same conclusion as I have, and before you start, who did you say wrote your document?'

'I don't believe Amber told you.'

'Who then? I want to know before I allow you to read the diary in my possession.'

He was about to blurt out Linda Richardson, but managed not to. Dave felt guilty at withholding as much information as possible, but with this man, they had no other choice – at least until they knew more about him, his backer, and how he planned to progress his investigation. Dave knew that behind any other motive Nathan voiced was an almost uncontrolled need for publicity, and behind that was greed and a lust for treasure. He suspected it didn't matter whether it was obtained legally or not. 'We have not been able to find the identity of the author.'

'Shame,' Nathan sneered. 'Luckily for you, I have this diary which will shed some light on that.'

Everything he said made Dave's blood boil. But he followed every movement as Nathan placed the case on the table and slowly removed a thick tome enclosed in bubble wrap. His internal seething changed in an instant to anticipation. He could not wait to confirm Amber's theory about the ripped-out page.

After carefully removing the bubble-wrap, Nathan produced a large, battered leather book with embossed gold lettering. As Nathan handed the tome over, he didn't stop staring, looking for Dave's reaction. The reinforced edges were even more worn than the rest of the cover. Dave carefully opened the book to reveal the first page. The dirty sepia-edged contents were thick and ragged, unlike sharp-edged paper. Without actually turning the page, Dave knew the internal sheets were burnished, wove paper. He ignored the malignant stare and concentrated on the volume before him. Dave noted the journal cover was in poor condition – split down the spine, the back and front covers frayed, bent, and damaged to the extent that the internal vellum board showed.

With all the respect due to such an old tome, he turned to the first page. It was handwritten and named Reverend Dalmont and dated 1727 to 17...

The end date was missing, as if the journal had never been finished.

Beneath these dates, Dalmont had written – *This diary will record my daily affairs, my travels, and all that befalls me in the times after my ordination into the Lord's clergy. It will be a thankful observation of divine providence and decency toward me and a summary of my life.*

He went to the next page and its first entry.

On the day of Our Lord, 9th March, 1727.

All the first 14 pages appeared to be entries from the Reverend's life journey to the part where rumours of Linda's sect began in his parish. Dave skipped its content but pretended to be interested in the text as he assessed the journal's size, the texture of the paper, and its colour. Everything looked right, the dimensions, the colour of the ink, and... In a full minute, he had reached the last page, and another revelation became apparent– there was more missing than only the page that had their stones illustration and the pages that Nathan had already copied and sent to Amber. Half of the diary was missing, going by the amount of ragged page ends that were still sewn into the spine. Then he noticed the final three page stubs had been neatly removed with a scalpel or pair of scissors. The last remaining written page ended in familiar text, and he read the last line. *I will tell no one, ever, for my word to the great priestess is my bond.* What had the Reverend needed to hide to force him to tear out the rest of the diary, and how had the Richardsons, and perhaps Linda, come into possession of the only other surviving page with its information and illustration? What had happened to the last entries? There must have been about 20 pages looking at the number of stubs. He felt sure Dalmont would not have stopped writing the diary despite his sudden loss of faith. Then he had a thought and leafed back through to the front. One more page had been removed halfway through the diary, and another bottom half of a page, had been cut away with a sharp edge, suggesting a knife slicing it away. The last line on the half page said.

So I have the Lord's blessing and will move to my own new parish. Bishop Rundle has recommended me to look after this church's flock, who he said are much in need of the Lord's guidance...

Nathan wrenched Dave's concentration away.

'I see you're puzzled as to why those particular pages were removed.'

'I am, yes.' It was time to see what else he could draw from Nathan without giving much in return. Surprisingly, he felt no remorse at using him; after all, it was how the man was treating Amber, and now himself.

'I take it you haven't got these or the other pages, Nathan?'

'Of course I have not! I wouldn't have needed to come to you if I had.'

'Some pages have been removed by a sharp knife or pair of scissors. This would suggest another hand was involved. Someone who had more time to carefully remove the pages rather than just tear them out. Perhaps it was you?'

'No. Not me.'

Dave gave him a long stare, but felt the man's denial looked genuine. 'I'd need time to read the whole of this volume to try to theorise what he did with the missing pages. Even then, it's possible he destroyed them, or they disappeared in the following years.'

'Dalmont removed them, I'm convinced, and the reason is surely obvious.'

Dave felt himself bristle but remained civil with an effort. 'How about you tell me?'

'The missing pages can identify the treasure's location. He's removing the whereabouts from any investigation by the Gloucestershire Sheriff or from people trying to trace the valuable items in the future. The pages may, of course, exist in an archive somewhere. One was certainly well preserved – the one in your possession.'

Dave froze. He'd worked it out. But of course, he would have compared the torn edge on the stone's JPEG to the spine of his document. Maybe it was Amber's error. She should have cropped the document tighter, but she had wanted it to look like the real page in every way. Now that Amber's little secret was out, he felt relieved. At least he would not have to talk around the discovery. 'Yes, of course I was about to get to that.'

'Reverend Dalmont must have been a meticulous and accurate artist; he'd have been a good colleague to have recording finds in a dig team.'

Thoughts and theories tumbled through his head. Why had Nathan said that when the drawing and text were by Linda? But Nathan had no idea that they had identified Linda as the priestess. Then the reason blasted through his head like a shockwave. Not possible, surely, he thought, and blurted, 'You think our Stones document and your diary were both written by the same hand?'

'Of course. I compared the handwriting. I'm a mean graphologist as well as my other talents, so I noticed the styles were identical.'

It had not been Linda who had written the text around the illustration, but Reverend Edgar Dalmont. How had he not spotted the similarity before? It was an obvious conclusion to draw. He, Amber, and Ben should have guessed before now. This was what Nathan was being so smug about and why he'd insisted on dragging him here straight from work. The vile man had also decided Dave was the project leader, not Amber.

His silence encouraged Nathan to lean forward so Dave could smell the coffee the man had just consumed. 'So now I've furthered your project for you. I want something in return.'

'What if Amber and I paid for a meal tomorrow night? Would that be recompense?'

'Of course not. I had in mind being a full member of your project with access to anything else you discover. For starters, I want a look at the original of the page you hold.'

'You can't,' he snapped. 'It's in a private archive. We were only allowed to photograph it without taking it away.'

'Then get me access to that archive.'

'Again, I can't. It was a private viewing allowed by its owner, who wants to remain anonymous.' The necessary lies seemed to build on previous lies and flowed out of his mouth as if he were used to regularly creating such stories. Dave felt guilty at deceiving Nathan and knew he had to offer the man something, but what that could be without handing him and his backer domination of their project was difficult to work out. He had just done more to progress their project than they usually managed in a week. But first, he had to discuss the problem and

Nathan's information with Amber and Ben. Perhaps the best way forward was to meet Nathan's backer and work out how much this shadowy figure was financing and controlling him. He could think of only one harmless thing to give Nathan. 'Let me put it to Amber and to the other member of our team.'

'The other person is...?'

'Ben Tarrant.'

'Ahh... I've never met him, but I believe he's a good all-around archaeologist with sideline skills in meticulous historical research. You've done well to get him on board.'

'We think so too.'

'Oh yes, I've just realised he's a member of the finds department in Amber's Trust. She must work with him every day. Is it on a friend helping a friend out basis?'

'Not at all. It's a professional arrangement.'

'Let's leave it at that,' Nathan leered at his own innuendo.

Anger flooded Dave's head, and he knew his face was turning crimson, but before he boiled over, the man clapped his hands on his knees and stood, scooping up the diary and re-wrapping it in one swift motion. 'I'll be off now, my friend. I look forward to hearing from you and Amber. Perhaps even from Ben.' He took two steps, then turned and, with a malevolent look, said, 'You owe me now – don't forget.'

Dave glared and said nothing. Then watched Nathan until he was out of the cafe and gone.

CHAPTER EIGHT

The drive over to her parents' home took longer than usual, as a crash had blocked the A40, so she had to detour with a stream of traffic along minor roads. She arrived late, tired, and hungry. Dave's Toyota was butting the garage door so that Ben's Ford could fit in next to her mother's Honda.

Amber parked in the road and walked quickly up the drive to get out of the cold November wind. Liz opened the front door moments after her daughter had walked to it. She gave her mother a quick hug, noting the dark, puffy lines under her mother's eyes. She had not been sleeping well.

'Everything okay, Mum?'

'Yes, dear, I'm fine.'

But she wasn't. Amber knew her mother too well and guessed the problems with her tormentor at the social club had deepened. 'Is that horrible woman giving you aggravation still?'

'Oh, you mean Cowpat?'

'Who?'

'I can't bear to call her by her real name, but I can handle the woman. I have many friends that'll take my side if she tries to take my place as vice-chair. I get the impression she thinks I'm doing a lousy job.'

'You were voted into the post and have done everything required of you – and I bet, to a very high standard.'

'I know, and I am meticulous. But you know… that woman is so, so…' She left the sentence hanging, her face showing her frustration.

'If I can help... you know, come along to a meeting and draw her to one side for a word.'

'No, it's all under control, Amber. Don't worry.' She smiled in reassurance.

Amber wasn't so sure but decided to press the matter no further and nodded, then told of her frustrating journey and asked if she could make her mother a cup of tea.

'No dear, I'll make you one and a sandwich, then watch this evening's soap instalment. The characters invented problems will cheer me up.'

Amber excused herself and rushed upstairs with the laptop bag, tapping against the banisters.

'Oh God, guys, you wouldn't believe the journey here. It was horrendous.'

'No worries,' Ben said. 'You're here now.'

'Have the comfy seat,' offered Dave as they hugged.

Amber relaxed into it, and they had a few seconds discussing the recent increase in traffic problems. Liz came upstairs, handed her a mug of coffee and a plate filled with ham and cheese sandwiches, and disappeared back downstairs.

Amber cradled the mug as Dave said, 'I have something of a problem to report.'

In a moment, he had the others' undivided attention.

'It's Nathan – he wants in with us. The vile man sought me out after work, and I'm sorry to report he's bypassed you, Amber.'

'The total shit,' she spat.

'He is,' Dave said with as much distaste. 'The problem is compounded further because he has provided us with some important background to our search, and I can verify that he did not fabricate it to suit his ends.'

'Okay. Most important facts first,' said Ben.

'I discovered our document was definitely ripped from a journal written by a Reverend Dalmont, which he began in 1727.'

'That was what I was going to announce. I also knew about the Reverend and the journal,' said Amber in astonishment, feeling deflated.

'I see,' said Ben, and his eyes looked distant as Dave saw him assessing the information.

'Nathan forced a meeting on me as I left work; the damned man accosted me as I walked through reception. He convinced me to accompany him to a cafe where he showed me the journal...' Dave explained his idea of checking the journal and seeing if their document fitted it. 'Then, as I was getting more annoyed with his imposed company, he dropped a bombshell – and unfortunately, he's correct. Our document is the work of Dalmont and no one else. However, Linda could still be the illustration's artist, but not now the only prime player in our research. I believe the Reverend is a main character as well.'

'Looks that way,' Amber muttered as she clicked up the email attachment of Nathan's pages on her laptop. 'Linda is still central to finding the stones, though. She is the head priestess, after all. It still stands that every ceremony conducted at the stones at that time was instigated and run by her.'

'True. It looks, however, that Dalmont may have been taking on a more prominent role, going by Nathan's journal's last entry.'

'I think Dalmont has thrown in his allegiance with the pagan cult,' Amber suggested. 'The first paragraph of our translated document has the words - and we must assume it's written by him. *Now I have cast aside my worldly existence and dedicated my life to that of guardian of this holiest of places.* Perhaps he wanted to protect them both, so he ripped the offending pages out.'

'Perhaps she dictated what she wanted him to say.'

That stopped the conjecture as they all thought through that possibility and other scenarios.

'Perhaps she couldn't write.'

'No, she was an educated lady from a well-to-do family. She would have had a basic level of literacy taught by her mother and then a private tutor to educate her further. Many families did this confidentially at the time so as not to suffer the public disapproval of a high society that scorned educating female children to the same standard as their male siblings.'

They lapsed into contemplative silence.

Minutes later, both she and Ben had reread Nathan's last text and had agreed with both her and Dave's assumption. The discussion progressed into what Nathan had demanded in return for the latest document.

Dave stood and started pacing the small room. It was a habit he could never get out of. His excuse was that it helped him think. 'I feel guilty about lying to Nathan about the source of our document, but we cannot allow him to attend our meetings and accompany us on any excursion to the proximity of the site. I mean, okay, we still don't have a clue as to its location until we get the last translation through, but I don't want to share anything until we meet his backer.'

'I've got it,' Amber said in an overly loud voice. Her smile showed the sudden solution she'd just had. 'We get a solicitor to create a legal non-disclosure agreement with Nathan, which will constrain him in writing not to disclose the stone's location when found, nor give any associated information to his backer.'

'Yes, excellent, an NDA should cover us,' Ben relaxed as he mulled her answer over. 'Agreed.'

'As I understand it,' Dave began in his slow, precise delivery as he paced, 'An agreement should state that an NDA is a legally binding contract that requires all people involved to keep confidentiality for a period of time. I think that period should be as long as we can possibly get to give us time to register the site and get a team in there to professionally map and excavate it.'

'That's how I see it as well,' Amber added. 'It's up to us to decide what would be considered confidential and what is not. I think a solicitor could draw this up, and Nathan and his backer, and we too, will have to sign it. That would stop Nathan, and whoever else he has behind him, from going public if we strike the archaeological find of the century.'

'Okay, it looks as if we can properly tie him down,' Ben agreed in a satisfied tone.

'I'm looking up what happens if he breaks the agreement,' Dave muttered as he stared at his laptop screen. 'Here it is... "In almost all cases involving an NDA transgression, you'll be able to pursue damages stemming from a breach of contract."'

'Good, I expect we could nail him with copyright infringement too, trade secret misappropriation, breach of legal duty, and any other violation I can think of,' Amber added, then realised she had let her anger show. 'Sorry, but he really is an annoying man.'

'Understandable, Amber, he must be as unpleasant as rumours suggest,' Ben consoled her. 'But we still need that last translation to see if it contains directions. If it does not, then our only other avenue is to try to trace the missing pages from Dalmont's diary and hope they contain location information, and that's going to be a tall order. I agree with Nathan that the pages must have contained sensitive information that the author wanted to keep anyone from discovering.'

'This all revolves around whether more pages still exist. I have a gut feeling they may be hidden, in the same manner our manuscript page was.' Dave felt a thrill course through him – it would be really interesting to begin such a specific document hunt.

Amber was still thinking about their illustration page. 'I should get our last translation through tomorrow – but it is Saturday. If it doesn't arrive Monday, I'll chase it up and say it's urgent.'

'I'll phone our family solicitor and discuss the NDA solution with him on Monday as well,' Dave said. 'Then we can give Nathan our conditions and see if he'll agree.'

'He will,' Ben added. 'I know this type of publicity seeker. He'll try to find some way of profiting from anything he's included in.'

'I really dislike the man,' Amber added again, as if stating her dislike would somehow make him easier to bear, but all that happened was that the anxiety over his inclusion increased further.

'It will all work out, my dear.' Dave massaged his daughter's shoulders. 'Let's move on for now and discuss Dalmont and see if we can fathom what made him tear out pages from his diary.'

'Sure,' Amber whispered, then stretched her arms out and laid them gently in her lap. The action seemed to reset her emotions, and she focused on Dalmont's long-gone story.

'It seems to me that something desperate must have happened for him to ruin his personal diary, Dave continued. 'Many educated people wrote diaries back then as a way of making sense of an uncertain life and to record personal tragedies as well as life's big events and decisions. With a religious man like Reverend Dalmont, it would also have been a way of affirming his beliefs and to give praise to God.'

'Yes, that's an accurate assessment, Dave. I've just reread, in detail, the extraordinary account Amber emailed yesterday. I'm wondering what Dalmont's motivation was for wanting to return to more ceremonies. It comes over that he, too, was smitten by Linda's beauty. She sounds quite empathetic as well. A good leader, I reckon.'

'I think, in time, it is possible that he will have tried to turn the pagans from their religion back to Christianity,' Amber suggested. 'But it must have been a hard path to tread; I suspect they may have got fed up with him and maybe offered him to their Gods as a sacrifice.'

'Human sacrifice is a flight of fancy, Amber,' Dave added.

'Maybe, but he saw fresh bloodstains on their butterfly altar.'

'Could be animal blood, not human,' Ben offered.

'We may never know the end to this incredible tale,' Amber felt let down thinking about the ice-cold 300-year-old trail.

'Unfortunately, we won't know unless we find the other missing pages. Historical research, without any other written source to draw from, often ends in dead ends,' Ben said sadly. 'I fear this is the last we'll ever know about the good Reverend. He most likely burnt the missing pages to stop the church authorities or the local sheriff from learning more.'

'But someone else could have ripped out the pages to protect a secret.' Amber spoke as the scenario came to her. 'I suppose, if he found out something this sect wanted kept secret, they could have murdered him, raided his rectory, and found the book...'

'... Then destroyed the pages. Whatever happened, we may never know.' Dave rubbed his hands together and then clasped them. 'How about if there are two people involved in removing pages? He seems meticulous, a man after my own heart, so he cut out those with a clean edge and later someone else hastily ripped out the others.'

'Very plausible,' Ben nodded.

Amber felt her heart rate increase in elation; their discussion had revealed important background. She felt an overwhelming need to find out what had befallen the enigmatic pair. 'Let's keep going. There are signs of being able to progress on this. We also have the translation of the last paragraph of our document to come.'

'Yes, let's not get our hopes up yet, though,' said Ben. 'I have a few, let's say, personal resources for wheedling out historical secrets. I'll see what they can come up with.'

Dave had resumed pacing; now he was stroking his beard as well. 'So, let's see if Nathan has any other information he can offer us. Email him the conditions for him to join our select group, Amber. Let's see if he agrees.'

'I'll do that tomorrow first thing,' Amber said.

They exchanged more conjecture on the stones' location and whether Linda could have kept her own diary, or even whether she had shared the Reverend's diary, and it was her entries that were missing.

'Interesting theories,' Dave summed up. 'Let's keep digging,' he decided in an upbeat tone, missing the pun he'd accidentally muttered.

Ben left, and Amber joined her father and mother in the lounge until Liz suggested her daughter looked as if she needed some sleep. Her parents stood at the front door as Amber waved from the open car window and then pulled out of their driveway.

As she drove home, Amber hoped the next few days would provide enough information to keep the project alive. She really felt the dedication the woman had for her cause. It was almost as if she were living Linda's story now.

***

The weekend passed without any of the three announcing further progress on the project. Amber emailed Nathan early the next morning with their conditional acceptance of his inclusion, clearly stating the NDA condition. That made her feel better, so she carried out household chores for the morning whilst checking her inbox constantly. There was no further communication from Nathan, Ben, her father, or from TransGlobal with their translation. She went for a catch-up with a girlfriend on Saturday evening. Sunday floated past in a similar relaxed fashion. The evening saw Amber in front of the TV with a glass of red wine and her feet tucked under her on the sofa. Later, her bed beckoned, and she slept soundly until her mobile rang. She groped for the device.

It was her father calling at 2:14 in the morning – that could only mean one thing – trouble.

'Hello Dad, you okay?'

'Apologies, Amber, I've some bad news. I'm with Mum in the hospital. We've had a break-in. But don't worry, she's alright, not hurt at all, she's just in shock and has some bruises from being tied up and gagged.'

'Tied up, gagged, oh my God. Oh no – what's going on? Are you sure she's alright? Oh no ... can't believe it.'

'Someone broke in when she was there and surprised her. Crept up on her from behind...'

Amber paced out of the bedroom, then back as she tried to catch up. 'Why... I mean, not you as well.'

'I've been trying to find a few minutes to get hold of you. We've been here since 12:45 this morning.'

'I'm getting dressed and coming right over. She needs my help.' As Amber spoke, she gripped the phone between her chin and shoulder whilst struggling into jeans and then grabbed yesterday's fleece top. 'Not your home as well... When did this happen? Where were you?'

'It was about 10 o'clock, an hour before I got home from visiting my old friend Reg.'

'Oh God, this is awful. I'm coming over now. Take care, Dad. Please. I'm leaving now.'

In minutes, she was accelerating her car down the road and onto the fastest route out of town. Luckily, at that time of day, there was little traffic and no police to catch her speeding.

Beneath her confusion and near panic, thoughts about the stones project tumbled over concern for her mother. She and Ben had insisted that all the circle documentation was hidden or deleted. It was good planning, she realised with relief. But Dave was so methodical with backup files, he may have left a duplicate file on a flash drive. She pulled over into a layby to phone her father, 'You still at the hospital, Dad?'

'Yes, love,' said the croaking, tired voice.

'Mum still okay?'

'Yes, she is. She's sleeping and I'm still here with her.'

'Good, that's the most important thing. I must ask – are you sure everything to do with our project is still secure?'

'I've hidden everything. Nothing's been stolen. I haven't left any files on the laptop, and I hid the external and flash drives.'

'Are you certain, Dad? I mean the manuscript itself ...'

'...Is still concealed in the Welsh dresser, and the drives are elsewhere where no one but I can find them.'

'Have you checked this hidden place?'

'Yes, while I was waiting for the ambulance. Don't worry, everything is under control, Amber.'

'That's good, Dad, I'm coming straight over to the hospital. But one last thing – how about your camera and laptop with their digital copies?'

'I had the laptop in the car last night when I was out at Reg's place. It wasn't necessary to delete its files; the thing is always with me...'

'And the camera?'

'I found it, damaged... scratched, but I still have it.'

'What about its SD card?'

'Oh,' the voice on the phone suddenly deflated, and Amber knew bad news was coming. 'I forgot to check that. We'll discuss this when you've seen your mother.'

The line went dead, and Amber knew what he was going to find later.

The journey to Gloucester hospital was on empty roads but in driving rain. Luckily, it was too early for rush-hour traffic. It took two hours with her car sliding and aquaplaning on surface water. As Amber drove, she battled with thoughts that all this trouble was her fault. If she had not given Nathan the section of the manuscript to translate, he would have never known they had a document to obsess about. But then, a normal academic would not be so desperate for fame that they would go to any lengths to obtain information. But he was clever. There was no evidence to say Nathan had anything to do with the break-ins. He may just have said too much to his unscrupulous backer. It was a good move on their behalf to insist on meeting this backer and get whoever he or they were to sign the NDA. As she negotiated the route through Gloucester, Amber sighed, What was done could not be undone.

It was almost six o'clock and still as dark as a bat cave when Amber pulled into the brightly lit area of the hospital's multi-story car park. Minutes later, she ran into the reception and was told her mother was still in a cubicle in A&E.

In minutes, she reunited with her parents. Her mother looked pale and had bruises on her face and raw weals on her arms.

'So glad you're here,' whispered Liz.

Amber sat on the bed to cuddle her. Dave sat on a chair on the other side, looking tired and worried.

An hour later, a doctor came round and, after a thorough examination, discharged her mother.

'Do you want breakfast in the canteen here?' Dave asked Liz.

'No, I want to get home. There's a lot of mess to clear up, and the police said they would be over to investigate this morning.'

'They only agreed to do that because of the assault,' growled Dave.

Amber didn't feel like speaking, so she just kept her arm linked with her mother's as they waited at the main hospital entrance for Dave to bring his car from the multi-story car park to collect Liz. When she got back to her car, she texted the situation to Ben.

Back at the house, they settled Liz into an armchair, made coffee, and then Dave drew Amber into the study, where he voiced his concerns. 'So, is it a coincidence that Nathan Daniels sought me out at my workplace yesterday? Then this has happened. I'm not saying he did it personally, but I think we must insist on finding out exactly who his backer is.'

'Agreed, and we want to meet him in person, not simply a PA spared from a busy schedule. I've heard all the excuses when companies pretend they want to fund an archaeological project, but are concealing other motives. I imagine part of Nathan's agreement is that he has to keep this mysterious partner fully informed. We should wonder what exactly the guy wants from all this.'

'How do you mean?'

'Well, if we find the stones, does the company behind the backer want to open it as a tourist attraction? Perhaps they'll lean on the landowner first to sell the land. I mean, we're being lent on in a very nasty way where each break-in gets more disruptive.'

'Yes, Liz tied up and bruised – what next? Perhaps we ought to warn Ben.'

'I've texted him. He's asking that we keep him fully in the picture.'

'I'm going to check the camera for its SD card,' Dave mumbled, and the distressed look on his face grew even more.

Cradling a mug of coffee, Amber went through to the lounge to stay with her mother. They sat in companionable silence as the sound of Dave moving around upstairs reached down to them. Her mother's social club problem never came up, and Amber thought it best not to add to her mother's upset. Amber looked at the time on her phone. 12:25, then noticed she had three missed calls from her line manager, Craig Dalgarth. She had forgotten to phone into the department. No one would have fielded phone calls from potential sponsors and contracts. Craig would have asked people if they knew where she had gone. She dialled him. He picked up on the third ring.

'Yes, Amber. Where are you?'

'I'm so sorry, Craig. I'm in the middle of a family crisis.' Her emotions were about to bubble over. Actually, saying the word crisis seemed to be the trigger.

'My God, Amber. What's happened?'

She told him as concisely as she could. By the end of the call, she was in tears, and Craig soothed her and said she'd missed nothing of consequence, and to only return to work when she felt able to.

'Thanks, Craig, I'm so grateful,' she sniffed, aware her voice was tremulous, her shaking hand barely held the phone as she broke the connection.

'I'm fine, dear, don't you worry about me,' offered Liz as she took her daughter's hand.

'Thanks, Mum. But what next? Is Ben going to be mugged on the off chance he has a related document on him? And what about Dad and you? Will they come back here again and hold you both hostage?' She sniffed again, letting the concerns out seemed to bolster her resolve. 'I hate that man,' she snarled as her mood turned.

'Which man, Dear?'

'Nathan Daniels. He's involved in this crime right up to his neck.'

'Is it all worth it? I mean, the whole document is a complete fantasy.'

Amber realised Dave had not kept his wife up to speed with Nathan's journal. The seventeenth-century mystery was building up to something – and she needed to know what was written in the missing pages. The Reverend was a competent writer, maybe he had done something to gain the displeasure of the pagans and they'd bumped him off, and one of them had ripped the evidence from the journal...

Dave chose that moment to arrive back in the living room. Instantly, she knew something was wrong.

'The SD card is gone. I've checked to make sure I hadn't left it in the laptop port or that it had not somehow fallen on the floor in the study. It's gone, I'm afraid, and now Nathan's criminal friends have a lead on us.'

'Oh no,' Amber gasped as she stared and took in the implications. 'They're going to realise I've doctored our document when they compare the two. Nathan will be asked today to translate the missing text. Damn, damn, damn – what are we going to do, Dad?'

'We need to know what those last lines contained, or we just become passengers in Nathan's discovery and his subsequent publicity. Phone Transglobal and say we need the translation urgently. Get them to email it straight away.

Then we can see if the content gives them a lead on us or not.'

'I'll do it now.'

'Can you two go upstairs to discuss your fantasy schemes? It's all giving me a headache,' moaned Liz. 'I'd be much happier if you dropped this silly game altogether.'

I really can't give this up now, Amber thought and walked away without consoling her mother. In moments, she was climbing the stairs and pressing the contact details to connect the call to the USA. It would be about 9:00 in the morning over there, she realised as she glanced at the time. The phone picked up on the fifth ring, and an American voice with a New York accent answered.

'Hello, this is Amber Dorsett here. I'm phoning over the translation I've asked for.'

'Wait a minute, Lady, I'll get your details up,' she heard sounds of a keyboard being tapped. 'Only just got the PC going, it's as cold in this office as it is out on the boulevard this morning...' the voice rambled on.

Amber remained quiet and kept her impatience to herself.

'Ah, here we are. You are fourth on the list. I'll get onto it late tomorrow.'

'I need it today, please.'

'Afraid I cannot comply. I have a language convention to attend on 43rd Street this afternoon.'

'Can someone else do it then? It has become very urgent. Someone who thinks the translation means something it probably doesn't has burgled us.'

'Well, possibly. I have a student who does piecework translations for me. Bethany is in her second year at Cornell University and is majoring in Latin. She is becoming quite adept at translating. For a further fee of 50 dollars, I'm sure she would leave whatever she was involved with to do an express translation. But she is not quite up to speed yet, so I can't guarantee her interpretation of various 17th or 18th century peculiarities is spot-on, and I won't be able to go through it for verification.'

During a few seconds of silence, Amber mulled it over, then decided she had no choice. 'Yes, alright, we can work around one or two vague points, I'm sure. I'll pay if I have to, but I want it in my inbox after lunch – your time.'

'Very well, Lady, you have my word. It'll be with you. Your credit card number, please...'

She paid and finished with, 'Please ensure the translation is with me. It's urgent.' There was something about the translator she didn't trust. He was only after an extra fee, she was sure, and doubted there was an assistant at all.

'Will do, Ms Dorsett,' said the voice and broke the connection.

It really was another mistake going to Transglobal. I must try not to make these silly errors, she berated herself. But how was she to know?

'That's all you can do, Amber,' said Dave, who'd picked up her side of the conversation.

'Let's give them until 6 o'clock our time, then I'll phone him again.'

'So how are we going to pacify Nathan. He's going to phone one of us when he finds out. I don't blame him if he turns nasty. We've misled him big time.'

'Let's see what the damn man has to say. I'll apologise to him if I have to, anything to try to keep him away. All is not lost; we still have the info on Linda and the origin of our document that he knows nothing about. Both will be good bargaining tools.'

'But will he beat us to the stones?'

'Get Ben in on this. We need a council of war.'

'That's a bit strong, Dad, but I get your point.'

It was 6:30 pm, and Liz was feeling well enough to help Amber prepare spaghetti bolognese for dinner. At Amber's urgent request, Ben had turned up straight from work, and she had made sure there was enough food for four.

'Thanks, guys, that's really thoughtful of you,' Ben said.

Amber thought he looked genuinely pleased. 'When would you have eaten, Ben? I mean, you couldn't have stopped off on the way here just now.'

'No, I guess I'd have got something later from that kebab van that hangs around the centre of Long Marsh.'

'That's not food, it's rubbish,' laughed Amber.

They sat around the table and began discussing general archaeological news. The whole problem with Nathan and their search for the stones became unreal, probably because of the two bottles of wine that Dave passed round at every opportunity. They chatted about nothing in particular and joked at every opportunity. Amber wondered whether Ben and her father were also fed up with the whole fantasy and thought it was time to forget the entire thing. Or, maybe, they were just releasing the tension with the alcohol and banter. She went along with the second option as she took another sip of Shiraz.

Then her phone pinged. One glance at the text brought their project back into focus. It was from Bethany at Transglobal.

Amber opened the attachment instantly and skipped the American woman's polite preamble.

CHAPTER NINE

She read the translation of the last long paragraph and gasped, 'Wow, guys, this is what we hoped for, listen up.' Amber cleared her throat and repeated in her best semi-sober oratory voice.

And so onto your journey. Take yourself to the good village of Colesford and hence into the woods surrounding Barkers End. Head northeast and you will, after two hours of enchanting journeying, observe a wooded valley filled with boulders clothed in moss and shaped like unholy monsters, these guard a multitude of ancient oak. Travel beyond this place to the sight of the Mountain God Tragarne's unusual rock, which can be observed on the eastern ridge at sunset. Go beyond this tree-bedecked ridge and circle round to the path worn by many creatures. Walk along this for two hundred steps to where sprites invite you to drink water pouring into their rock-pool. Follow the stream into a small depression with a wooded knoll at its centre. The Priestess has called this place Saintlow, which amuses the whole congregation as the name itself denounces their old beliefs. Then walk along this encircling watercourse clockwise to the two entrance pillars. Proceed within, then walk anticlockwise uphill until two large elms are framed between Goddess Deidre's two stones. Wait here for all the Gods to acknowledge you with the last rays of sunset. Then behold, you are within the temple, and wonders will be visited on you in great abundance. I will await you there to endow you with these great riches and instruct you on your future service to the all-knowing Gods.

'I'll get a road atlas,' Dave said and strode to a kitchen cupboard and fumbled with various cookery books and old, bent, and stain-covered 'How To' DIY books. After rummaging for a minute, he removed a large-format road atlas. Amber smiled as she realised the wine had affected his usual precise movements.

'Colesford is only an hour's drive away,' gasped Amber. 'Don't know Barkers End though.'

Ben bent over one side of the atlas as Dave opened it on the two pages showing the Welsh borders, Gloucestershire, and Herefordshire. Amber managed to view it through a gap between their heads. It took her a few moments to realise she had an arm around each of their shoulders as she peered down. It felt good, and not just around her father's shoulders, so she left her left arm around Ben, too. He didn't seem to mind. With an effort, she focused on the map.

Colesford was situated on the western fringe of the Forest of Dean and not far from the town of Monmouth, Barkers End was not on the map. Then Ben indicated a name in the smallest size type. She could just make out, in minute type, a small village called Barkend. 'That must be its modern name,' Ben muttered.

'I'm thinking it's near the famous Puzzlewood,' Dave said. 'That's a place of ancient woodland with caves and strange rock formations open to the public. It features loads of trails, so it's very unlikely to be the location for an undiscovered circle. It's a mass of moss-covered rocks and weirdly shaped trees as well, so going off-trail there will be hard going.'

'I know the place; they filmed a lot of TV and film sci-fi stuff there.'

'I'd also be surprised if our circle remains are anywhere nearby,' Amber added. 'It would have been discovered and listed years ago.'

'I've got their website up,' said Ben, as he showed them his phone. 'The rock formations look as if people have positioned stones in narrow ravines and gaps in the scowls.' He showed them the picture.

Amber read the blurb, 'Oh yes, scowls are rock formations, but none of these pictures look anything like Dalmont's stones illustration. We've got to look for somewhere outside the Puzzlewood location.

'I think I have an Ordnance Survey map of the area,' Dave stated.

'Can you lot carry on with this upstairs and leave me to load the dishwasher in peace?' asked Liz with an irritated note to her words.

Amber knew her father had a drawer full of OS maps in a cabinet in the living room, and suspected he would have that map. It would probably be indexed in proper alphabetical order. She and Ben could download the appropriate map to their phones later.

The two of them took the road atlas upstairs to the study and looked over it as they waited for Dave. The Forest of Dean covered quite a large part of one side of the double page, with a few villages breaking up the blanket green.

'If we go north from Barkend as the directions suggest, it brings us to...'

'Let's wait for Dave's map. It's only a big splodge of green on here,' Ben smiled. 'Or I could get the OS site up on my phone...?'

'No, give him his moment, he hasn't quite embraced the full scope of modern technology, I'm afraid,' Amber laughed, and they fell into a few minutes of conjecture before Dave returned ten minutes later with a map in one hand and a refilled glass of wine in the other. Amber envisaged him trying to focus on the map titles even with his reading glasses on. She laughed aloud at the thought and covered her mouth up hastily.

'You okay? Ben asked.

She managed a serious face and slurred, 'Of course.'

'Here we are. It's map OL14,' Dave said without noticing his daughter's amusement. 'It's always easier to view the real thing rather than look it up online.'

With a faint smile, Ben unfolded the map until it covered the whole desktop.

They poured over it with fingers tracing various trails and paths from Barkend.

'There, look,' exclaimed Amber. 'The name Saintlow Inclosure from the translation – and there's a stream nearby...'

'...Called Perryhay Ditch – it fits. That's our circle's location, I'm certain,' said Dave in triumph. 'I knew it wasn't all a fantasy. I knew it. We've got to get there before Nathan does. I'm going over there to walk it tomorrow.' With a finger, he traced a green-dashed line. 'There's a public footpath called Spruce Ride that looks as if it runs nearby.'

'You're working tomorrow, Dad. It's Tuesday.'

'I'll phone in sick.'

Amber raised her eyebrows in surprise, but said nothing, It was unheard of for her father to feign a sickie.

'Stop right there, Dave,' said Ben quickly. 'We have the Nathan problem to discuss first. The burglaries must be linked to our research. I mean, he will have been sent the pictures from the stolen SD card by now.'

'I've a plan to sort this. Why don't we come clean with the guy and invite him along? We don't want him going over there with dubious people delegated by his backer. It'll be best to have him where we can see him – with us. Getting him on our side is surely best now. I've got to soft-soap him with an apology too.' Amber surprised herself with her solution, although it meant not only talking nicely to Nathan but winning him over, too.

All three looked at each other, and Amber could see the two men balancing the risks of including a manic self-publicist on the trek with them, as opposed to the obvious problem of having him find the circle before they did.

'We need to know who his backer is, and if he's the one who is going to represent Nathan. I've a bad feeling about this anonymous financier. If they can break into both your houses, what else are they capable of,' Ben said.

'We don't know how deeply involved that bugger Nathan is in all this criminal activity, either.' Dave snarled. 'He certainly rubbed me up the wrong way. Nathan could be capable of anything dodgy, even trying to help someone force information from us.'

'He wouldn't dare try that on me,' Ben snapped with fists clenched.

It was the first time he had confirmed to Amber that he could take care of himself – and hopefully her and Dad too. Good, she thought, that's a confirmation of another reason why I wanted Ben in on the project.

'Why don't I phone him now and sound him out?' she suggested with growing resolve. 'We can wait to walk the area until Thursday, surely. With Nathan on board, I'm sure he won't try to organise his own search before that. Also, I'm sure I can get that day and Friday off,' Amber persuaded.

'Alright, phone him now Amber.'

'Do it, Amber,' added Ben.

She stabbed at her phone and strode into her old bedroom for privacy. Opening the door, she sat on the bed, psyching herself up, and took deep breaths to clear her Shiraz-fogged head. She examined her surroundings. The bed was made up neatly by her mother, and looking exactly as it always had. She had spent her childhood sleeping in this room and subsequently still stayed in it occasionally, especially during the traumatic months of legal hassle with her and Timothy's divorce proceedings.

Finally, she was ready and pressed the green connect symbol and heard Nathan's phone ring.

'Yes,' said a gruff voice three seconds later. He didn't sound happy.

'Hi Nathan. I've phoned to give you an apology and also to invite you along to something.'

'Apology? What are you on about, Amber?'

He sounded tired and, quite rightly, annoyed.

'First, I want to apologise for the RAW file format I sent our document in.'

'Why, it opened fine. It was completely legible.'

This wasn't what she expected him to say. He must have noticed something wrong with it, surely. 'Has your backer sent you another file of the illustration, probably yesterday?'

'Wha…?'

'A new file, or one including his translation.'

'Not heard any … … don't know why he would retranslate what I've done- …'

'He sent it to you today, then?' In the resulting silence, she imagined the unknown financier saying, why do I have to get to the truth for you. You've allowed yourself to be hoodwinked by this Dorsett family. So far, you have failed to find the hidden chalice, the ceremonial dagger, and the other artefacts. Get your act together.

'Wha for, you shent it to me. I sent him a copy of it.'

Her mind raced. It sounded as if he hadn't been sent the stolen, original file. What was Nathan saying? – It appeared he hadn't even been leant on to get results either.

The man sounded really drunk. He was clearly unhappy about something. She wondered whether Nathan had been threatened with something like, get some results pronto, Daniels, or you're toast. It was her turn to sound puzzled. 'You've had no communication from your backer about our document, then?'

'My backer has turned into a real arsehole. He accused me of incomp... etence and failing to get reshults amongst other shitty comments.'

Nathan slurred his next words so badly that they became incomprehensible. Amber heard the sound of a bottle being upended and gurgling liquid, probably emptying into a whisky glass. It could only be good news for her, Dad, and Ben. She dared to hope they could regain the advantage. 'What does he want from you now, Nathan?'

'Too much,' came back the miserable but clear response. 'They've given me a location where they believe there are... buried artefacts or some treasure. I've been told to get over there and check the place personally.'

'I'm sorry to hear they're leaning on you, Nathan.' Her mind raced as she spoke. The dodgy backer must want Nathan to pillage the site for purely financial gain or to find, then add, the chalice and the other items to a private collection. They had the correct photo and had the missing passage translated already. She, Dad, and Ben had a real problem now. Also, it appeared Nathan had no idea where the backer had got his information from and appeared to know nothing about the break-ins. She decided to question him without revealing anything about the stolen SD card and its contents.

'Can we please return to the photos of the document I sent?'

'...Amber, wha did you think was wrong with the file you sent me? I mean, I opened it fine, and it was in focus... competent drawing of a stone circle too. Can't be real...' he giggled and belched. She heard the slurping, gurgling sound again as he upended a bottle of spirits into his mouth.

'Sorry, Nathan. I thought I'd sent you a blurred low-res shot and that you must have struggled to read it. Dad said he took the first pictures by pressing the shutter without putting the camera on a five-second timer; then he took the accurate one without touching the shutter button.'

'Why do it that way, juust take the picture.'

'Because without the timer on, pressing the shutter causes camera-shake.'

'Thatsh okay Amber, it wosh good. When we going out for an evening again? I need some company.'

'We'll arrange a date if you tell me who this backer is and where he or they got this information about the circle's location from.'

'I don't know the answer to boff questions. I'm working through a second party... Receive a monthly cheque issued by Photon Venture Holdings. Tried a search engine or two with the name, but no reshults come back. Can't go scavenging around in woodland; but they told me I've got to.'

'What is the location they want you to search, Nathan?' It was the million-dollar question, and his answer would confirm their suspicions.

'It's shumewhere called Perryhay Ditch, near a place called Saintlow.'

Her heart skipped a beat. That confirmed their worst misgivings.

Nathan sounded really miserable, and she didn't have the heart to pressure him further. It was still better that he came along with them rather than search the location himself and give any finds to whoever was behind this holding company. 'Sorry to hear that, Nathan. I don't know how indebted you are to them, but look, we have a lead on the circle's location, too. How about joining us? We could then let you have your share of the resulting acclaim, and you could cut out your backer from this.'

'Thank you, Amber, thatsh appreciated. I don't want to fall and break a leg on my own. But I owe them. I can't afford to pay back the finances they've ploughed in.'

'You only owe them for work on this project. That must be a small fraction of the work you've completed for them – surely?'

'Thank you, Amber. That is a good argument. I'll use it in an email in response to them. The bastards... wish I never...'

She heard the sound of the bottle emptying into his mouth, followed by incomprehensible slurred words.

'Can we arrange that date now, Amber?'

He sounded really miserable. Despite her negative feelings for the man, she felt sorry for him. 'Okay. How about a Friday evening soon, 8 o'clock at the Stainton Eatery near me?

'Okay, tell me when.'

'I'll let you know. Just need to rearrange my diary.'

'Fankyou,' Muffled thumps and bangs came from her phone as he fumbled to break the connection.

Back in the study, Amber related the conversation.

'Interesting to see how the idiot's let himself be used just for the love of money,' snarled Dave.

'I'd say it's lucky he doesn't know of your deception, Amber. You were right to invite him along, though. Otherwise, he could have blundered around, and if by chance he found anything, he'd have either turned it into a publicity extravaganza or just looted the site if there was anything of removable value. My concern here is the depths of illegality this backer may be prepared to stoop to.'

'We need to persuade Nathan to fob them off for now,' Amber begun as she thought a solution through. 'We'll get him to sign the NDA, so he's legally bound to silence. If we find the stones, then Nathan will have to tell his backers we're still searching. It will give us a chance to schedule the site legally and come to an arrangement with whoever owns the land it's on.'

'Providing the land owner plays ball and keeps quiet, too,' Dave added. 'And providing it's not on common land too.'

'Common land is always owned by someone, like the local council.'

'Correct, but people usually have the right to walk on it or graze animals.'

'Good point, but back to the topic. This guy behind Photon Venture Holdings may hire someone else to look independently, then loot the site,' Ben added.

'I'm sure the stones will have fallen, over the years, and have become shrouded in brambles and ivy. They won't be able to shift any fallen stones manually without large lifting gear, either. So what is there for them to steal - only the unlikely possibility of buried ancient ceremonial items? Okay, we know it's possible for the chalice and other treasures to be buried there, but...'

'The stones may have been torn down and carted away for building stone by locals or the sheriff's watchmen. So the site will not be obvious without ground penetrating radar to find the sockets.' Dave said. 'We know of many sites that once had stone or timber circles, and their locations have only been discovered by a geophysical survey. There's no longer any evidence of them above ground at all.'

'Let's wait and see when we've found the site, Dad,' Amber felt the beginning of a thrill as she always did when field-walking a new archaeological site.

Ben looked up from his phone, where he was adding in a GPS location from the OS map. 'I'd like to trail along too.'

'Of course, I took it for granted you were going to be with us,' said Dave.

'I might have field-walked many locations, but I've never been on a speculative hunt like this,' Ben said with excitement giving his words an edge. 'But the thought of spotting a stone is tantalising. I don't expect to see upright stones, of course; they would be too huge to remain hidden. The whole jaunt is like some kind of real-life Boys-Own adventure.'

She tried to look serious. It was hard to keep her feelings from showing. Ben, with her and Dad – two of her favourite people together and doing what she loved; field-walking, chatting about archaeology, fantasising about the finds to come – perfect.

'You're on, guys. It'll be a kind of preliminary expedition,' she managed to sound professional. 'We have GPS on our phones and can add notes, discuss boulders that look like fallen stones ...'

'...Okay, hold on,' Dave interrupted. 'I'm 55 years old, so don't go marching off, and also remember to include me in your discussions if I'm puffing along behind you.'

'Sure thing, Dave,' Ben laughed, 'But I suspect Nathan won't be as fit as you.'

'You'll be fine, Dad, but we must make allowances for Nathan. One good thing, we have Thursday booked, fewer walkers around then.' Amber said, not wanting to think too much about Nathan plodding along and moaning about blisters or being scratched by brambles. She reached over to Dave's laptop and brought up Barkend on Google Maps. It showed a pub just outside the village that would be a good rendezvous point for them to begin the search. 'Here we are, guys, we meet here,' she pointed to a pub symbol. Amber's phone labelled it the Rising Sun. 'We can drive in one of the cars to the footpath start point and walk from there.'

They readily agreed, and she thumbed her phone to let Nathan know, and got the voice-mail service only. Nathan must have slumped into an alcoholic doze on his sofa. She left him a voice message. 'Hello Nathan. We'll meet you in The Rising Sun Inn just outside Barkend at 10 o'clock, Thursday this week - prompt. Bye.'

It was just before 10 o'clock before they were all parked. She and Ben transferred to Dave's 4x4 Toyota to chat and to drive the short distance to the footpath start.

'We can take the lane from here toward Cinderford,' Ben said as he checked the sat-nav on his phone. 'The Spruce Ride footpath bisects it.'

Nathan was not on time. With rising impatience, Amber left the front passenger seat and paced around the car park, and only got back inside the 4x4 when a yellow Ford pulled up. Nathan was almost an hour late before he tramped toward them.

'Sorry, sorry - traffic,' he mumbled and heaved a rucksack into the Toyota's boot.

'Okay,' she said, and Ben nodded.

Dave glared and stroked his neatly trimmed beard. 'Before we go, sign this NDA agreement.' He thrust it behind him from the driver's seat.

'No thanks.'

'You will, or you can get out and we'll drive off and leave you here.'

Reluctantly, Nathan grabbed Dave's clipboard and pen and scrawled his signature and date where shown.

Dave handed him a copy. 'Read it and abide by it.'

Nathan looked dazed and disappointed, but managed a nod.

With a smile, Amber noticed her father had even thought of placing a carbon copy sheet between the two documents.

'Introductions,' she began, ignoring the minor confrontation.

Nathan interrupted, 'I've met your father, and I watched a video of a presentation Ben gave last year on Roman kiln firing techniques. Could have tapped in a few points, but you seemed to get it over well, so didn't bother.'

'Thanks,' Ben said and returned to his sat-nav.

Why was it that every time this man spoke, it made her bristle? Perhaps he's more human when drunk, she thought unkindly.

'How far before we get out and walk?' Nathan asked. It sounded more like a moan than a question.

'Not far,' said Ben. Amber and Dave didn't bother to reply as Dave drove slowly along a single-track lane bordered by conifer and sycamore woodland. The sun was out and low in the late November sky. Last night had gone down to minus two, and even now the dashboard thermometer only showed plus-four. She had on her rainbow-coloured woolly hat with hanging tassels, bought from a stall at Glastonbury festival a few years ago when she and Tim were an item. Her hair was tucked inside the hat, and Ben commented on her, looking like a regular ego-warrior.

'I've no studs and earrings or body art,' she responded.

'You don't need them,' puffed Nathan.

How am I supposed to take that comment? she wondered and ignored the man. It was getting quite claustrophobic in the Toyota, with the heater on full blast and three men sitting too close to her. Two minutes later, they passed footpath signs pointing to a gated path on either side of the road, so Dave parked on a grassy verge close by.

It took ten minutes to put on thick jackets and for Dave to change from his driving shoes.

'Which way?' Nathan asked, and Ben pointed to the east path. 'I'm going to make a head start. You can all catch me up easily.'

Amber hoped they would cut cross-country from the path before they reached Nathan. He was bound to be plodding along and missing anything off-piste that looked worth investigating.

The cold was biting, but soon, trees around the footpath closed in and cut the icy breeze out. She had on her thick thermal mittens, the gaudy hat, and a padded shower-proof jacket. Dave had a woolly hat with a pom-pom on top, a thick waterproof done up tight round the neck, and a heavy rucksack. Ben didn't seem too bothered with the cold, with jeans, summer walking boots, and a thin fleece. But he also had a loaded rucksack, which Amber thought must contain waterproofs, food, and drink.

The path wound through trees, sometimes through marshy areas, and once over a stream still covered in ice. They all tried to peer through the shadows, where beams created by the low sun masked the woodland depths, to spot anything that resembled a fern-covered embankment concealing a ditch and a collection of fallen stones. They came across Nathan stumbling along around a sharp left bend shielded by shady conifers. He had mud splattered up the legs of his baggy black sports trousers. She was amused to see more wet mud on his backside and lower jacket, the obvious result of a slip.

'How are you coping?' she asked him with a note of sympathy as she viewed his sweat-streaked face.

'Slipped twice, grabbed a branch, got a splinter,' he mumbled.

'You'll soon get into a rhythm,' Ben said.

'You lead the way, Nathan, we'll go at your pace,' she suggested and realised he would be no good at looking to either side for any interesting features.

They stopped to turn right into trees where a ridge appeared to lead to a sharp drop onto lower ground. It became their first disappointment; the lower ground was devoid of trees and full of marsh grass. There was no sign of any ancient construction, and certainly no fallen stones. Back on the path, a left-hand turn found the track meandering downhill before being swallowed by more trees as it progressed uphill into the deep shadows of more conifer forest. They stopped for a break on a fallen tree trunk to eat sandwiches and drink cups of hot chocolate from a thermos flask.

'Another half hour and we'll have to turn back toward my car,' Dave said. 'We don't want to risk getting lost in the dark.'

Later, a sense of disappointment kept them all quiet. They had turned round on seeing the distant houses of Lower Soudley begin to appear beyond the thinning forest. Only one other hiker had passed them, and apart from that, they'd been alone as they searched. Amber's enthusiasm sunk to a new low, the whole trek had been fruitless.

'I always think the landscape looks different on a return journey,' Ben stated, hoping to keep their spirits up. 'Sometimes the trees open up to reveal distinct features we didn't spot before.'

'Fingers crossed,' she said, and Dave grunted.

Nathan sighed. 'Wild goose chase,' he whined.

'There's no choice but to walk the area, mate,' Ben responded.

'No, very true. I checked out the whole area from the aerial view on Google maps,' said Amber. 'The deep contrast of the trees hid almost everything beneath. Any visible open ground failed to reveal anything of interest.'

'I know. I've spent the last couple of evenings doing the same thing,' Ben added.

'You can't beat footwork in these investigations,' Dave added.

'It's all crap,' puffed Nathan as he staggered along, now with a slight limp. 'LiDAR survey would have shown anything interesting.'

They returned along this easy-to-follow route for an hour, stopping twice to look either side of the track at items of interest. One was a natural collection of boulders that interrupted the trees over a slight rise in the terrain, almost hidden by lengthening shadows.

It was soon pitch black, and their breath frosted the air as they heaved rucksacks into the car.

'We'll try the west track next time,' stated Ben unnecessarily.

No one replied. It had been a disappointing day.

'Shall we walk it on Saturday?' Amber broke the silence as the car stopped in the pub car park.

'If I have to,' said Nathan.

'If you don't come along, your backer will have something more to say. You won't get even a sniff at the acclaim when we've found the stones either. Going by everything you've said and some supposition by me, you could even end up with an arranged roughing up from them.' Ben lowered his voice to a more conciliatory level.

'Locating any archaeology is never easy and quick, as you well know. '

'Of course I know that,' Nathan spat. 'Okay, okay, count me in again.'

'It may be worth detouring into the surrounding trees more often,' Dave ignored the exchange. 'Maybe when we're off track, more hidden features will appear.'

'Well, we're on common land, so it's worth spending the extra time and effort,' Amber said in a tone that was full of false optimism to give them all a boost.

CHAPTER TEN

Matt pulled up in his narrow drive, relishing the clean-up job and the detail it would reveal. Luckily, it had been a straight-forward journey, as he was so deep in thought the car seemed to have driven itself. He was desperate to get the find onto the kitchen table so he could carefully disentangle it.

Gathering his gear from the car boot in one sweeping movement, Matt rushed indoors and through to the kitchen to start the job. He savoured the fantastic thought of discovering what would appear from the clod of soil. He laid the dank-smelling lump onto newspaper on the table. With unsteady hands, he used a small screwdriver, a wooden spatula, and an ordinary cutlery fork to separate earth from metal. He was used to brute force as an auto-engineer, but this was an altogether different job at the opposite end of the scale. Late into the evening, he had the necklace unravelled and was surprised at how long a careful separation of the necklace's elements within the thick soil had taken. He had seen this meticulous unpicking done on TV and knew it was even slower when done with great care by experts. He was not one of those, so it had taken a mere five hours with a break for something to eat in the middle. He was again surprised to find the necklace was still intact apart from the missing clasp end.

About midnight, he finally laid it out to get an overall impression of what he had found. Most prominent was an oak leaf made of gold. This was in the centre of the braided gold chain. Either side of this was two silver leaves of a smaller size and shape. All four were as finely textured as the oak leaf. He couldn't identify the four identical leaf shapes, so he googled UK trees on his phone. A few minutes of research, and he found a site that showed a small painting of a leaf against the appropriate tree with some information. He discovered the silver leaves were rowan, a tree that was common throughout the UK.

The chain was woven, with exquisite craftsmanship, from delicate gold strands. On one side, the gold was wound around a beautifully crafted rose shape, then continued six centimetres to a hook. The other end of the chain was shorter with torn ends to the strands; he guessed this was where another rose shape, six centimetres of chain, and a clasp would have been. Another hour, and careful cleaning with a soft cloth resulted in a shine to the silver, and most dirt removed from the gold. He left a sheen of compost in the weave of the gold chain and in the finely etched veins in the leaves; he had thought it best to show evidence of its recent retrieval from the ground.

The next day, Matt forgot to go detecting, and spent the daylight hours staring at his treasure, wondering what to do next. He decided to hide it for now, as you can't be too careful these days. He had a space he'd constructed beneath the garden shed floor a few years back. It was a project that had kept him busy after his wife's traumatic passing. He wanted to hide her family heirlooms, some of which may be worth something. He kept a few more items in this makeshift safe, like his mother's silver brooch, his father's Rolex watch, £100 in cash, and his apprenticeship indenture certificates.

It had been an interesting carpentry project. He had cut the floor-boards, then made a supporting wood battened structure beneath. He designed it so the whole thing came up with leverage at one point, using a large screwdriver. He had then used a spade to dig a hole beneath the floor and line it with plastic. Then a steel box he'd found in a junk shop held his valuables. He lined that with more plastic so no damp could penetrate. He had finished with an extra layer of protection. He emptied the old, heavy work-bench, to make it light enough for him to drag, if he kept his back straight. One leg sat squarely over the centre of the cut timber floor, the rest of it sat against the wall. Satisfied he had planned and executed the extra security well, he then refiled the workbench drawers. It was back to weighing a ton and unmovable again, he had thought in satisfaction. The final touch gave him further gratification; he had dragged his smaller, wheeled, hydraulic jack in from the garage, settled it under the bench leg, then, bracing himself, he heaved on the handle. The bench gradually rose up eight inches, level with the large window. Matt locked the jack in position. Then, with his screwdriver, he checked that he could lever up the modified floor panel and reach in to open the metal box.

It had worked perfectly, and he remembered his feeling of satisfaction – no one would be able to get into that hidden, safe place.

He placed the new treasure in this secure hideaway, refitted the floor and bench, and locked the shed door. He would rather have left it indoors on his mantlepiece, or next to the telly, where he could admire the treasure whenever he looked that way. He knew that it was unwise to even contemplate doing so, as burglaries were not unheard of, even here in the small village he lived in. The Forest of Dean was a popular place to own property, and criminals took advantage of that.

It was all done, and the excitement abated, but he ached to tell someone about the treasure he'd found. So that evening, he went for a stroll and ended up in his local, The Queens Arms. He knew most of the clientele, all of whom liked a good discussion whilst propping up the public bar.

'Evening, Chris,' he tried a thin smile at the landlady.

'Hi Matt. Haven't seen you for a while. Your back finally improved then?'

'It did, but I have to be careful. It could happen again, according to the consultant. I'm continuing with the metal detecting. The walking involved is a good fitness regime.'

'Great. What have you found then?'

'Well, up until this week, not a lot.'

The comment seemed to go over her head. 'Ring pulls and bits of barbed wire then!'

'Well, sort of, but not on Tuesday.'

This was more difficult than he thought.

'What're you drinking tonight?'

He pointed to a pump. 'That new IPA would be nice.'

Noddy sauntered over while he paid Chris. Matt had seen him at the other end of the bar, wheeling and dealing like he always did in here.

Noddy nodded to Matt twice, hence his nickname. He always seemed to be in agreement but in reality, nodding was a sort of habit that he couldn't stop doing.

Chris walked off to deal with another customer, so Matt took a welcome gulp of his pint.

'Hey, good to see you again, Matt Bradley, my boy. Yer back good now? What've you been up to then?' He nodded as if Matt had already answered.

'Doing well now, Noddy. Been doing a lot of metal detecting. I got a permission from a farmer over Symonds Yat way.'

'Really, I've heard that's the way to do things. Legal like.' So, what 'ave you found then?

'Well, until Tuesday, just junk or interesting but valueless items.'

Noddy leant forward, obviously interested, and wobbled his head. 'What then? Anything I can buy off you?'

'Err, no. I mean, yes, it's valuable. Definitely. Maybe classed as treasure. Not sure though yet.' Matt knew Noddy only gave rock-bottom prices for anything.

Noddy's head bobbed so much that Matt gave up trying to make eye contact.

'Come on, what is it?' Noddy leant closer, as if ready to start some price haggling.

'A gold braided necklace with a large gold oak leave in the centre and two silver leaves on either side that are definitely silver. The silver leaves are shaped precisely, finely detailed, and match a rowan shape. A small rose on one side, and the other has something missing, another rose on a bit of chain, perhaps. I think the thing's very old, and really valuable. I've got to find out what to do next.'

'I'll sort it for you.'

'No, you won't. I think I need to tell someone official. At the local museum or something. You've any idea where the nearest museum is, Noddy?'

Noddy shrugged and changed the subject. 'Seen Bonzo recently?'

'What's this, my friend? I'm interested in antiques.' A new and gruff voice interrupted from behind Matt.

With a start, Matt turned round. A man in his thirties was near enough to hear his conversation with Noddy. He looked really fit and overly alert. He wore a dark two days of stubble, double denim with an open shirt beneath the jacket, and thick-soled boots. He didn't look like an antiques dealer, but could be ex-military.

He stared intently at Matt, 'Where did you find that item?'

It was more of a demand than a request, and Matt turned to stare back. He thought hard for a moment, perhaps saying that where he found it didn't matter. Then, with his mind racing he realised there may be other items to find nearby. He should go back and check the surroundings out properly. 'It was over Milkwall way. About five miles west of Barkend. You know the S-shaped copse in that sheltered valley. It was in there.' The lies flowed out with ease. He remembered one of his first detector searches, and it had been over Milkwall way. He had found nothing there, just as well, because it was after that he read he should have got permission from the owner to detect in the field.

'And you found nothing else at that location?'

'No. I searched the rest of the day. You a fellow detectorist then?'

'I'm not. Just have an interest in what you people find.'

'I'm quite experienced and know my way round all my detector's foibles. I cracked up my detector's discrimination to check the signal before digging, as I normally do to save bending and digging up canslaw.' He added a few terms he'd memorised from a TV sit-com he'd grown to love. He had no idea what they meant, but thought it sounded interesting and knowledgeable.

The man looked blankly at him. Matt thought his eyes looked emotionless, almost dead. The stare began to chill him; this guy has killed others, was his next thought.

He felt another hand on his shoulder and started, spilling beer from the glass he'd forgotten he was holding to his chest. Socialising was not something he was used to in the last few years.

He turned to a smiling face. It was another pub-local called Roger the Dodger. He was also on benefits and hadn't worked officially for years.

'Good to see you again, Matt mate.'

He tried to swop pleasantries, but the military guy had disturbed him. The conversation with Dodger was strained. The military guy's eyes still seemed to bore into his back. Matt turned back to the guy involuntarily; he was in no condition to defend himself these days should the man pick a fight.

The man had gone. A quick scan of the bar failed to spot him.

'Who was that guy at the bar?' he asked Dodger.

'A sort of security guard or bodyguard or something. Comes in for a pint occasionally. Must live nearby. Works away a lot. Maybe ex-special-forces, rumour has it. Cold bastard, doesn't do conversation much.'

After a few minutes more of idle chat, Matt left without telling anyone else about his find. The experience with the military guy had left him unnerved. He suddenly realised he had been foolish to boast of it. His thoughts switched to the find and where he had found it. He should have gone back to the woodland above the river and carried on searching. If the item was there because of a mugging or a fall from a horse, then there could be more to be found including the other end of the necklace.

He arrived home and sat on his old sofa. There was more he should do. He needed to inform the authorities. The necklace had been with him for five days now, and he wondered if it was too late to inform the local museum and the farmer. It wasn't as if he wanted to break the law, it was just that he didn't want to part with the object that had changed his life. It was so incredibly beautiful; he could almost imagine it around the neck of a Celtic princess – not that he knew what such a beauty would look like. He had never really had much of an imagination, hence why he had joined a main dealership that would put him through a car repair engineer's apprenticeship.

Examining his small phone screen for information was becoming frustrating. Why restrict myself, I have another option, Matt remembered. He hesitated for a moment, then sighed as he realised now was the right moment to use Dianne's laptop. He had never done so before; it was still hers, and he had treated it that way ever since that terrible day. He needed to look up a lot of information, and the internet on a larger screen would be easier. If she were watching over him, she would approve, he was sure. Matt pulled the laptop from the bedroom cupboard drawer where he had placed her other personal items. The battery was flat after all this time, so he plugged it into a convenient socket in the kitchen and stood crouched over the worktop.

He didn't know her passwords.

Reluctantly, he went back to the drawer and carefully moved items until he found her notebook. He remembered it as the one she'd written all her passwords in. It was her private book, and he had always respected that. He hesitated again, then whispered, 'Sorry, love, needs must,' and opened it to pages of details he tried hard not to read. Her passwords were on the last page, so he memorised the one needed. They all referred to her beloved dog, Diamond, the Red Setter. He replaced the book under other items and slowly closed the drawer.

Back in the kitchen, he entered her password into the laptop and found the internet link. 'Thanks love,' he muttered and felt his eyes water. It was more comfortable researching on the larger screen, so he sat, slouched forward, ignoring the physio's instruction to keep good posture at all times.

He described his problem in a search and clicked to expand what appeared to be the best-informed answer. It was on the local County Council's website. It stated, Our Finds Liaison Officer will assess any finds and record suitable artefacts on the Portable Antiquities Scheme. If the Finds Liaison Officer believes the item could be treasure, then the Officer will make a report to the coroner on the finder's behalf, and the item would be judged under the amended Treasure Act 2023. Matt looked up another site and saw he had 14 days to do this in. It was a great relief not to have kept his treasure for so long, it had become an offence. He decided to ring the officer tomorrow, and carried on learning about the legal side of metal detecting. Soon, he came across an organisation called The National Council for Metal Detecting and on their beginners' guide, he discovered he should have got Edgar Woodrow to sign a Search Agreement Form, which spelled out the exact agreement between the land owner and the detectorist. It didn't seem too much of a problem, but he decided to print two forms so he and Edgar could each sign a copy tomorrow.

Then he decided to phone the farmer and inform him. He tapped the number into his mobile and got an answerphone. 'Edgar, I've found something valuable on your land, a real beauty. I'm going to report it to the Finds Officer at the council tomorrow. Phone me back and I'll tell you more. Oh, and don't worry, it'll be fifty, fifty, if it ends up as treasure – and it's so beautiful I think it will be.'

Matt put the phone down and tried to concentrate on the drama acting out on the telly. It was impossible; he resisted the temptation to remove his treasured find from its hiding place. In the end, he got another beer from the fridge and started to plan tomorrow's outings.

Ten minutes later, his ringtone pierced his fantasies of finding more treasure.

'Matt, me old butt, what you found me then?' Edgar sounded really curious, but maybe his voice was laced with a note of disbelief. Matt thought the farmer had considered that a beginner detectorist like him wouldn't be capable of finding much.

'It's treasure mate. I mean real treasure…'

'Come on. What?'

'A gold necklace with a chain woven together with gold. A golden oak leaf and silver rowan leaves hang from it.'

'Where exactly did you find it?' Edgar snapped.

'Down by your last field and into the woodland there.'

''Where exactly? You're a bit vague.' Edgar was clearly panting.

'I'll have to show you where tomorrow, and you can have a gander at the necklace after I've shown it to the finds officer.'

'Hang on, you mean he's going to let you keep it?'

'Don't know. I'm hoping he'll just register it and take photos.'

'Course he won't, they'll want to keep it to assess its worth to the nation. I want to see it first, though.'

At that point, he didn't trust Edgar not to snatch it from him, especially if he went over there to show him the thing. He had the strangest feeling Edgar was involved in the necklace in some way. Did the farmer know about it already, or did he want to sell it for quick cash? Matt knew the necklace needed special protection, but not Edgar's kind of attention. It really felt like his now, and he only wanted to hand it over to someone trustworthy, and that would not be Edgar.

'Meet me at the Council offices tomorrow. You can see it when I hand it over for inspection. I may have to book an appointment; I'll phone them first thing and then let you know.'

'Pah, they'll keep it. Okay, if you insist, I'll see you there. Send me a photo now, I need to examine it somehow.'

'Ah, yes, I'd best take a photo of it before I forget.' It was a good excuse to go and record his beloved treasure. It would also be a kind of insurance policy to show he was the finder. Perhaps a selfie of him holding it up would suffice. A thought occurred to him, maybe he should have photo'd it before he separated it from the soil clod and before he'd cleaned it up. He dismissed the thought; it was too late now. When it had been registered as treasure and he'd had its value officially confirmed, perhaps he could sell his story to the papers. He needed the cash, but only a legal payment.

'Make it nice and sharp.'

'Why?'

'I just want to examine it properly, seeing as I can't see the real thing.'

'Huh! I'll do my best.' He rang off.

The shed was freezing cold, and wind whistled through a few gaps in the panelling, but Matt ignored the discomfort, switched on the light, and latched the door closed. It took an hour going through the bench moving procedure, photographing the necklace carefully from all angles, including perching the camera on the workbench top, setting the timer, and creating the selfie with him holding his treasure. He reluctantly returned it to its hideaway.

The next morning, Matt was up early. He spent an hour on the internet learning about the subject in general. He checked out the local detecting clubs – they were all full and not taking on new members. Maybe they'd accept him as an experienced detectorist once his exquisite find was known about. He went on to research all kinds of treasure finds, metal detecting best practice, and UK law and the Treasure Act. Then, finally, metal detecting techniques until 9:00 when it was time to phone for an appointment. He was put through to the correct person within a minute after explaining about his find to the receptionist.

'Good morning, Mr Bradley. I'm Derek O'Brady, the Finds Liaison Officer. I understand you may have found something rather special. Using a metal detector, I'm guessing.'

'Yes mate. Best thing I ever bought.'

'Could you describe it, please?'

'What the detector?'

'No, the find.'

He did, and a minute later, he had an appointment to take it over that afternoon at 3 o'clock. The man had sounded impressed. He would be met in reception by O'Brady.

Surprisingly, he got through to Edgar on the first ring. The farmer said he would be at the council offices early, so he didn't miss anything.

Matt tapped disconnect and sat feeling a little deflated. The whole incredible discovery was soon going to be taken over by bureaucracy and historians. He was about to be merely the finder. The thought that his share of the necklace's value might make him well off didn't placate his mood.

He couldn't resist going to his shed to retrieve the treasured necklace from its hideaway. Just one last examination before it was taken away. Within a few minutes, the beautiful artefact seemed to smile back at him. He stroked the gold oak leaf and realised he could hardly bear to part with it. The thought saddened him, so he placed the treasure back in its tissue-filled box and returned it to the hideaway.

He decided the best thing to do to cheer himself up was to go detecting for the morning.

And there was only one place worth going to.

He arrived at the end of the bumpy, potholed lane an hour later and parked on the verge. It took moments to assemble the detector and put on his rucksack. Looking up to the dark cloud rolling in from the west, he guessed he had a couple of hours before rain. He climbed the gate and jumped down the other side as if he were a teenager. His back twinged, reminding Matt that it was still not healed and probably never would be, as the consultant had warned him.

It was a five-minute walk across the field to the woodland and then over the broken barbed-wire strung post into the trees. On the way to the find's location, he swung his detector in a continuous arc; you never knew if a surprise find would be directly in his path.

He found the spot of freshly dug soil and paused for a moment to look around. He felt something unusual come over him. He saw a beautiful woman, the Celtic princess of his dreams, on a horse, followed by a man on a smaller horse. They wore simple clothes, dark green gowns and breeches with gold edging and leather ankle boots. She had flowing locks of tangled hair blown behind her by the forward motion. Her horse looked covered in regalia. It hit a small hole and stumbled. Its sudden cessation of forward momentum threw her forward. The woman screamed as she hit the ground, and Matt came back to reality with an echo of the scream. What on earth was that? He blinked and looked around. Nothing there, just a rustle in the trees and birdsong. He was cracking up, or he'd just had some kind of mystical vision. He went for the former explanation, but didn't want to actually hear anything else untoward, so he put headphones over his ears and returned to sweeping.

He scanned slower and more methodically than normal, not wanting to miss anything. In minutes, he had another promising signal. He dropped the detector and dug with his lightweight shovel. This time, the item was more elusive; he swept the detector over the spot again. The signal beep was a different tone than before. Not gold then, but worth continuing to dig. He used the pinpointer and tried it over three clods of soil. One blipped loudly, and he broke the soil apart with his fingers. A small crescent shape appeared. Bronze or brass, he thought as he rubbed it clean. It appeared to be a representation of the moon with a circular loop in the top and bottom. Matt guessed that these holes were to tie it to something. He wondered if it could be a horse brass. He'd have to research it when he got home.

After putting it in his finds bag, he carried on but only found ring-pulls and other assorted junk. Time flew by, and his phone bleeped its programmed-in deadline of one o'clock. He stopped, sat on a stump, and finished his food and drink. Not an unsuccessful morning, he thought, and then pondered his vision as he strode back to his car. What if the woman had really fallen from a racing horse, and as she fell, ripped the horse brass from the beast? Then, on hitting the ground, the necklace had been torn from her neck, and she couldn't find it. Or maybe she just found the torn end. He imagined her disappointment; he would certainly have been upset if it had happened to him. It was all conjecture, but part of his growing fascination with this amazing and hopefully lucrative hobby. He wondered how long ago the drama had happened and how mortified the woman must have been.

Idly, he also wondered why Edgar gave the detectorists club permission to search his land. It had seemed the man must know something about the necklace – he was so keen to examine the treasure. Was it merely that it had been found on his land, and he had had no idea it was there all his life?

Soon, he was home and parked in his narrow drive. After he took his detector and other gear indoors, he made a coffee and relaxed with a snack. At least today's search had shown there were no more items of value near the necklace's location, he consoled himself. Soon, it was time to head off to the council offices for his appointment, so he unlocked his back door to go to the shed and retrieve his trophy.

After one step, he froze. There was something wrong outside. He looked and stared. A sudden panic came over him as he saw the shed door had been ripped from its hinges. In an instant, he knew what to expect, but hardly dared think it. His heart thumped; his stomach knotted, and his legs shook as he ran to the wreck.

One look inside and the scene seared into his mind. The bench drawers and their contents were strewn around in complete chaos. The bench was not where it should be, and the car jack had been moved.

The floor was ripped up.

The metal box lay torn open in the shed corner.

He reached it. The box was empty.

Matt fell to his knees and wept.

CHAPTER ELEVEN

It seemed that as soon as they had made Saturday the day to continue the search, the weather forecast uncannily changed the arrangement. A storm was coming in from the Arctic, bringing freezing temperatures and blizzards. It was expected to be short-lived, but meant the weekend was only suitable to hunker down and keep indoors. Dave consoled himself, it was the end of November now, so these weather conditions had to be expected. He finished his usual stint in the warehouse offices and got home Friday evening as the snow started.

After two hours of indecision, he was about to phone Amber and then Ben to reschedule the search when his phone rang. Amber's voice cheered him in an instant; she'd decided to sort it all out for him. They rearranged the expedition for Monday. She had already soft-soaped her department head, and Ben had done the same by saying they were following up on intriguing private research. Despite Craig Dalgarth's curiosity, they had kept the story so vague that he had lost interest.

One of Liz's little passions on these wintery days was the living room's log burner. A warming blaze meant she could snuggle down in front of it on the sofa. Sometimes she had a new best-selling novel and read for hours, at other times catching up with admin or programme arrangements for her beloved social club. It was Dave's job to ensure he fed logs into the blaze at regular intervals. In between this task, he took to sitting next to her and browsing the internet on the laptop in his lap. Occasionally, he glanced out the French doors at the ever-deeper snow. It was the 22nd of November, and snow was early for a British winter. He found himself wishing the rest of the winter would be the rain and dark skies that were more usual in these days of global warming. The laptop's warmth and the log fire made him feel more relaxed than he had felt for a long time.

Saturday progressed in a cosy haze. He looked online for various threads that might help progress his, Amber and Ben's project. Then he ate whatever meal Liz prepared, apologised, left the kitchen table, and made an excuse to return to trawling the internet. An inkling made him search antique furniture websites for information on hidden compartments. The searching fed this growing intrigue in the methods used by unknown ancient cabinetmakers to create the secret compartment in his and Liz's dresser. He had not even attempted to start renovating the tatty old piece because he had more respect for the dresser's age now that it had produced their captivating document.

Researching the subject online for most of Saturday gave Dave a lot of the background he lacked. An apparently ordinary piece of furniture could be in its owner's home for years, or even generations, only for secret compartments to be found when it was sent to an expert for reconditioning or valuation. Hidden compartments in furniture could be incredibly well concealed by the high level of skill employed by cabinetmakers. He became fascinated by the abilities of the craftsmen and clicked on a picture of a beautifully preserved secretaire. It had a well-hidden false back that was invisible to casual inspection. In order to discover the piece's secret, you had to remove the bottom right-hand drawer and pull out a hardwood fillet, which was tucked in flush with the side. A bookcase could hide a single space, but a sideboard could hide a whole host. He looked at pictures of a sideboard with a hidden lever that sprung away the exterior rear panel. What looked like internal bracing for the frame was revealed, but each hairline rectangular shape concealed an inner drawer that fitted into a recess above the drawer on the outside front of the piece. It also had a hidden ledge suitable to store necklace or ring cases that could only be reached with great difficulty.

With sudden inspiration, his mind superimposed their old and tatty dresser over the image. What if he reached up behind the cavity where their document had been hidden? He hoped to find a ledge. It was worth a try. He pounded down the stairs from the study through the kitchen to the garage, walked over to the dresser, and heaved it away from the wall. In moments, he had sprung the compartment open and then sprawled onto the floor on one elbow so he could best reach up inside. His hand felt around inside and encountered only smooth wood and cobwebs. After a thorough, groping search, he gave up and got up onto his knees to give his aching back and arms a chance to recover.

He went back to the laptop and stared at the secretaire picture with its multiple drawers. That gave him another idea – the dresser had drawers too. What if he removed them and had a look behind?

It was plausible that the cabinetmaker had built in more than one secret.

The left-hand drawer came out easily. He laid it on the floor and tried the right-hand drawer. It seemed to stick, and he reached into the space where the other drawer had fitted. There was an obstruction at the back of the right-hand drawer. He groped his fingers into the narrow slot and pushed and prodded. The drawer came free suddenly with a dull click. He took it out and looked in at the large space behind. It was raw, unvarnished wood and appeared solid. There was a slight darkening to the wood where he had released the sticking drawer. He prodded the area, and a rectangular section of the back moved out a fraction. Dave pushed some more, and a gap appeared big enough to get his fingers into. He pressed on the panel, not wanting to snap the ancient wood. It came away and revealed a space. The space was filled with something that looked like a long buff coloured cylinder.

Dave's pulse raced. He knew what it was.

It would have been a struggle to insert the item in lengthways unless the other drawer had a compartment behind it as well. He went to the left-hand space and prodded. This wood panel sprung out more easily. He put it on the floor and stared at the cylinder. This end showed a rolled wove-paper edge.

His heart was racing now, and his hands felt clammy. It took him a moment to realise he was panting and sweating. Then, with a rush, he strode to the desk to get his camera with its new SD card – everything should be recorded.

He took two quick JPEGs. That would suffice, he thought. Then he removed the thick paper roll. It was tied with a yellow ribbon. He took another JPEG of that as well. The bow untied with ease, but the paper still retained a cylindrical shape. Carefully, he unrolled the wove paper, anchored the edges with two paperweights, and viewed pages of handwritten sepia text. With the paperweights holding the corners down onto the desktop, he examined the whole document. Its size was the same as their document and Reverend Edgar Dalmont's diary. It had a ripped edge where it would have fitted the spine of the diary.

His heart was still pounding as he put on his reading glasses and became engrossed in what the Reverend had written in his spidery hand all those years ago.

It is with a labour of love that we have created this illustration in celebration of our wondrous temple. It intrigued me to indulge Glenys in allowing her to practise her command of Latin and to give me the words to surround her illustration of the temple. It will mean that only a well-educated man or a scholar can read this, but for those willing to study this page, many delights await you. This is a record of a truth that was once known by all, but now we fear it will never again be so. I finally understand the glory in celebrating deities that rule the woods, the plains, the mountains, and the sea — they are to be treasured and not blasphemed and ignored, as my fellow English gentlemen are inclined to do.

The great Priestess has created the most worshipful of polytheistic ceremonies to honour them all. Each season and each God has a ritual, and as the congregation dances, we sing hymns in an entrancing harmony that weaves them into the very depths of our being. Now I know these celebrations so well that they fill my heart with simple truths. The most memorable hymn was taught to me by my Priestess wife, Glenys, after our fifth meeting. This was our first shared joy and is also central to the dance of Deidre, Goddess of the moon, and Smalran, God of the night. To my surprise, she has told me of the Priestess before her and the one before that who wrote the beautiful hymns scribed below about one hundred years ago. So I repeat it here as it fills both our hearts and minds, as it surely does every soul in our congregation.

We rise to dance and sing.
Around the stones we do ring
Like bright moths fluttering in the light
We dance to banish the night

Gods of family and brethren, through you we start
To know the love that with others we share
That which comes back to us when they too do care.

The Priestess will collect them again soon

The Priestess Stones

To return to dance beneath the silvery moon
Forever we will praise the Gods of leaf and stream
And together our union will fulfil the dream

I feel wonderfully relieved of the duties of my parish, so much so that I have sent a letter of resignation to the bishop. I go now from this rectory forever to a small cottage in the woods. It has been secretly procured by my dearest's father, to whom I am much obliged. He obtained it from Messrs Browning and Browning, brothers who had it built as a holiday retreat. Archibald Browning being a sponsor of our small religion. It is there in this hidden abode that my dear Glenys will join me. I am further fortified with this, our ancient chant — it never leaves my mind and extinguishes all my theological training, leaving a new purpose and joy. I feel some wondrous revivification in the hymn written below, as if many generations of guardians who have cared for these stones all look on and uplift my energised soul.

The ring shapes our rite
We are creatures of night
Fox and owl, stars and moon, we are
Stream and soil, trees near and far
Soul and eyes, foot and hand
Are as one
Are as one
Are as one

My heart is full of the kindest emotions. I am fulfilled. I can think of no greater reverence than to record our glorious service and our devotions. It cleanses my soul, and I am repeatedly assured that I am at one with the land, the streams, rivers, and rain, the sun and the moon, and all the creatures that live beneath the life-giving light. I worship the ancient Gods and am one with Glenys at all times. I harmonise with the sweet sound of her voice as we sing in our cottage when alone, but most often under the stars with our loyal flock, as we all offer our veneration to the great ones. To honour this worship, I write below all the other sacred hymns and ritual chants.

Glory be to the Gods of this land, forest, and river.

There followed eight more hymns and four more chants. Dave read them all twice, enthralled with the scenes and ceremonies they evoked. The Reverend's handwriting was really fine, small, and closely packed. It needed to be, Dave nodded in admiration, to fit so much information into each page. Then he sat at his desk, stunned at what he had found. He stroked his beard and analysed what he had just read. Looking objectively, there was nothing there that added anything to their search or that made the stones any easier to find. But this continued story of the Reverend and his love for Glenys was a fascinating and moving tale. It didn't take any great deduction to work out that Linda and Glenys were the same person. Linda had embraced life in her new role as Priestess of this rich but secret cult. As she had become integrated into the cult's rituals, it had made sense for her to drop her previous identity. That would have made her safer and less traceable to the authorities and had probably ensured her ongoing freedom.

But people, and possibly the authorities, must have eventually traced the couple to their cottage. The Reverend may have gone into town to buy food and clothing, and other necessities, and been recognised. Then Dave wondered whether other members of the sect would have done all these chores for them to allow the Reverend and his Priestess lover to remain incognito.

That brought on another train of thought. Had the two gone through a marriage ceremony, or had they lived together? It would have been scandalous in those days to live in sin. Then he realised a pagan marriage would have been blessed in a pagan handfasting by a prominent member of the sect and not a minister of the Christian clergy. He rubbed the top of his nose and his eyes; it was conjecture that may or may never be known about, unless he could find more pages of this diary.

It was time he informed Amber and texted Ben. The easiest way was to take a photo again and email them. But he wanted to have a few moments of glory, to impress his clever daughter once more with his deductive skills, so he decided to phone her.

'Hello, Amber,' he began as she answered. 'I've discovered something ...'

'What? I'm all ears!'

'I've been researching and found an unexplored avenue.'

'Come on, Dad, don't be so deliberately vague. Okay, you've been clever again. Now tell me.'

'I've discovered another hidden compartment in the dresser.'

'Really,' her voice rose in pitch with excitement. 'Come on – you found what in there?'

'Two more sheets of the diary.'

'Oh my God, that's brilliant. No more tantalising hints, don't make me draw it out of you. I presume it's in English. Read the whole thing – now.'

So he did, and when he'd finished reading, there was silence broken only when Amber gasped, 'Wow. Just wow! That gives us an incredible insight into what happened to the Reverend.'

'I feel fired up by their story. What incredible background this would be for when we announce the find of a major new stone circle.'

'We still have to find its remains. I wonder whether the watchmen would have torn it down in a fever of Christian rage.'

'I know, and I hope not. I'm trying to remain positive. But this associated story is an incredible background for the entire project. I'm going to spend my time trying to find more of this diary. It could be secreted away in other furniture.'

'Or it could be in another compartment in the dresser.'

'No, there are no more hidden spaces in the piece, I'm sure. I believe other furniture that is, or once was, in Springborough Manor will hold more. I'm going to book an appointment at the manor to look around, perhaps to see if they have any other old furniture that may still be there from the time of the diary. If I put in a good case, I hope they will let me examine the pieces.' He spoke as the idea came to him without prior consideration. 'I wonder if the dresser could have been in the servant's quarters – it is nowhere near elegant enough to have been in the main house.'

'Good idea. Perhaps other old furniture survived – thrown into a junk room, perhaps. But don't get your hopes up, Dad, people make a living out of searching unused storerooms for old furniture and damaged junk to restore or sell on. I hope they haven't got there before you.' Amber said.

Dave agreed and rang off with a casual, 'Bye for now.' Then he took photos of the document and emailed the best of them to Ben. It was almost 11 o'clock before he went online and found an admin email for Springborough Manor and typed an enquiry.

Dear Sir or Madam

I am a retired archaeologist with an interest in historical research who is exploring a project connected to an intriguing character called Linda Rourtier, who lived in Springborough Manor in the late 17th century.

I wonder if I could make an appointment to tour your storerooms and old servants' quarters. I am hoping you have some old unused furniture stored that may relate to that period. If so, could I examine this furniture in detail? Also, could I ask if you have an archive of documents from that time and whether I could have permission to peruse items of interest?

Look forward to hearing from you.
Kindest regards
David Dorsett

He sent the query and then settled down to a late evening coffee and another examination of the diary pages to see if any further information could be extracted. At 12:30, he decided there were no additional leads or insights to be extricated and retired to bed.

He rose Sunday morning to a bright bedroom that was reflecting light from a blanket of snow outside.

'Cold,' mumbled Liz and drew the bedclothes tighter. He went downstairs and prepared breakfast, loading a tray up with tea, cereal, milk, and toast, as he often did for Liz on a Sunday morning.

He went back downstairs to prepare his own breakfast and, while passing, glanced out the porch window. To his surprise, he saw two sets of footprints in the snow. One set came to his front door, and he could see the same size print reversed as the person had left. He went to the door – nothing had been pushed through the letterbox. He opened the door and stared. An object lay on top of an inch of snow. It was a sheet of aluminium cut to the shape of a swastika, where the symbol was reversed, with its ends all appearing to point anti-clockwise. This was a symbol taken over by the German Nazis before and during World War 2, but it had previously been used by various civilisations throughout Europe and pagan religions before then. He felt a shiver go up his spine – a swastika made this way round had negative connotations and could only be some kind of warning. To reinforce this idea, on top of the swastika was a bottom-jawbone looking like it once belonged to a sheep or goat. He knew little about pagan curses, but enough to know this was also some kind of warning.

Dave put on a pair of Wellington boots and picked up the two objects. He was about to fold the thin aluminium up to put it in the recycling bin when he saw red lettering on the reverse of the swastika. He wiped icy snow off and read a line in red paint. *Stop searching, or it will do you no good.* With a frown, he folded the metal and placed it with the jawbone into the appropriate refuse bins.

Back indoors, he ate cereal and toast with little appetite and then helped Liz with a few chores. As he swept away snow from the path to the front gate, he decided not to tell his wife about the threat and upset her further. This historical search should have been straightforward, but was now being tainted by the greed for treasure. He could only think treasure hunters thought the gold chalice, torc, bracelets, gold and silver leafed necklace, and goblet must be buried at the lost stones. An obstinate streak told him to carry on and not be intimidated. He shook his head and sighed. He would continue with his searches, regardless of any provocation.

Later, upstairs in his study, he started his laptop. Deep in thought, he pondered the significance of the doorstep objects. It was a warning to stop searching for the stones, to be sure. But who had left it? Nathan was too wrapped up in his own misery to try a stunt like that, and anyway he had too much to lose now, he had sided more with them than his aggressive backers. There was only one other real possibility – Nathan's mysterious backers. They had enough information to go on and had decided there was a real treasure, one worth retrieving. They thought Dave, Amber, and Ben were also on the trail of the chalice and the other ceremonial items. He decided not to worry, Amber, and Ben, with the implied threat either. By now, he had also dismissed any idea that the swastika and jawbone had been placed as a kind of curse on him and his home. It was ancient mumbo-jumbo, and he had no time for it.

The day went peacefully enough as the snow melted outside. He spent the morning on the internet, but could find nothing else to do with the Reverend or Linda. He switched to the archaeological sites and searched for any reference to people finding evidence of henges, standing stones, or fallen stones in the Forest of Dean. Again, he found nothing apart from pictures of people standing with their favourite ancient monuments and giving their own interpretations of the surrounding landscape.

In the afternoon, he, Liz, and Amber left the Red Lion after Sunday lunch for a brisk walk along the lanes around Little Piycombe. Then it was the evening, and he prepared his rucksack and walking boots for the next day's exploration near Barkend.

Once again, he parked in the car park of The Rising Sun Inn outside Barkend at 9:55 and waited for the others.

The car's thermometer said it was a mere plus one outside. Amber and Ben drove in one after the other, and they all waited in Dave's 4x4 Toyota for Nathan again.

He arrived 15 minutes later and emerged from his car. The passenger door opened, and another man got out. He was muscular and sported two days' worth of stubble and signs of long, dishevelled, greying hair emerging from a head-hugging woollen hat. His appearance was completed by army-style walking boots and a thick blue winter anorak.

'Sorry, sorry, it was traffic again.' Nathan mumbled. 'This is Ken Davies - my colleague and keen metal detectorist. He's my right-hand man when it comes to searching specific areas for potential sites. Don't worry, I've sworn him to secrecy.' The man nodded slightly and said, 'Good morning to you all,' in a commanding tone.

'Okay.' Dave turned to Nathan, 'I must emphasise again, please do not discuss our search with anyone else.' He stared at Ken. 'And I will require you, Mr Davies, to sign an NDA, of which I have a copy in my car downloaded from my solicitor's documentation.'

'You could have asked us first,' Ben spat at Nathan.

Amber glared and said nothing. She admired her father's foresight in bringing additional NDA copies with them.

'I will not sign,' Ken said icily.

'If you do not agree, we will not do this exploration with you today, or any other day.' Dave stated in an official and precise tone; his words sliced the cold air.

There followed a freeze-frame scene as if time had paused.

Dave and Ben glared.

Ken stared back, expressionless.

Nathan looked at the ground.

Ben took two steps toward Ken Davies.

Amber fidgeted from one foot to the other and stared from one man to the next. Her eyes came to rest on Ben. She wondered who would give way.

'Very well,' Ken held his hand out for the paper and pen.

No one spoke in the awkward silence.

Without another word, Dave walked to his car and returned with a clipboard holding the NDA document. Ken scrawled a signature, printed his name, and dated where Dave indicated. He wacked the pen onto the paper as he signed in a show of annoyance.

Ben signed to witness the signature.

Amber realised her heart was pounding and released a large breath into the frozen air.

The two men squeezed into the back of Dave's car with Ben.

'We'll take the lane from here toward Cinderford again,' Dave said as he checked the sat-nav and thought over the sudden development. For Davies's benefit, he said, 'we're going to go back to the parking spot where the Spruce Ride footpath bisects it.'

'Let's hope the west path gives us more luck this time,' said Amber.

It was just before 11 o'clock when they parked up. This time, Nathan stayed with them and kept pace without falling behind. Ken stayed a step behind his colleague. Dave thought Nathan seemed quite buoyed up with the expectation of finding something. Occasionally, he commented to Ken. His companion merely nodded as if he were listening to an employee rather than a partner.

Oak, ash, and sycamore lined the westerly path with stands of conifer in between. Underfoot was slushy with melting ice, and deeper hollows were still filled with an icy layer. The trees filtered a sharp breeze that made Dave's nose run, and he puffed along behind the others. They took regular trips off the path to explore any slight rise in the ground amongst the trees. On two occasions, the view over the treetops below allowed him to comb the surroundings with binoculars. The distant view was, however, mainly flat, and no landscape features gave even a hint of concealed archaeology.

They passed four men, three in their thirties and one a little older, walking the other way. All looked fit enough to be army special forces on a yomp and wore large backpacks to match their camouflage trousers. Ben nodded in passing. Amber said, 'Hi.' Ken ignored them. The four men carried on as if they had passed no one. Lunch time came, and they stopped on another fallen bough and drank hot soup with bread rolls. Ken walked off to attend to a long phone call.

With his large-scale OS map unfolded, Dave checked their position, then consulted a compass for a bearing.

'We're about parallel to the B4226. I suggest we walk to Buckholt Inclosure, circle back to the B-road, then walk the road until we hit the path back to the car.'

'In my experience, that south-facing high ground there is worth investigating,' said Ken as he prodded the map.

'Alright, we'll do that,' Dave agreed as he examined the map. 'It's right alongside the path, though, so I doubt we'll see anything that hasn't already been spotted by generations of walkers.'

Six unproductive detours later into promising woodland rises and open areas, and it was getting dark with jet-black clouds looming. There was no evidence of ditches, embankments, or fallen stones anywhere, even on the higher ground Ken had pointed out. Then the snow started again.

Ben was tracing the route on his phone. 'We've no time to fit any more in. Further detour or delay will mean that if we find anything, it'll be pitch black, and I don't want to walk these paths to the car then.'

'Give up for today,' puffed Nathan, sounding desperate.

'I vote for the Phoenix hotel on the B4226 and a hot meal, then a taxi back to the cars,' Dave suggested. 'It's only a mile along the road.'

'Okay,' Ben, Amber, and Nathan agreed. Ken stood to one side and didn't contribute. They set off again at a brisk pace, which warmed Dave up slightly.

It was hard walking, broken by constant stumbling and splashing through puddles and mud. Black night had descended by the time they reached the road; still a mile to the hotel and four to where they had parked their car. Only two vehicles passed, both spraying frozen slush from their tyres. Then the snow fell in wind-blown sheets, and the temperature continued to drop. They walked the first quarter-mile along the road in silence as they all processed the disappointment. Dave saw the steam rising from the other's fast breathing and realised he was struggling to keep up. The cold seemed to be eating into his lungs and was making breathing difficult. He looked at Nathan and noticed the man was limping and visibly shivering. It was soon almost impossible to keep up, and Dave hobbled along getting further behind. In front of him, Nathan stumbled, then limped every step, and Dave caught up with him. The man looked all in and was shivering. Ben was in front and slowing down. In the gloom, Dave focused on Amber as she strode behind Ben, her face strained, and her cheeks and nose turning red from the wind-chill. It had been a gruelling day, and their need to find evidence had driven them on too far. This second fruitless trip had sapped their energy to the point of exhaustion.

Ten minutes later, the snow stopped, and the shape of the hotel loomed, looking uninviting without outside lights or lit-up signs to show it was open. They walked through an entrance porch and had to leave their muddy boots in the reception area. A disapproving manager stood by the main door and pointed to a large sign that said, *Notice to walkers. Please remove your boots.* He was a neatly dressed elderly man with a comb-over partially covering a bald head. He glared at each of them and appeared to resent their arrival. An elderly woman looked up from the reception desk, appeared bored, and resumed examining paperwork.

'I'm going to book a room for the night and get a taxi back to The Rising Sun tomorrow,' announced Nathan.

'The same for me,' Ken added. 'I'm completely done-in.'

'Could we book two single rooms, please?' Nathan asked.

The woman sighed, stared at each of them, and muttered, 'We're expecting a large coach-load to arrive, so all we have are two small rooms at the back, which were the chef's and a maid's quarters.'

'I'll take whatever, as long as it has a bath and hot water,' Nathan replied.

The woman clicked a mouse for a minute, then thumped a credit card reader onto the counter without another word.

They sat in the lounge until the shutters were raised on the bar. The barman was a little friendlier. 'Don't see too many people at this time of year. You must be dedicated walkers.'

The manager said you had a coach load coming, Dave remembered. This guy sounded like he was being more truthful. He ignored the previous falsehood and tried to formulate a reply. He was still warming up, his face still felt cold, as if numbed by a dentist's injection. 'We'd have gone indoors anywhere to get out of that cold. Thirty percent chance of snow showers, the weather said.'

'Turned out to be 95 percent,' added Ben, and ordered a brandy, then took a large mouthful.

Amber gave a sickly smile and hobbled off to find a seat.

The lounge bar was empty except for four fit-looking men looking quite like the backpackers they had passed earlier that morning. Dave noted all had trimmed beards, one had a red scar running under his left eye and a shaved head, and another was older, appeared bald because of a close crew-cut. The man turned to speak to one of his companions, and Dave noticed he had a blue and black eagle tattooed across the back of his head in such a way that the bird's wings touched the base of his ears. He hadn't noticed this on the walk earlier, as the man had worn a knitted hat. He looked away as he, Amber, and Ben ordered from the bar menu and then sat down in comfy armchairs near a log fire burning in a large, blackened fireplace.

'Thank you for allowing me to join you today,' Ken said. 'I will spend the evening examining my map in detail. I'm sure I can produce some more promising areas to search. I've had a lot of success finding items for clients in the past.'

So, Ken was an employee, Dave realised. But his attitude to Nathan earlier didn't seem to match. Davies had acted more like an employer and was not respectful of his client's opinions. Dave decided to keep a close eye on the pair tomorrow and in the future if Ken accompanied them on another search trip. He nodded acceptance of Ken's statement and noticed Ben looking sharply at both men, then his face formed a frown before relaxing. There would be time enough in the taxi to discuss Ben's reaction later, he decided.

'You take on metal-detecting work for a living, then?' Dave asked.

'Well, occasionally. Mainly looking for people's lost rings. I have other priorities too.'

Dave nodded; he was too tired to quiz the man further.

'I'm really looking forward to a soak in my bath,' Amber announced. 'But where the hell do we look next?'

Nathan mumbled. 'No stones, no progress. We need new ideas. That is why I invited Ken.'

'Next time, ask us before inviting more people,' Ben spat.

They all became lost in their thoughts as Dave mentally reviewed all they had discovered of the stones and the pagan cult that had once worshipped there.

'We may need to admit we're looking in completely the wrong area,' announced Amber. 'But first, I think we should strike north toward Great Kensley Inclosure.'

Dave could tell she was wondering if the translated directions must have been deliberately wrong to put people like them off the scent.

'The OS map shows a lot of uninterrupted woodland, only broken by the B4226 road. We need to go off track there a lot more if necessary.'

'We are still right to assume that the stones are around here somewhere and hidden in thick woodland, so that looks like our best remaining bet,' Ben decided.

'Lucky for us, it's all common land. Don't want to trespass,' mumbled Amber.

'Yes, I agree,' Dave said. 'We still have a lot of searching to do northward, maybe detour further from the path in a specific area and try not to cover as much distance as we did today.' Dave felt himself reinvigorate as he spoke. 'I'll create proper square grids so we can explore each one thoroughly. You can use the GPS facility on your phones, I'm sure, but that tech is a little beyond me.'

'Yes – let's be better organised. That's good,' mumbled Nathan.

Dave could see that Amber was easily keeping up with his thinking, although she looked worn out. The discussion ambled along without further new decisions. The food orders were carried in, one plate at a time, from a sullen waitress who only grunted when Ben asked for mayonnaise. They all ate quickly and ravenously. Nathan and Ken excused themselves and went up to their respective rooms. Dave felt as if his limbs had dissolved with fatigue. The roaring fire in the nearby hearth soothed his aching muscles but seemed to add to the numbness. 'We've got to go,' he croaked and finished his lager-shandy.

Ben had already ordered a taxi, and it dropped them back at Dave's 4x4 at 9:15. It was coalmine black in the pull-in, surrounded by tall conifers as they piled the rucksacks into the back. As he got into the driver's seat, he noticed a slip of paper under the wipers. Getting out again, he retrieved it, but the night was so dark he had to get back in to read under the car's cabin-light. *Carry on searching, and nasty accidents often happen in dense woodland.*

'What's that?' Amber said and yawned.

'Only advertising rubbish,' he muttered and scrunched the paper into the ashtray, then looked to Ben in the rear seat. Ben stared back and nodded. He wore a grim look that said he had read the note over Dave's shoulder.

We're being watched, Dave's thoughts screamed at him. Who were they up against? It could only be Nathan's mysterious backer. That made two break-ins, witchcraft totems with a scrawled warning, now this...

As he slipped the car into gear and drove onto the road, he thought about their two days of searching that had accomplished nothing. He kept the communal silence as he negotiated the tree-lined bends back to drop Ben and Amber at their cars. Then he reminded himself that in all their miles of walking and exploring, they had only passed one group of fellow walkers. He remembered they looked like the group in the hotel lounge. There had been no sign of anyone congregated in a particular area - in fact, there had been no activity anywhere to draw their attention. He would have thought that another party searching as they had been would have been noticeable -

unless they had found the stones already and were employing nighthawk metal detectorists to search and take away any finds. He hoped that even more treasure hunters had not taken up the search for the stones if his SD card information was being given to other unscrupulous people. They may be searching the correct area already, hence why he had not spotted them. The lust for gold and artefacts was far more important to them than a tumbled-down circle. But he doubted even if the night-hawkers had worked out where the ceremonial treasures were, then they would leave the site untouched for Nathan. Maybe Nathan would be told where to go later, and would then go into overdrive with his own lust for publicity and acclaim, and he, Amber, and Ben would be too late to benefit. But he couldn't do that, the NDA would stop him. He sighed to clear his head and force himself out of the conjecture – it was getting him nowhere. It was a complex puzzle, and he decided to wait and hope none of his conjectures arose.

With the problem still tumbling around at the back of his mind like clothes in a washing machine, he reached the pub car park where Amber and Ben's cars awaited them. He didn't want to trouble Amber with the problem as she sleepily kissed him on the cheek. He smiled and settled down for his drive home.

Ben had already closed the rear door and was standing next to his driver's side window. Dave wound it down and Ben lent close. 'I'll be in touch to discuss the next step,

Dave, and that note on the windscreen too.' He nodded knowingly before striding off.

He watched Ben wave to Amber as she returned the gesture to both of them before driving away. He frowned at the note's contents and Ben's proposed discussion of it, then decided to give it no more thought unless Ben brought the matter up.

The drive home seemed short despite having to drive slowly in plummeting temperatures and a thick frost. They could not search again until the next weekend; he resigned himself to going to work and spending his spare time thinking of research and how to get more angles on the whereabouts of the stones or the rest of the diary.

He got up early the next morning, and the day appeared to be like any other until the phone rang after breakfast. A police sergeant introduced himself and said there had been a serious mugging at The Phoenix hotel, two men were in hospital, and there was internal CCTV footage showing him, David Dorsett, with the victims in the bar.

The Sergeant's next words chilled Dave to the bone. 'You will need to explain yourself and all that you know concerning Nathan Daniels and Kenneth Davies.'

Dave croaked an inarticulate reply and stopped himself pressing the red disconnect as he realised it was not a hoax call. He slowly drew the phone away from his ear and checked the caller display as if it were a live bomb, then just stared at the wall in disbelief. The caller fell silent as if expecting Dave to fill the space.

'I err… What's that, Sergeant? They are alright… Or are they?'

CHAPTER TWELVE

'How did you trace me?' he asked the sergeant, as curiosity overcame the initial shock.

'We obtained your name and address from the credit card payment for your evening meal yesterday. Also, one of the victims, Nathan Daniels, was conscious and managed to give your name before his condition worsened.'

Although Dave had not taken to Nathan Daniels, he felt for the poor man. But the Sergeant had just said Daniels was conscious. Was being past tense. Did that mean... He asked, dreading what he now knew the reply would be.

'Unfortunately, Mr Daniels is now in a coma and in intensive care.'

Nathan did not deserve what had befallen him. 'That's appalling. How is the other victim? I'm guessing it's Ken Davies?'

'He's also in intensive care and in a bad way.'

'Oh my God. I'll assist in any way I can, Sergeant.'

'A colleague, Detective Constable O'Malley, will be over this morning to interview you. Please do not go out until you've seen him.'

'Yes, I mean no, of course I won't,' Dave said and clicked disconnect as he tried to assimilate the latest bad news.

The bad news seemed to be piling up. This had been a simple field walk of their target area. Now it had turned into a serious crime. The shock of the incident made him pace the room faster as he thought about what they should do next. His immediate concern was for Amber, and he phoned her. The line was engaged.

He paced up and down the living room, then down the inner hallway. This had all happened because they had stolen his SD card. He hadn't thought to hide it, and now this terrible assault was because of his incompetence. He continued pacing; it was his way of assimilating a bad shock. He tried to contact Amber again. This time, she picked up.

'Dad, I was about to call you. The police have been on the phone with terrible news.'

'I know they phoned me. Are they interviewing you too?'

'Yes, this afternoon. I said I had to work, so they're seeing me there.' There was a pause in which she croaked something unintelligible, then finally said, 'What's going on, Dad? Have we got ourselves mixed up in some kind of criminal gang without any scruples who'll stop at nothing to find buried artefacts?'

'I wish I could get to the bottom of it.' As he spoke, Dave thought of the valuable items listed in the Reverend's diary – at least one gold goblet: a ceremonial chalice; a gold torc worn by Linda for ceremonial purposes; a silver dagger with a hilt encrusted with jewels; possibly her wrist and ankle bangles as well. Last, the gold oak and silver rowan leaf necklace sounded stunning. The list solidified a decision in his mind. 'I'm going to level with the police and tell them what we believe is the reason behind all the break-ins ...' He was about to mention the witchcraft symbols and scrawled threat, but stopped himself in time, '... and how they're connected. Nathan will have some serious questions to answer when he's recovered, and I'm going to make sure the police ask them.'

'But Nathan's been attacked. He's seriously hurt, so he's a victim. How do we equate that?'

'I don't know. Perhaps it was a punishment for not delivering the goods.'

'And Ken Davies. He was assaulted, too. So he can't be part of this unpleasant backer's crew either.'

'I know, it doesn't add up. I hope the police can get to the truth, that's all.'

Just before midday, Detective Constable O'Malley sat himself in one of Dave's and Liz's lounge armchairs. He settled deep into the padded fabric as if all he really wanted to do was to have a nap. Going by the dark folds under the man's eyes and the two days of stubble, Dave thought the man was worn down with his workload. O'Malley produced his notebook, then a mobile phone, and mumbled about new technology not being better than writing in a traditional notebook. He stabbed at the mobile and set in down on the table between them. Dave realised it was recording the conversation.

'Mr Dorsett, I take it you've been informed that Mr Nathan Daniels died at 11:18 this morning?'

'Oh God. No, I didn't know. That is terrible news.'

O'Malley nodded grimly, all the time watching Dave's face for signs other than sheer horror. After a long moment's silence, for Dave to recover, he began his interrogation by asking what Dave and his friends had been doing before arriving at the Phoenix Hotel.

'I'm a retired archaeologist; my daughter Amber and Ben Tarrant are currently employed by an Oxford archaeological trust. Nathan Daniels is, err... was a self-employed researcher and historian. His colleague Ken is a metal detectorist, but only as a hobby, I don't know his profession or business interests. I, my daughter Amber, and Ben Tarrant have been researching the whereabouts of an unknown Neolithic or Bronze Age Stone Circle.'

'Could you clarify, so the record of this circle is understandable to laymen like me?'

'It's a type of earthwork from the Neolithic period or Bronze Age, usually consisting of a circular bank with an internal ditch surrounding a central flat area that may contain ritual structures such as timber or stones set usually in a circular arrangement.'

'A sort of Stonehenge.'

'Nothing near as grand.'

'So you have found this structure?'

'No, we haven't found a thing, and if we do, it will probably only be tumbled-down stones amongst bracken or trees.'

'It must be worth the effort combing the Forest of Dean, though.'

'Of course. Documents we have from the 17th century show there was once an impressive structure somewhere in the area we were searching.'

'Alright, so you had a good reason to be in the area. When you left the Phoenix Hotel, all three of you got a taxi to your car – a 4x4 Toyota Land Cruiser, I believe, and left without wandering around.'

'Yes, we did, we were worn out after the day's walking, it was nighttime, pitch black, and freezing cold.'

'So why do you think your companion Nathan Daniels was attacked?'

'I have no idea.'

'And Ken Davies, what about him?'

'I have no idea why he was picked on either – how is he, by the way?'

'I believe he's going to pull through. Mr Davies has been transferred to a private hospital. We are at present contacting them for an update on his condition.'

'Did Nathan give any indication as to why they were attacked?'

'They told him to stop searching, but still took his wallet.'

'So, were they only petty muggers?'

'Maybe. But they warned Mr Daniels off.'

'Have you a description of them?' Dave thought of the four cold and unfriendly men on the walk and then in the bar.

'I normally ask the questions, Mr Dorsett.'

'Sorry, but I want justice for our colleague.'

'His room faced the back of the car park on the second floor. Later that evening, he heard a commotion outside the window and went down to investigate. He found Mr Davies lying unconscious on the concrete outside the fire-escape. Then he was beaten from behind with a metal bar. He didn't see his assailant. Can you think of any reason why these two men were assaulted?'

'I can only give you some background on recent criminal activity and two incidents, threats which may sound unrelated, but I believe they could be connected.' He went on to detail the break-ins, the witchcraft symbols, and the scrawled threat.

'You have no idea who was behind these incidents, I suppose?' asked the sergeant, who now looked even more tired. Dave could only guess because he had added to the massive workload the man was juggling.

'Well, maybe, but it is little more than a theory.'

'Go on...'

Dave related all he knew about Nathan and his mysterious backer, and how the information on the stolen SD card from his camera had given this mystery backer the rough location of the stones.

O'Malley rose from the armchair with some effort. 'I'll give this info to my colleague, who can ask Mr Davies if he knows the name of Mr Daniel's backer.'

'He didn't know. We've already asked him.'

'We'll see about that,' O'Malley said as his finger scrolled his phone. Then he put it to his ear and walked off to face the French doors.

Dave raised his voice; he was beginning to get irritated by O'Malley's brusque manner. 'You should know that my daughter forced some information from Nathan Daniels. He's working through a second party and receives a monthly cheque issued by Photon Venture Holdings. It's a front for someone; we've all tried Googling the name, but no results come back.'

'Thank you,' O'Malley said and turned back to the view from the French doors.

Dave occupied himself with messages on his own mobile and tried to ignore the muttered one-sided conversation behind him. Six minutes later, O'Malley redeposited himself in the chair. 'Can you give me more information on Ken Davies, please?'

'I know nothing about him; he was imposed on us by Nathan Daniels without prior discussion.'

'So he displayed the kind of behaviour you would expect from someone with an interest in your profession?'

'Yes, it was obvious he knew the sort of location we were searching for. He helped spot a couple of possible likely areas of ground, too. Nathan told us he was a keen metal detectorist. I can only assume he was above-board.'

'Above-board — what does that mean in regard to this matter?'

'That he was not a treasure hunter who would keep valuable finds and not report them to a coroner. As you know, the coroner has powers to declare finds as treasure-trove and has powers to stop finds from being sold on. I do wonder, though, whether Ken Davies is what we call a night-hawker that robs new sites of any valuable finds, usually under the cloak of darkness.'

'He was not an above-board detectorist then?'

'I don't have any facts to support that other than his association with Nathan Daniels, who has, I mean, had a reputation for twisting facts, discovering vague clues and then forming them into populist sensations merely to publicise dodgy archaeological theories.'

The detective constable frowned, and Dave could see he was assessing what he had been told. The man looked up. 'I think that will be all, Mr Dorsett. But we will need a formal statement tomorrow, at the station, now this is a murder enquiry.'

Dave nodded. 'Yes, of course,' he muttered in a daze.

He showed O'Malley to the door and watched him drive out of their drive.

'This crazy quest you and Amber have got involved in is going too far now, Dave.'

He was unaware that Liz had been standing behind him; she must have been listening to the whole interview.

'There's so much going on, and a concerted opposition must mean there's something worth finding. Why should the illegal treasure hunters win? We must make another determined effort to find this site and save whatever is there for the nation's heritage.' He surprised even himself with his fierce defence of a project that still only existed on pages of a long-dead Reverend's diary. Then he felt for Liz. She'd put up with a lot recently. To her, the whole thing was a resurrected manifestation of the ordeal they'd both gone through after Volgrum's Last Stand. She thought that his stone circle project would lead to another unpleasant example of the badly paid profession they'd left behind years ago. He walked to Liz and put his arms around her shoulders and drew her to him. 'One more day's searching over at Barkend and then we'll call it a day. I'll go back to online research only. There can be no danger involved in that. But look on the bright side – we're zeroing in on the site, I'm sure, Liz. Next time out, we'll hit the jackpot. There's only this one area left to search.'

'All this trouble for a few old tumbled-down stones, Dave. If it wasn't for Amber being as obsessed with it as you, I'd have demanded you forget the whole thing. Our safety as a family is at risk, and that worries me. I have enough of my own concerns as well.'

'You mean Cowpat at the social club?'

'Who else? She's lying about me behind my back now, I'm sure.'

'One more day's search, Liz, just one more, and if it yields nothing, I'll forget the whole thing. Then I'll intercept Cowpat as she goes into your next meeting. I'll demand she ceases her behaviour.'

'You will promise me this about your project, Dave. I don't want you interfering with my troubles, though. I'm worried you or Amber will be the next victims to end up in hospital or a mortuary.'

'I promise, Love. If we get no results, then the fieldwork is finished and done.'

'Not only the physical fieldwork, Dave, forget the whole fantasy.'

That was something he was reluctant to do. 'There's no harm done in searching Springborough Manor storerooms or to researching the subject in libraries or online. It'll only be a hobby after a look round Springborough – I'll promise you that, Liz.'

She stayed in his arms for a second more before sighing and drawing away. 'Alright, I expect you to keep to that promise though, Davey.' The pet-name was the one she used to call him when they first met.

'Thanks, my dear.' Then he thought to try to raise her spirits a little. 'But what about if we find the circle next time out, and if the circle's there, then there will be evidence of the ditch and embankment too? We could really boost Amber's career with that find.'

'At what cost, Dave? Think of all you went through thirty years ago. Is it worth it?'

There was nothing more he could say to convince Liz. He knew the project was worthwhile. Finding tumbled down stones and a suggestion of a ditch and embankment would do a huge amount to promote not only Amber's career, but Ben's as well. He shrugged and stretched his arms in a gesture that said, who knows? Liz gave him one long look and swept from the room.

Dave sighed and wished he could say more to reassure her. He had to admit to himself that he was far too obsessed with Linda's life, her ceremonies within the circle, and their search for the site. He opened his laptop to check his emails, something to take his mind away from the unpleasant events happening around their project.

In a moment, he was absorbed again – he had a reply from a Jayne Bateman at Springborough Manor. He noted her title was events manager, and she engaged him instantly with what she had to say.

Dear David

Thank you for your inquiry, which has fascinated me, especially the tantalising snippet regarding Linda Rourtier. Yes, I have consulted Mrs Christie, and she is happy for you to look over any old furniture we have in storage. I will accompany you to show you the two rooms where most of the disused furniture is stored. We also have a cupboard in the drawing room containing some old documentation. You are welcome to peruse the library, but we have no proper archive.

Will Thursday, December 7th at 10.30 be convenient for you?

Kind regards

Jayne Bateman

Could this search lead to a breakthrough? Dave hoped he could uncover further documentation that would pinpoint the location of the circle. He allowed himself a moment's daydream where he, Amber, and Ben walked directly into the forest and found the stones hidden somewhere where no one else had stumbled across them. An ancient oak had fallen and exposed its roots to the daylight, and something within had a golden glint. He snapped back to reality – wishful thinking was pointless. He had to examine any old furniture for hidden compartments and see if he could spring a hidden latch again, then maybe some document of importance would be revealed. Dave went online and spent an absorbing hour learning about all the old master-cabinet makers techniques for concealing such things.

That evening, over the phone, Amber showed him how to take a video conference call on his laptop. She was still upset and croaked. 'I went to the hospital to see Nathan. It was too late, and he was already dead. The detective who interviewed me said his arms and legs were all broken and he had a serious concussion from multiple blows to the head. It was a miracle he came round to say anything before he lapsed into a coma.'

He consoled his daughter as best he could, but she disconnected the call when talking became too much. Half an hour later, she reconnected and had brightened; he decided to continue briefing her. So at ten o'clock, he sat awkwardly in front of a split-screen showing himself, Amber, and Ben. He informed them of his appointment at Springborough and tried to tie them down to a date for the final search for the circle, and asked whether they were happy to commit to this one last exploration.

'I'm free this Saturday, but are we sure about opening ourselves up to the possibility of assault?' Ben began, 'I mean, I'll take the risk. I can look after myself, but what about you guys? I'd hate to think of either of you or Liz coming to any harm.'

Dave remembered Amber telling him that Ben was a martial arts fanatic. 'I'll take my chance, but I don't think you ought to open yourself up to more risk, Amber.'

'Don't think I'm going to stay at home and let you two make the find of the century,' she snapped back.

Ben laughed and added, 'I knew you'd say that.'

Dave kept a straight face. He still felt a sense of guilt at having drawn both her and Liz into a venture that was proving more hazardous than they could have envisaged.

'I cannot cast the project aside without knowing whether there is anything to find,' he said with determination. 'If these people really think there is treasure to be found, then we have a moral duty to get there first and retrieve it for the nation.'

'Well put, Dad,' Amber said. 'I'm not to be left behind, I'm as committed to this project as you.'

'And the nation deserves the stones as an addition to all our heritage. So it's Saturday for one last search, then?' Ben added.

'I'm up for it!'

'No lowly criminals will stop me,' Dave finished, with his face inches from the camera.

'I'm not a dentist, Dad, move back a bit.'

'Sorry, this technology is new to me.' All three laughed, and Dave felt a glow of pride toward his dedicated team. 'I'll hopefully brief you on my successful search at Springborough Manor soon. Until then, look after yourselves.'

With an affirmative, they all broke the video connection.

The next few days felt as if they went on forever, like the time preceding a much-anticipated holiday.

Then Thursday 7th, came around amidst a return of snow showers and leaden December skies. By 10.00 in the morning, his 4x4 had skidded and slithered to the ornate entrance pillars and wrought-iron gates of Springborough Manor. He got out and found a voice-com security system and pressed a button for assistance. A digitalised voice asked him to state his name and the reason for his visit. He replied, his words accompanied by a frozen cloud of breath. A security camera on a nearby post refocused on him, then the gates clicked and swung open.

He parked at one end of a long sweeping Cotswold-stone shingle drive. The manor towered above him with its intimidating colonnaded portico, making him feel very small, at the same time, in awe of the magnificent structure. Its frontage loomed up for four stories, each level broken by eight white Georgian-style windows with a multitude of small panes of glass. The west wing was smothered in large-leaf ivy, which in the cold winter morning shone a fluorescent green against the cream-painted surroundings.

Opening the car boot, he removed his old briefcase, which contained a 14-megapixel camera, a small tablet computer for entering notes, an assortment of pens, pencils and disposable gloves, A5 paper notebook, a magnifying glass, and his reading glasses. Carefully closing the boot to avoid making too much noise, he walked up the centre of 16 steps that had been thoughtfully salted to prevent slipping on the ice that coated all other horizontal surfaces. He noticed a row of icicles hanging from the edge of the portico roof; they reflected the yellow light issuing from the windows on either side of the two dark blue front doors. One swung open, and a woman stood silhouetted in the light emanating from within.

'Mr Dorsett, welcome, please come in,' she said in a crystal clear, well-bred English accent. 'I hope your journey was not too eventful?'

'No, it was fine, fortunately the gritting lorries predicted this morning's temperatures,' he lied – his journey had been a nightmare of spinning wheels and lost grip as ditches loomed alongside every corner. He stepped over the threshold into an enormous reception area.

'Shocking weather, a taste of the Christmases of yesteryear,' the woman continued, then held out her hand. 'Charlotte Christie.' Noting his look of surprise, she added, 'I decided to show you round myself. Jayne forwarded your email, and I'm curious about Linda Rourtier and how our old discarded furniture can further our knowledge of her.' She gave him one of those smiles that the British upper-class female specialised in. It said, You can trust me and I'm enjoying this unusual appointment with someone who has less in life than me.

Dave felt warmed by her words and obvious interest. 'I must ask you to keep my interest in Linda Rourtier, your furniture, and archive confidential, Mrs Christie. We have a slightly unsavoury opposition group also searching for what we're working on.'

'Of course, you have my word. It sounds intriguing, can you tell more?'

Instinctively, Dave knew he could trust her, so he carried on to tell more than he had previously decided to. 'I, my daughter and one other have uncovered an extraordinary 18th-century tale of witchcraft thwarted. Pagan ceremonies officiated over by Linda. A love affair with a Christian man of God, and above all this, there is the possibility of an undiscovered Neolithic or Bronze Age circle somewhere not too far away.' Dave left out the possibility of valuable artefacts and more exact locations; he didn't want to give everything away. He could see he had her complete attention.

'Fascinating, David. Some marvellous folk history, and potential to further our knowledge of ancient history.'

As they walked through a long, well-lit corridor lined with tapestries and ornate busts, she broke a friendly silence. 'I gave myself a luxurious evening yesterday to see how much I could find out about Linda - and what little I discovered in two hours was fascinating. What an independent and self-willed woman - to think she walked these floors and looked out onto the same views. I would like to hear more of her and how you linked her to your search, please, Mr Dorsett.'

They strode into a less luxurious area of the mansion, and he gave her a brief rundown on the old Welsh dresser and its secret and the initials on the seal, but stopped short of telling her about the Latin on the wove-paper illustration.

'Extraordinary,' Charlotte said as she opened a door and clicked an old round bakelite light switch. 'This was the Butler's lair,' she laughed. He followed her into a room illuminated by a single bare ceiling bulb and with walls that were stained with a century of grime. Junk and some more substantial furniture had been piled high around a small soot-stained fireplace with a wrought iron grate. An old oak kitchen table had peeling paint and crudely cut boards for a top, but was still strong enough to support piles of boxes brimming with discarded junk. In the far corner, an old writing desk was similarly cluttered. Another cabinet was revealed behind an ancient clothes horse and a large, broken picture frame.

'This is a good starting point for me, Mrs ...'

'... Call me Charlotte, please, Mr Dorsett.'

'Thank you. I will.'

'Good, now let's get stuck in, David. I have allocated the whole morning to this fascinating indulgence.' She rolled the sleeves up on her expensive blue cashmere sweater, revealing a high-priced, feminine Santos De Cartier jewelled watch. He hadn't expected personal help, especially from the well-heeled owner of Springborough Manor. 'Err.... okay, we need to clear the boxes from around the desk. I would like to remove the drawers and check for hidden compartments, latches, and the like.'

An hour later, they both had hands black from grime, and he had nothing to show from their efforts. 'We've drawn a blank here, I'm afraid, Charlotte.'

'Well, we have one other room to forage in, and then I shall leave you to search the library and the concealed cupboard in the drawing room.'

A concealed cupboard certainly sounded as if it would hold items of interest, he thought, as she opened another door at the end of the short corridor.

'This used to be a maid's room,' she said as she clicked another Bakelite light switch.

The room was similarly piled with junk and had even more cobwebbed furniture laden with boxes. From these protruded old candle stick holders and tangled electrical cables. The rest of the room was filled with ornate plant stands, two old chests of drawers, another table with drawers under the top, a collection of four cream-coloured old bedside cabinets with carved legs, and even a moth-eaten rocking-horse. 'Not been in here for ten years,' Charlotte muttered.

He prodded and picked at every hidden surface in the furniture and hauled it all away from the wall to do the same to the rear panels, but to no avail. Despite the furniture being old, stained and unloved, they found nothing unusual apart from some fifty-year-old magazines in a drawer, some old bills and a road atlas from 1938.

'That's me finished in the storerooms. Thank you, Charlotte.'

'Oh well, I'm afraid there are no other rooms containing old junk, David. It's time I left you to your task,' she said with a note of disappointment as they left the room and retraced their steps to the entrance hall. He followed Charlotte through a series of opulent reception rooms. She pointed out a bathroom where he could wash the grime from his hands. The elegant woman led the way into another enormous room with four large windows; an elaborate plastered ceiling, and a wall covered in old portraits enclosed in ornate gold frames. She showed him to an expensive-looking, highly polished mahogany table and four crimson padded chairs in a large bay-windowed alcove. 'This is our east wing dining room. I have arranged for you to have a light lunch in here. I'll get Jayne to show you the library and drawing room at 2 o'clock, but I doubt you will have much success. Five years ago, I gave her permission to look through the books and documents, provided she listed them all on a spreadsheet. She included anything of interest, but found nothing, I'm afraid.' Charlotte held her hands out as if suddenly realising how grubby they were. 'Please make yourself at home.' She turned to go with a last comment. 'I'm so sorry I could not offer you any interesting discoveries, Mr Dorsett, but I hope you have better luck this afternoon. Jayne will keep me informed. It's been nice meeting you,' she held out her hand, and as they shook, he thanked her.

Charlotte nodded, and with a slight smile, closed the door behind her.

He cleaned up in the bathroom, and 15 minutes later, a young woman with unruly russet hair brought a cheese and ham salad, with hunks of bread and homemade salad-garnish, followed by cake and fruit, with a large pot of coffee. Dave assumed she was a housekeeper or cook. 'That looks lovely. I appreciate you all looking after me so well today.' The woman nodded and looked stony-faced at him, then walked away. Dave noted she wore what, these days, was known as 'traveller' fashion. In his time, she would have been called a hippy. It takes all kinds to run somewhere like this, he guessed, and concentrated on the food. As he ate, her face lingered. She had worn her red-auburn hair in dreadlocks gathered behind her neck with a bright band and had had a long hand-woven jumper beneath an apron which didn't match the rest of her fashion statement. She looked familiar, as if they'd met before, but he couldn't place her.

He sat and doused his disappointment with the wonderful flavour of expensive coffee. With anticipation of a successful afternoon, he turned and cast his eye along the portraits. Most had brass plaques screwed into special recesses in the frames. He stopped at one that had no identification. It was smaller but still stood out from the others. Underneath and on the wall was a framed note that said. "This unsigned portrait of an unknown woman is believed to be an estate worker from a cottage belonging to the Rourtier family."

Dave stared in astonishment at the familiar features. It was Linda Mary Rourtier.

CHAPTER THIRTEEN

'The artist is unknown,' a feminine voice behind him said, 'but painted in an extremely accomplished manner and in the techniques of the 17th century.'

He turned and saw a petite young woman in a thick sweater, a carefully knotted scarf around her neck, a long grey skirt, and shiny black shoes. Her hair was tied back in a blonde ponytail, and she smiled a welcome. 'Jayne Bateman.'

'David Dorsett.' They shook hands, and he immediately noticed she was a little more hesitant than her confident employer. 'Thank you for allowing me here today.'

'We're all intrigued by the connection we have with your research, David.'

'Thank you, although I'm afraid I haven't made any further progress this morning.'

'Yes, a shame. Mrs Christie has informed me. I'm afraid I can't guarantee any luck this afternoon either. I have an interest in our library's old documents and leather-bound books. In my spare time, a few years ago, I recorded everything it contains. Still, the best of luck, I'd love you to find something I've missed.' Jayne turned to the painting he was examining. 'I see you have an interest in this enigmatic portrait. We believe it was painted circa 1700. It was found two years ago in a boarded-over alcove in one of the lofts when Mr Christie was supervising replacing some rotten roofing timbers. He decided to get it restored, properly framed, and hung in here. Whoever the model was, the artist must have been captivated by her beauty to have painted such an accomplished portrait. We all here have fallen in love with the painting.'

David stepped back and stared at a familiar and imposing woman. Linda was pictured sitting on a plain wooden chair with a stone-framed window with leaded stained-glass in the background, on the sill was a bunch of tulips in a pottery jar. She was probably in her thirties with the same unruly, curly ginger hair escaping from a different lace bonnet. She had been painted wearing a plain blue blouse with a darker blue shawl draped over one shoulder, which, in this portrait, led down a longer dress of darker blue. The only ornamentation on the figure was a simple red rose pinned to the shoulder.

'I have a tale or two to tell about this woman – It's actually Linda Mary Rourtier. I must inform you that I believe this could have been painted by William Hogarth. It has the style of his early years, about when he first became known and appreciated. I see here some elements included in a little-known painting of his that's stored in the British Museum, also of Linda Mary Rourtier.'

'Really? That's incredible. We need to do some more research on it,' she stared in appreciation at a portrait she obviously had great affection for. 'It must be valuable.'

'I'd get an art expert in, perhaps from one of the major auction houses.'

'Yes, I'll inform Mr and Mrs Christie when we're finished today.'

'Could I take a couple of pictures of her?' he asked as he reached into his briefcase for the camera.

'Of course,' she stepped back so he could get the full portrait in his camera lens. 'But please don't publicise this until we get it authenticated.'

'Of course. I will ask my two fellow researchers to keep it confidential as well.' He stepped back after taking the photos. 'I'm wondering how it came to be hidden in a boarded-up alcove. Obviously done on purpose as if someone was trying to hide any reference to Linda.'

'She was wonderful. It's hard to understand, isn't it?' Jayne looked visibly puzzled. 'I've given many an hour to pondering that without coming to any conclusion.'

'Maybe her parents were too upset at her fall from grace, and wanted to avoid any questions when visitors viewed the painting. That's the only reason I can think of,' Dave said as they both stared in admiration at Hogarth's masterly painting of the beautiful woman.

For a couple of minutes, Jayne appeared deep in thought whilst tapping her lips with the mobile phone she was holding. 'I've had an idea... about your search. I'm wondering if you would care to search the mezzanine area above the stables. There's very old stuff piled up there that's really worse for wear. I was up there with our groundsman two years ago looking for something for Mr Christie, and there was some very old furniture at the back that could have come from the old servants' quarters. I believe it's all been there for years, well before my promotion to this post.'

All Dave's despondency lifted in a moment. 'Thank you, Jayne. That sounds promising. Can we go straight over there?'

'Of course. I'll contact Jeff and his assistant groundsman, and they'll go over and help us move the junk around up there; it's a chaotic jumble.'

'That sounds fine; I was expecting really old furniture to be somewhat inaccessible. I'm very grateful to you for this.'

'Consider it some recompense for your identification and advice on the painting, David.' She turned away and spoke into the phone. A voice replied immediately and agreed to meet them at the stables.

While he had spent the morning inside the manor, the rain had melted the thin layer of snow and ice, turning it to slush. They walked quickly to the stables to avoid the chilling wind driven rain. One side of the main stable doors was open, and Dave could hear voices inside. They went into a room lit by an occasional bare bulb hanging from exposed rafters. Dave glanced around and took in individual bays for 12 horses, only five of which were occupied. The animals were in an assortment of colours and breeds, which snorted and stomped, excited to see people. Tack was hung on wooden pegs all around, and one side of the stable was filled with bales of hay. A middle-aged man in a waxed green jacket was manoeuvring a wooden ladder up toward the mezzanine level. He was being assisted by a teenager who looked almost asleep. He had long brown hair and wore a retro denim jacket and ripped jeans.

'Hi Jeff, you got here quickly,' said Jayne breezily.

'Not much we can do outside in this weather, Love. We were only cleaning tools and suchlike.'

The ladder was in place in moments, and Jeff stood on the end, tried unsuccessfully to wobble it, and then declared it safe. Jayne introduced Dave, and the groundsman nodded in response. His assistant looked too worn out to reply.

'You wanna go up first mate and tell us what you want shifted,' suggested Jeff.

After testing the ladder to see if it would take his weight, Dave carefully rose one rung at a time. Above him, a worn and bent wood railing fronted the mezzanine, held together by old rusty nails. He grasped the rail to heave himself up onto the wood boarded floor. There was little room to move. The area was full of all manner of junk from broken wheelbarrows to various signs screwed to stakes announcing, *Open Day Today* and *Keep off the Grass*. He shifted a roll of plastic barrier fencing and then a wooden crate filled with worn, snapped halters and harnesses, frayed rope, and other equestrian debris. Behind a stack of carelessly stored wrought-iron railings, he spotted the first piece of furniture, a bedroom drawer cabinet with open drawers from which spewed old sheets of newspaper and a few bottles of dirt-coated garden chemicals. Behind that, he could see a dressing table whose sides looked to have been crudely repaired with black painted timber. A wooden crate and four cardboard boxes bulged with plastic pots, and other wooden containers sat on the dressing table and towered above his head. He shifted a collection of old boots and broken tools to get to this pile before realising he was now in danger of trapping himself amongst the junk. It was a major clearing operation.

'Okay, guys, I give up. We need to take a lot of this stuff out and temporarily store it down below – if that's alright Jayne?'

'Certainly. Come down, Dave, and we'll leave Jeff and Marty to shift it.'

'Not too many spiders, I hope,' muttered Jeff as he revealed his phobia.

The two men began to lower the pile of junk into a corner of the lower stables, amidst grunting and heaving. Jeff stopped occasionally to swear and brush his jacket. 'I hate the damned things,' he said, as another large spider scuttled away. They refused all offers of help, which secretly pleased Dave. Any heavy work left him with a sore back that made him feel his age these days. Jayne took him over to the horses, who all knew her well.

'I ride this guy, Toblerone. He was a great racing thoroughbred, retired now as he's an old boy,' Jayne said as she stroked the horse's muzzle. Dave was introduced to the other horses, a mix of Welsh Mountain and Highland ponies.

Whilst stroking Toblerone's muzzle, Jayne paused and looked directly at Dave. 'Could I ask you a very small personal favour, Dave?'

He came instantly alert, wondering what was coming. 'Of course, Jayne, you've been of great help to me already.'

'I and my daughter Raven have become very keen metal detectorists. We were isolated together during the Covid lockdowns, and both of us loved a certain TV sitcom series about metal detecting enthusiasts created a few years ago. We have a large garden - a great place to practice, so I bought a couple of second-hand machines on eBay. After many hours of finding bits of metal junk, Raven found a brooch with a garnet in the centre. Not worth much, according to a jeweller friend. It was right at the bottom of the garden near the field boundary. It really cemented our relationship and hobby.'

A worthwhile find, Dave remembered his grandmother had a similar item. He nodded and waited for her to continue.

'I found a small Georgian thimble and a recently dropped pound coin.'

Dave nodded, 'How did you identify the finds?'

'Put them into one of those photo apps that identify anything. And it found accurate matches. Not the pound coin though,' she laughed and continued. 'We're not very good at asking permission from local farmers if we can sweep their fields, though. In fact, we're so inexperienced we're embarrassed to ask.'

'I understand. Some farmers are agreeable, especially when they know any finds would be split fifty-fifty.'

'I know, we've looked up the legal side.'

'You could join a local detecting society for experience.'

'We have our names down for the two local groups, but at present they're full.'

'I'm not surprised, Jayne,' Dave sympathised. 'Since Covid and the ongoing publicity following the increase in valuable finds, it's become a very popular hobby.'

'Yes. So many people suddenly had time on their hands. I guess it's not surprising they took it up. So I was wondering …' Jayne hesitated.

'How can I help?' Dave prompted.

'Well, if your search involves needing an area swept. Could you consider me and Raven for the job?' She looked intently at him, hopefully even.

It obviously meant a lot to her. If he included her in a detectoring sweep, then he would be there to supervise, and each promising signal could be investigated together. A local society and its experienced detectorists and the permissions they obtained for searching private land were really the best way ahead for her, though, Dave realised. She could not know of the valuable ceremonial artefacts that were associated with their research, so she couldn't be angling to be included in that search.

'I'll log your interest, Jayne, and if we need your services in the future, it would certainly help us both. But at the moment, our quest is more of a historian's project with absolutely nothing in the physical landscape to warrant such a search anywhere. And if we do find a need for a detectorist search, we would of course need permission from the landowner. By then, we would have to declare the location of such a historic find to official circles. They would have specialist archaeologists experienced at metal detecting within a team they appoint.'

'I understand, Dave. Just thought I'd ask. You've already taught me a lot from just discussing our new hobby.'

'I won't forget your request, Jayne. Sometimes these searches do warrant a quick detector search to confirm something unofficially. I'll keep you and your daughter in mind.'

'Thanks again. I appreciate you speaking frankly. I still have a lot to learn.'

'Yes, there is a lot to know about. And not just the identification of items you may not recognise as worth keeping. Whatever you do, if you're lucky enough to find gold or anything you think is remotely valuable, report it to the local Finds Liaison Officer or the Coroner within 14 days. There was a jail sentence handed out recently to two people who tried to sell a coin horde privately.'

'Thanks, yes. In the unlikely event of us striking valuables, we'll definitely keep within the law.'

'Good. Any question I can answer, just message me and I'll do my best to help. My daughter Amber and her colleague may be able to help too if I can't.'

Jayne nodded, accepting all that he had said. 'That's all I can ask. Thanks, Dave.

'No problem.'

He frowned inwardly as a thought entered his head, 'Have you ever heard of a detectorist, who may be a local, called Ken Davies?'

She thought for a moment, 'Sorry no. The name rings no bells with me. I'll ask Raven tonight.'

'No, it's not important. He was someone I met briefly recently. It just occurred to me that I didn't know whether he was local.'

The unexpected conversation had taken up 50 minutes. It was interrupted as Jeff shouted down, 'Okay, that's got you to the furniture, Mr Dorsett.' The groundsman didn't even seem out of breath. Marty sat on a straw bale, yawning.

Jayne sat next to Marty and started tapping on her phone. Dave hoped she was just reporting back to her daughter. Jeff produced a flask and two cups, one of which he handed to Marty. In moments, Dave was up the ladder and checking which piece of furniture looked most likely to contain hidden compartments. He went from one set of drawer units to another, then to the dressing table, and onward to an assortment of rustic single cupboards. None looked well enough built to contain secret compartments, so he started to open doors and drawers. An assortment of contents spilt out of each. After an hour of searching, he'd found many old magazines, candles set in rusty stands, empty boxes of matches, two Victorian photo frames still containing faded sepia photos, ancient newspapers, an old shawl, a pair of moth-eaten laced boots, and an assortment of bent nail files, scissors and combs.

The last piece of furniture was wedged in the darkest corner and covered in a century of cobwebs. It was an old drawer unit about three feet tall and four feet wide, and was painted a revolting and peeling dark green. The piece had four drawers, each with two plain wrought iron handles. The whole piece appeared well-made but battered with many years of use. On opening the top two drawers he saw they contained balls of rotting string, an old rusty penknife, a broken jewellery box, and an unused hardback notebook which fell apart when he picked it up, and finally the skeleton of a mouse. In minutes, he had got to the last drawer at the bottom of the unit. This one was frozen solid. He tugged, tapped, and twisted the drawer by its handles, but whatever he did, it would not budge.

He shouted downstairs, 'One last drawer to check out, and it's jammed! Have you got a screwdriver, Jeff, or something else to lever it open?'

'I have everything in my pockets, Dave,' he joked and came up the ladder as if he expected a horde of rats to attack him. Unbelievably, he had a large penknife with a screwdriver and an assortment of other built-in tools. He had found a broom and proceeded to brush the cobwebs away. After 10 minutes of levering with the penknife, Jeff also admitted defeat. 'Almost as if this bugger has a false front,' he muttered.

Dave took the possibility seriously – it was possible. He crouched down to examine the door front. One end had sagged slightly or maybe it was so crudely made that the drawer runners weren't level. He shone his pen-torch into the crack and thought there were drawer sides within. 'No, I think it looks like a real drawer, Jeff. It's just jammed.'

Marty, unknown to Dave, was leaning on the balustrade behind him. 'Rip the bottom plank off at the back, mate. You can look inside and see what's jamming it.' The lad was beginning to get involved, as if he was finally recovering from a hangover.

'Hey, good idea, Marty boy. I'll rip it open from its back.' Jeff immediately hauled the drawer unit out from the corner as spiders scuttled back into the shadows. 'Nip back to the workshop, mate, and grab a crowbar, hammer, and a strong spade. We'll have these old planks off in a jiffy.'

Marty disappeared at a run. Dave thought the boy had fully woken up now, probably in time for the next night of booze and partying, he assumed. It seemed a shame to ruin such an old item of furniture, but Dave placated this feeling by imagining another 100 years before anyone set eyes on the piece again.

The three of them sifted through some of the junk while they waited for Marty. Jayne put a picture frame to one side. 'The photo looks to be of the housekeeping team from the early 1900s. Mrs Christie could keep it on the ballroom bar as an item of interest for the next party bookings.'

Jeff commented on a few items, but nothing of interest to his search. Dave opened the drawer above the jammed one; it opened fully but there was a plank base beneath it, obscuring the bottom drawer top. He stood to one side and tried to work out why the bottom drawer was so jammed up and concluded that the frame of the piece must be warped either from damp or being manhandled up here all those uncountable years ago. Perhaps it really was a false front, as Jeff had suggested, as the unit showed no sign of incorporating any kind of sophisticated release mechanism. The back of it also looked as rustic as the front and sides. It was obviously a very old piece and would have been in the bedroom of one of the lowest grades of servant in the manor's workforce. Perhaps even a stable-hand that slept in here, he surmised. His thoughts were interrupted by Marty, who climbed the ladder crashing a spade into each rung as he did so. He handed the tool and a selection of others to Jeff as he levered himself up onto the wooden platform.

Dave thought the spade was too crude a tool to use. He moved to the back of the unit and against the wall so he could supervise Jeff to make sure the man would not destroy the back of the drawer unit completely. 'Not too enthusiastic, please – I hate the idea of unnecessary damage. Looks like woodworm could have weakened the whole back, anyway.'

'Sure thing, Dave. Picture of restraint, me.'

Crouching down, Jeff hammered the end of a crowbar into the edge of the bottom plank where it was nailed onto the unit's back. He grunted and heaved on the plank edge, to no avail.

'Careful.'

'I am being,' Jeff snapped back.

'Try the other edge.'

'I was just going to.'

Dave thought it best to say no more.

The other edge of the backing plank was equally hard to remove, the nails that held it appeared to have rusted into place. Even Dave was getting impatient now.

Jeff hit a hammer hard on the centre of the plank, which bowed and sprung back. A cloud of dust rose from the joints.

'No good. It's going to have to be brute force,' announced the groundsman.

'What do you intend? I'm sorry, I was an archaeologist, and forcing anything is still a complete horror to me.'

'I'm going to bend the middle and get Marty to force the spade into the top of the damned plank in the middle of the unit, then use it as a fuckin' lever.'

'I suppose that'll create a large enough gap. I'll use that large screwdriver and try to force the edge away as you do that.'

Marty was with them in a moment, and Dave noticed the boy looked alert, with his wide eyes showing excitement over the sudden, violent, forced entry.

In moments, they had grouped round, and Marty forced the spade in. Jeff hammered the crowbar's metal edge into the groove. Marty tugged and Dave levered while Jeff hammered. Suddenly, the left edge of the plank popped out under the crowbar. Dave dropped the screwdriver and tried bending the plank outwards. Marty also grabbed an edge, and it came away with a crunch and another cloud of sawdust and dirt.

In moments, they had the debris cleared away, revealing the back of the drawer. It was not a false front.

'I'm going to kick the fucker forward now,' panted Jeff.

'No, take a bit more care.'

'What for? It's jammed fucking solid. It needs a well-aimed kick.'

'If you must,' Dave gave up on his principles.

Jeff sat facing the back of the unit, and using his boot heel, he kicked hard.

Dave winced at the resulting crunch. The drawer front protruded a centimetre.

Another kick, then another. Marty grabbed two drawer handles and tugged. Both the handle's screws ripped out, and the boy fell backward.

'One more kick.'

Dave winced at the resulting grating sound. The drawer flew forward with a grinding sound. Dave stooped and examined the drawer sides and runners. 'There's the reason for the jam,' he announced and pointed. Someone had driven thick handmade nails into the runners at an angle so that the drawer could be shoved closed but not reopened. He was looking at the stub of a broken, headless nail and then the other side of the drawer, which had a similar nail now bent sideways.

'Thanks, guys. My apologies, it was the only way to open it in the end,' he said, looking at the two groundsmen. They moved away to allow him to get to the drawer, and he bent and rested a knee on the floorboards to look inside. It was only filled with decaying cloth - an old blanket. It may once have had a tartan pattern, but now looked various shades of threadbare grey under a layer of grime. Disappointment filled him, but there was only one more thing to do before giving up for the day. Carefully, he removed the blanket and placed it on the floor. A large black spider scuttled into a fold. Jeff screamed and took two steps back. Dave ignored him and looked into the bottom of the drawer, which was filled with a flat, brown leather folder. A ragged, buff coloured edge protruded.

In a moment, he knew what it was and grunted his excitement.

Jayne stooped next to him. 'A document, surely,' she gasped.

Dave took great care to remove the leather folder and placed it on top of the unit. Then took his camera out and photographed every detail.

'I'm not leaving till we've seen what it is,' Jayne stated with conviction. Then she turned to Jeff and Marty, 'Thanks for all your help, guys. It is much appreciated.'

Jeff gave a small salute with fingers to his forehead as if he'd once been in the armed services and turned to go. Marty looked disappointed but followed his boss down the ladder.

Finally, Dave lifted the leather flap. Three pages of wove paper were revealed, full of handwritten text. This time, the familiar hand was revealed to be shaky and with lettering plastered in inkblots. The top page had many crossings-out and alterations, but it was still the hand of Reverend Edgar Dalmont. Dave felt huge elation; the whole day's search had been worthwhile. But this new batch of pages had been harder to find than the previous ones. He wondered whether these three sheets would be the last he would find. He opened the folder and pored over the text as Jayne pressed against his shoulder to read.

Dear diary, it is with the greatest devotion that I create this document, and it is fitting that this writing shows my veneration to the Gods, who cast their divine hands over our lands. It is also apt that this devotion be written on a page of the diary I once kept most faithfully. This was once devoted to my previous worship of another God, but has now been blessed by the King of the Gods, Woden.

Our thriving church is no more. We have fled to pastures anew and left behind our glorious temple. Glenys, my beloved High Priestess, and I are destitute and rely on the charity of others now that we are exiled from the earthly dwelling of the Gods.

The cause of this sorry tale must now be explained. At least one of our fellowship allowed his devotion to escape his mouth, and soon his talk spread until it became too much for the dreaded watchmen of Gloucester to bear. He was not a treacherous fellow, merely one under the influence of one of our mankind's many vices. I am told this poor man was prone to spending his pennies on copious quantities of ale, for which he had a greater devotion to than our church. One evening, he was followed after boasting about our holy temple to all who would listen. He was heard to say that he had travelled many times to attend a rich and heavenly gathering in distant woodland. Being in a permanent state of inebriation, he remembered none of our rules, and caused a great noise as he sang and blundered straight to our ceremony.

We had barely a minute's warning from our one lookout before a multitude of watchmen thronged amongst us. Our loyal follower Archie Woodright ran with myself and my dearest Glenys, and so being forced to dispatch two chasing watchmen with merely a strong bough. I and Glenys had to run to a prepared and blessed hide to bury there our sacred chalice, ceremonial jewellery, and other treasures. I will tell more of their location later in this account. I believe dear Alfred, Daisy, Agnes, and Cuthbert lost their lives as they defended us, our sacred altar, and beloved circle of stones. I am told that apart from Archie, all the others of our congregation were arrested and taken before the mercy of magistrates or slaughtered. I myself received a sword thrust to the shoulder as I defended our Glenys from harm. My beloved then received the strength of Sampson and became like a woman possessed, for the power of the Gods was within her. She hauled me away and, somehow, we evaded the watchmen.

When my freedom is further threatened, I will leave this journal with a good friend, him being Lawrence Thorpe-Wellington. I must here declare it was he who rescued this journal from our cottage and smuggled it to me in our woodland retreat. He is now under instruction to keep this valuable and true record safe for when I deem it right to pass it on to the next custodian of our circle. He will further hold it till my daughter Willow reaches adult years. She will then be allowed to examine this record of her parents' devotion and observance of divine providence. These are precautions I must take for Glenys, and I have great fear for our lives. The watchmen are still in search of us, and we must be gone to wander the forests and live with the woodland God Thralen in his leafy abodes.

Our dear Willow is with us, for now, as we go from one hideout to another. These are small cottages and shepherd huts, some heated with fiery hearths, others devoid of all comforts. We have good friends who still serve to clothe and provision us to keep starvation at bay. But there are days when we merely eat berries from the trees and what meat our animal traps provide.

This has been a fall from our lofty status, but we will continue to worship the true Gods. Why did the great ones not come to our aid when we needed them too? That is only for them to know. I suspect we were found unworthy in some manner. You will undoubtedly ask how our unfortunate situation came to be. It was to do with the bigoted councilmen and clergy of the local wards who believe in only their single, all-encompassing God and will allow no other. So they sent their watchmen and constables against us and we were too peaceful in our intents to prevail.

My and Glenys's beloved temple is a thing of the past, and we can now only pay homage to the great Gods in small clearings within distant woodland. Our small ceremonies are filled with devotion, and we three sing heartily, which returns the Gods to us for a while. Occasionally, we are joined by devoted followers when they are sure their absence will not be noticed. We bless these temporary places of worship with woven effigies and other offerings to placate the great Gods, so all is not lost. We are blessed with Willow, our daughter, who is our acolyte in training and sings with a wonderful, youthful voice. We three still dance, sing, and joyously praise the great ones, for no one can take our beliefs from us, and no one can say the great Gods of old do not still watch over us. The Priestess has served our masters with great devotion, and I am convinced they hold a special place for her by their sides.

But the intolerant watchmen and their masters still search for us in the hope they can incarcerate us in the deepest, dampest, and most forgotten dungeon. They will not succeed because, like the Goddess Morrigan, we can change our disguises at will and are able to become invisible in the depths of the woodland.

'Is this a continuing story? I mean, a saga from the 18th century?' Jayne gasped.

'Well, yes, it is turning into quite an involved and tragic tale.'

'It's almost as if they employed an ancient magic to make themselves invisible. Surely not? I mean, how did they evade capture?'

'No, it's not magic, just the style he wrote in. He's using fantasy to upgrade and applaud the skills of his beloved wife. I and my colleagues are hoping to find the location of this pagan temple. That's the main purpose of my research.'

Jayne looked at him as if trying to assess something he said. 'Such a sad story. I'm not surprised you are keen to recover more.'

'I fear these may be the last pages to be found. It's thanks to you, Jayne, that I found this batch.'

'Thank you, and I really hope there is more of this tale hidden somewhere.'

Jayne looked completely fascinated, and Dave trusted she would not use social media to blurt out their find. 'It's too late in the afternoon to carry on searching back in the manor house. Can I make an appointment to come back?'

'Of course, I'll check with Mrs Christie, but I'm sure the beginning of next week will be fine.'

'Many thanks, and could I ask you to keep this find in confidence, please?'

'I will, and I'll give these pages to Charlotte later. She will be fascinated with your find, David. Would you like to photograph them first?'

Dave thought quickly, his small camera was not up to accurate on-the-spot snaps of important documentation. He needed to set the pages up at home and use his DSLR camera and proper lighting to get accuracy and clarity. 'Do you mind if I take them home to photograph properly? I'll bring them back next time I'm over.'

Jayne thought for a moment, 'Feel free to take these pages with you for now. Mrs Christie will want them returned though.'

'Thank you, and yes, I understand.' Dave hoped that next week's appointment was not too late and Mrs

Christie, Jayne, or someone else would not conduct their own search of the dining room cupboard and the library. He believed it a possibility that further pages could have been hidden within large old books, and he intended to carry out a very comprehensive search.

CHAPTER FOURTEEN

Matt had no idea how long he sat distraught. Eventually, he moved to stare into the box until the sun moved around and shone through the shed window directly at him. It was as if he'd just lost a close family member and was grieving. Idly, he shifted an old tennis ball from one hand to the other. About twenty minutes later, he was starting to shiver with cold and shock and managed to sift through the debris in the hope of finding the necklace. His shaking fingers and watery eyes found everything else, his mother's brooch, his father's Rolex, the money, the certificates - but not the necklace in its box.

He sat with his back to the shed wall and thought and thought.

First, he had to report the item stolen. Provide the police with the photos, then ring the Finds Liaison Officer to tell him the terrible news. Then he had to phone Edgar, which was another thing he needed to think hard about.

He phoned the police and was given a crime number and the email of someone who was designated to investigate the theft. The officer asked if he had any idea who knew where to look for the artefact. Matt couldn't give a single clue and exclaimed irately, 'How could anyone have known it was my private garden shed that held my hidden safe place? No one looking from neighbour's windows has X-ray vision, and my fence is six feet high and secure as well.'

The officer grunted and tapped away on a keyboard. He wanted copies of the pictures, so Matt went indoors and started his laptop, then attached and emailed the photos.

The Finds Liaison Officer was trickier. He wanted the crime number and the name of the officer dealing with the case. Matt gave him all the information. He asked the same questions as the police about where Matt had left the necklace and got the same answers. Matt stated that he had no idea where it was now.

'Can I send you the photos, as a record of the find in case someone else offers it to you?'

'Yes, Mr. Bradley, that would be advisable. But I've never heard of a thief offering a stolen item to the country.'

'Sorry, it's all I can think of to help.'

'I understand. Thank you for informing me. I hope the police can resolve this.'

'I hope so too.' He broke the connection.

After the call, Matt was left thinking that O'Brady thought he'd made it all up, going by the man's impatient and annoyed questions. Matt then realised the man may think the necklace had never existed; or maybe he thinks I've sold it illegally, was his last desperate thought before refusing to debate with himself further.

After fielding all the upsetting questions, he started to focus on real possibilities. Matt slammed his mobile phone onto the table and started thinking hard. No neighbours could see in, of course, but someone eavesdropping from the field boundary at the bottom of the garden might have worked something out. He wandered outside to the hedge boundary and stared up at the old horse chestnut tree.

Someone climbing up there could possibly look down into the shed window. But who would know where he lived to be up there spying on him? Then he really started thinking. Edgar had also shown a very strange interest and had asked more direct questions than appeared normal. He had sounded irritated and was so adamant he wanted to see the treasure, it was almost as if he was trying to confirm something he already knew about. The farmer also probably knew where he lived from years ago. But he wouldn't be capable of climbing the tree; he was surely in his early sixties. With a disturbing thought, Matt realised Edgar was very fit because of his job and could have climbed the tree. He would have had to have had a huge motive other than simply selling the necklace for easy cash; perhaps the farm was going bankrupt? Matt stopped there and refocused. There must be other suspects.

Then it hit him – the dead-eyed military man had heard his description of the treasure and had been very curious. Noddy had used his, Matt's name whilst speaking. The military man heard that vital info and had the ability to find his address online. He was fit and could have climbed the tree with ease.

Matt forced his way through a thin part of the hedge and into a field where wheat shoots were starting to appear. He needed to find evidence to inform the police about, to show he could have been under surveillance. He started by examining the soil and grass verge around the tree. The field soil had been scarified to a fine tilth and was undisturbed. He looked closely at the tree trunk, a large root spread above ground into the field edge, and the finely ploughed soil was very close to the root, but no footprints disturbed the surface. He spotted three broken twigs on the ground; they were freshly snapped with golden horse chestnut leaves still attached. There was also a footprint under the largest twig, it showed clear indentations with tread patterns. The intruder had walked along the grass until the large tree root allowed him to climb up the tree, but had also forced him to step on the soil. Maybe the police can use the tread print to identify the make of boots worn, he hoped, so he photographed the footprint using his phone. Matt then noticed disturbed soil and the shape of what could have been a hand. He wondered if the intruder could have tripped over the root, which would imply that whoever it was had been there during nighttime hours. Matt envisaged the man staring through the holes in the hedge at his shed and the back of the house as he walked and had simply not seen the root.

Then Matt had a disturbing thought. He had last viewed the necklace in daylight this morning and would have seen an intruder. But it had been late last night and pitch-black when he came outside to take photos of his treasure. He had turned the shed light on; whoever it was could have seen everything he'd done illuminated by the light from the shed. The bench would have been in full view and the necklace also on it. If he'd resisted a final examination of the necklace, no one would have known where it was.

Matt decided to be sure he was right first before doing anything else or telling the police. He would have to climb the tree. The lowest branch that would support a slightly overweight adult with spinal problems was about six feet up. He decided to get his aluminium decorating steps out to make the ascent easy. He was back ten minutes later and propped the stepladder against the tree without opening them out. They became firmly wedged, so he tested his weight on the first rung. It was solid and would not move. The climb was easier than he thought, and Matt managed to heave himself from the top step onto the branch with relative ease. The view inside the shed was very clear from his elevated position. His heart raced with frustration – why in damnation had he bothered to admire his treasure last night? It was a really stupid thing to do. He hit his forehead on the tree in frustration.

Do I go and confront Edgar or start checking out the military man? Matt pondered as he trudged back indoors to get his car keys. The quickest response would be to tackle Edgar. He knew exactly where to find the farmer. Decision made, he swung the car into the road and raced through the gears.

As he drove, he recapped Edgar's responses to the find. He had been so insistent on seeing a sharp picture. Surely the guy didn't want to examine it that closely. Unless he was looking for an inscription that he, Matt, hadn't spotted, that is. The thought went off in his head like a bombshell. What would it have said, "All my love, Edgar", perhaps. Edgar had been married to Deidre for almost 40 years, and the loss of the beautiful find would have been a severe upset. Surely, I would have seen an inscription, though. He continued pondering. Then wondered if it was somehow written finely on a stem that joined a leaf to the necklace. He decided that scenario was unrealistic, then another reason came to mind. It could also have been a family heirloom that had been lost in the woodland by his mother or grandmother, and the sorry tale had been handed down in the family for generations. It was reason enough for Edgar to steal it back, he decided. 'I have to force an answer or two out of the man,' Matt snarled aloud in anger. 'I want it back from you,' he shouted. Edgar knew something more; he became convinced of it.

In record time, he screeched to a halt on the cracked concrete yard of Edgar and Deidre's farmhouse. Matt jumped from the car and slammed the door. Edgar's tractor was parked in front of the barn. Matt marched to it; the engine was warm. He ran into the open barn and shouted, but there was no response. In seconds, he had turned and reached the old weather-beaten front door of the farmhouse, and began to hammer on the tarnished brass knocker.

No answer as usual. He hammered again, then lifted the letterbox flap and shouted. 'Edgar, I know you're in there. I need to speak pronto or I'll kick this door down.'

He heard a rustle, then signs of movement. The sound of creaking stairs receding announced someone had decided to keep out of the way.

He decided to find a back door.

He found it through a side gate, around the rear of the dilapidated farmhouse. The door to a glass porch with peeling paint and weatherboarded sides was open. An internal door had an ordinary metal doorknob. He turned it and marched in. He found himself in the kitchen.

Edgar was seated at a large wooden kitchen table, calmly eating his evening meal.

'I need a word,' Matt snarled.

Edgar looked up, then took another mouthful. 'What about?' he asked with a mouth crammed with beef.

'You damn well know.'

'No idea. You've broken into my house without permission. You try telling me.'

'My necklace has been stolen.'

Edgar's mouth hung open. 'What?'

'You heard.'

Edgar slammed his knife and fork down. 'That was important to us. I suppose you left it where it could be seen, from a window or something.'

'I did not, it was well hidden.'

Matt took three steps toward Edgar and put his hands on two corners of the table opposite Edgar and leaned over, despite his back twinging. 'You already knew something about the necklace, didn't you?'

'I don't.' Edgar started fidgeting and picked up his fork and pointed it. 'I don't. Not in the way you think anyway.'

'You do know something then. It was not a normal interest you showed, was it?'

Edgar sighed, and his eyes appeared to look inward. He said nothing and Matt just stood leaning toward the farmer. Eventually one of them had to say something so Matt shouted, 'Spit it out. You've got thirty seconds.'

'Okay.' Edgar sighed in defeat. 'I'll tell you what I know.'

'Then afterwards, you can tell the police.'

'It's not that kind of knowledge. It won't help retrieve it.'

'Tell me, and I'll decide.'

'Many generations ago, my ancestors came to this country as slaves. The first recorded information comes from a local stately home, Bedringham House, where the once slaves had been given their freedom and were known as Bondsmen. My ancestor in the early 18th century was called Archie Woodright. He came from the same Jamaican family who were originally slaves a hundred years before his grandparents were freed by the family. He was known as a Serf or Bondsman, as he could not be sold but stayed with the family as a 'free' man. He worked there as the head groundsman and gamekeeper. He had special privileges as it appears the family was fond of him; they even taught him to read and write. There still exist letters from him in the Bedringham House archive.'

'How do you know all this?'

'My wife Deidre. She loves researching our family history. Fifteen years ago, the owners of Bedringham allowed her to go through the archive, and she photo'd a few letters and accounts from Archie. It appears he had a lot to do with a local pagan sect and barely escaped the lawmen of the time.'

'So what does this have to do with the necklace?'

'I think you'd best read the letter he sent to the Lord of the manor. I'll get her to bring up the photo on her laptop. She stored it there, I think, before she typed my family history. You can read the letter written direct from Archie.'

Matt thought about it and realised he had been too harsh on Edgar. He didn't like apologising much to anyone, but in this instance … 'Sorry, Edgar, for interrupting your dinner. I overreacted. This whole thing is turning into a nightmare. I think the Finds Liaison Officer at the council thinks I've sold it illegally and he's going to report his suspicions to the police.'

'Okay, Mate. We'll try to get to the bottom of this. Take a seat.' Edgar disappeared up the stairs in the hallway.

Matt sat and recapped what he'd just learnt. So, the necklace probably didn't belong to Deidre, but someone in Edgar's family from hundreds of years ago. He waited another ten minutes and heard the ceiling above creak as someone moved around up there. Then muffled voices and steps sounded on the stairs.

'Here you are. Read this. She's got the original faded ink pen letter up on the screen. Our son managed some electronic wizardry to make the words more visible.'

Matt leaned over the table and to the laptop. It looked like an old document, damp stained and yellowed. The type stood out enough to make the flowery writing style legible, and he began to read.

My dearest Lord Drailton

Please forgive the length of this letter, and I pray it does not inconvenience you.

I fear it is a necessary correspondence as I returned yesterday afternoon rather dishevelled and Lady Constance observed me and asked to my health.

I beg now to report to you of rather sad goings-on in woodland nearby. I believe the Sheriffs may approach you for information, but I hereby assure you, I am guilty of no offense.

Two days ago, I was beyond our land's boundary, and tracking poachers, when I came across my friends and most wonderful people, the once-Reverend Edgar Dalmont and his wife Glenys.

They have asked me to do a service for them and would I entrust a confidence, for which I readily agreed. As you know, they are being searched for by the lawmen, and also that their place of worship is no more. So I must ask you to keep the following in confidence.

They were running from a search party on high ground over Symonds Yat direction yesterday. It was an unfortunate encounter and the Reverend was mortified he had not kept better watch. He told myself that Glenys had tripped whilst fleeing through trees above the river. He helped her up, and they evaded pursuit. Unfortunately, her gold necklace with its silver and gold leaves had become torn from her neck when she tripped, and they were unable to search and to recover it for fear their pursuers would apprehend them.

I must now come to the crux of this account. They implored me, in the name of the woodland gods Malthren and Thralen, to search the area for this necklace. The treasured item was handed down to her, in her past life as Linda, by her grandmother. I, being a gamekeeper, would be expected to roam in woodland, so would register no suspicion. I agreed and hope to find this item, beloved by dear Glenys, very soon.

I myself was then yesterday apprehended by a Sheriff and at sword-point asked to explain my presence there. Although I was searching for the above item, I informed him I was tracking poachers, but he still believed I was one of these misguided criminals.

I was requested to prove I had knowledge of my profession, and was able to show the traps I had just dismantled. He agreed that had I been a criminal poacher, these traps would have been set instead.

Sir, I took the liberty of referring them to you, hoping you would confirm my credentials beyond any further suspicion.

I respectfully ask if you could do so, as they will be riding this way shortly.

Your loyal servant
Archie Woodright

Matt read the account twice; he had no knowledge of any of the information or characters in the letter. The necklace and the location certainly checked out. After he spent a further five minutes deep in thought, he managed to relate it all to Edgar's behaviour and his innocence in the necklace theft. 'So, Archie never found the necklace, but you believed it to be on your land, hence why you allowed the detecting club and me to search there. I take it you didn't tell them what you hoped they'd find either?'

'No, of course I didn't want them to search for anything specifically. I didn't want to make the necklace public knowledge and have them return endlessly. I may have been pestered by other metal detectorists or treasure hunters as well. If one of these unknown characters had found it, I doubted I would ever get to see it, let alone get it back.'

'Okay, let's move on. Has Deidre found any other documents relating to the necklace?'

'This was the only item I was interested in – it was on my land somewhere, so how could I not be?'

'I guess, the words, 'running through trees,' gave you and the previous detectorists enough clues to narrow the search area.'

'Not as simple as that, there was a lot more woodland on the steep banks up from the river in the 18th and 19th centuries. A lot was cut down to build wooden-hulled ships, and more during both world wars. Hence, they had a larger search area than the letter implies.'

'Okay. I'll go along with that. So where do we go from here?' Matt asked.

'We find the shit that stole the necklace from us.'

'Us?'

'I own half. I don't need to remind you. I was also hoping I might retain custody of the necklace as we know its history and links to my family, but the picture shows it's extremely valuable. I think the British Museum may even be interested, but then I'm not an expert. Back to this pressing matter, and tracking down the culprit. Did you see any kind of suspicious behaviour that evening?'

'Of course not, I was indoors with the curtains pulled.' Matt felt a lot more conciliatory now. 'I have one other possible culprit, now I can discount you.' He related what had happened in the Queens Arms the other evening. 'I know what you're going to say. I was stupid to mention the necklace openly in such a den of iniquity.'

'Do you know which of the buggers heard, and do you know his name?'

'No, to both questions, but I'm going to try to find out.'

'No wrong. We're going to find out.'

Matt was so surprised; he lost his train of thought for a moment. It was actually good to have a partner in this search. Someone with whom he could exchange information and conjecture with. Someone who could help formulate plans and then carry them out with him. 'Okay, partner. Let's pool ideas.' He briefed Edgar with the whole of the unfortunate conversation in the Queens Arms.

'So, Dodger thought he lived locally. I'll ask Zed Halane, he lives in Lower Rainstock too.' Edgar finished his cold dinner as he spoke.

'I'll drop in on The Dodger.' Matt added, not to be outdone. 'He's always in, unless he's secretly keeping fit in his back garden when I knock him up.'

'Secretly. Why?'

'He's on the social. They catch people like him who scrounge off the state. He's capable of working for sure.'

Edgar grunted and took the plate to the sink. 'Want a cuppa?'

'Please.'

They lapsed into silence for a minute, then Edgar returned with two steaming mugs. 'I don't think we have a lot of time until the bastard exchanges the necklace for easy cash. I'll phone Zed in a minute.'

'I'm going up the pub to see what I can find out about the guy, then I'll drop over to Albert Narbett's place. He tells everyone he's always exercising and taking long walks out of boredom. May have seen something, and after dark's his favourite time.'

'I'm gonna go off at a tangent here. I wonder where this pagan cult met? I mean, I've never seen evidence or heard of a cult. I have heard that such things still go on, but I, or Deidre, have never caught anyone on our land at night dancing naked round a bonfire.'

'They may have been more sophisticated than that. Perhaps it was a secret society kind of thing. Let's see what we can find out about them. In the meantime, I'm gonna chase the military guy down at the pub.'

Half an hour later, Matt was in his car and arriving at the Red Lion. The journey had been interrupted by Edgar phoning. He informed Matt that Zed Halane had no information to help.

'A dead end then,' Matt responded, and hoped there wouldn't be too many more.

The pub's car park was full as usual, more so than a lot of the remaining pubs were in the area during the winter months. During the summer, a lot of tourists bolstered their trade, mainly for food and one-off visits, but it was too late in the year for that. At least the Red Lion was still frequented by the local community as well.

He bought a pint off a young barman he didn't recognise and went straight over to Noddy and Rodger, who were deep in discussion with another local nicknamed Rippo. Matt had no idea what the man's real name was. He waited for them all to shake hands in some dodgy agreement. Two other guys Matt knew were deep in conversation at the bar. He remembered one of them being nearby when he'd stupidly mentioned his treasure to Noddy. One of the guys at the bar was Mart, someone to be avoided; he'd done time. Rumour had it that the offence he had been put away for was serious, but no one knew what that was.

'Hi Matt lad,' Noddy, Roger, and Rippo said in unison.

He turned away from Mart's back, nodding while maintaining a serious look. 'You guys seen anything of that military guy with the deadpan countenance?' he asked. 'The one at the bar that spoke to me last time I was in.'

'Strange guy. He doesn't speak to me about anything except always questioning about strangers,' nodded Noddy. 'Seems to be suspicious of everyone as if he's guarding someone or something.'

'Bodyguard,' Roge the Dodger nodded as if catching Noddy's habit. 'Doesn't seem to miss much while in here. Must have radar ears or something.'

'Just very large ears, I reckon,' Noddy laughed as his head bobbed.

'I've seen him elsewhere recently,' Rippo announced when the laughter had subsided. 'Why, what do you want with him Matt? He looks too bloody dangerous to mess with.'

'I found a valuable item while metal detecting. Hid it in my shed for safe keeping. Someone spotted me doing it and nicked it overnight.'

The guys all gasped and hissed in a chorus of swearing and astonishment.

'Supposed to be a quiet backwater here.' Noddy added. 'I'll keep an ear out for anything unusual offered for sale, and let you know.'

'Looks capable of nicking stuff and probably murder. As I said, I saw the bugger,' Rippo said.

'Where was that?'

'I was walking Bessie down Eastland Lane, and she tugged toward a gate, like she does when something excites her. The bugger was there watching two metal detectorists combing a field. He saw me coming by and still shouted to 'em to ask if they'd found anything. They looked at him and carried on with the detectors, so he shouted louder, a bit aggressive like. 'You found anything?' The nearest one stopped and walked over, lowered a jacket hood, and took off the headphones. I was a bit surprised; it was a teenage girl. I remember the conversation because he then asked to see their finds.'

Matt interrupted. 'When was this Rippo?'

'Last week.'

Matt wondered what the military man was looking out for. Could it have been other valuables? It was before his treasure went missing.

'What happened then, Rippo?' Matt asked.

'He asked who they were and what they were doing there. Think the girl said something simple like, 'detecting,' and the arsehole got angry. 'What are you looking for?' he demanded and the girl called her mother over. The mother explained the two fields were the first they had got permission to search in and they were really excited, having found two coins and a strange bit of cogwheel-shaped metal. 'Tell me if you find anything special,' he demanded. The woman said, 'Why?' He got edgy and said, 'cause I need to know. He darted a glance at me and said, 'Here's my number,' and handed them a card. I went over at that point and asked if everything was okay? The git just walked off. The girls didn't look too bothered.'

'Jeez!' exclaimed Noddy. 'What a weirdo.'

'I saw him get in his car. It was a big black 4x4. Range Rover, I think.'

There was a lot of info there, Matt realised. 'You seen the women detecting there again?' he asked.

'Yes, two days ago. They're okay when you speak nicely to them. Jayne, the mother's name is. Works over at Springborough Manor.'

Twenty miles east of us, Matt realised. They were a long way from home unless she travelled a long way to work like a lot of people did these days. A plan started formulating as he assimilated the account. The bloke had to live somewhere on that route to be driving along Eastland Lane, it was very narrow with few passing places, and it wasn't a shortcut most people used. He decided to drive that way tomorrow and see if he could spot the Range Rover parked up outside a house, or spot the girls on the way. It would be interesting to meet others with the same hobby. From what Rippo said, they sounded like novice detectorists, the same as him. But the forecast had stated the weather was taking a turn for the worse with minus temperatures and the chance of snow showers. He doubted anyone not committed to detecting would risk pottering along in a field and getting freezing feet in the process, let alone managing to get a spade into frozen ground.

He sipped his pint and listened to the conversation as it shifted to deals and then politics. His mind was still on the military man and the loss of his treasure. He excused himself and headed for home and his bed. It had been a wearing day full of unexpected twists.

Sleep for Matt had always been restorative, and at times, he woke refreshed and knowing the solution to a problem. He woke that morning and a line that Rippo had said entered his conscious mind, "Here's my number,' and handed them a card," the military man had said. So all he had to do was meet up with this Jayne and ask for the man's number, then phone it and see if he could get information from him. That left a series of new problems he needed to resolve. How could he get the man to give him his address in these days of numerous scams played out all over the internet, phone calls, and cold-calling? The man was probably more experienced at this kind of trickery and would just put the phone down. Matt couldn't give his name or reason for calling for obvious reasons, and he couldn't think of a reason to pretend he was phoning on behalf of anyone else. There was probably no address on the card either; he guessed at the name, phone number, and email only. He thought hard as more sleep became impossible; no other excuse came to mind that would convince the guy. Matt lay in bed and pondered further. Maybe the man had given Jayne more info than Rippo remembered. He decided to phone Springborough Manor and ask to speak to her.

An hour later, he got dressed and prepared for the day. He wondered if it would it be another day where he didn't know what direction he'd travel in or what location he would end the day at.

The first phone call didn't get him anywhere. Someone answered the phone who sounded very educated and in control.

'Hello, could I speak to Jayne, please?'

'Who is calling?'

'My name is Mathew Bradley, and I'm a metal detectorist. I understand she is too, and I wondered if she could provide me with information regarding a man who appears to be interested in any finds we discover.'

'I'm not sure. Are you not meant to declare finds to local museums?'

'Sorry, yes of course, and all above-board detectorists, like me, report valuable items to Finds Liaison Officers. Jayne was talking to this man recently, I'm told, and I thought we may be able to share a problem concerning him.'

'Very well, I'll let her know. Can she phone you back on this number?'

'Yes, please. And err… thank you.'

'You are welcome. Good day.'

The phone disengaged, and Matt wondered whether Jayne would even get the message.

Maybe he could find her phone number a different way. He fired the laptop up and entered Springborough Manor in the Google search box. To his inexperienced surprise, a web page URL came up near the top, and he clicked it. He looked along the list of pages and to 'contact', he clicked, and there it was. A line said, for all enquiries, contact Jayne Bateman, Events Manager. A message box was shown below, with small print stating, 'Maximum 56 words only'.

He couldn't think of what short message to enter that wouldn't convince her he wasn't a time waster.

Matt wondered if he put her full name under another search, whether he would get a contact number come up. He tried the modern Directory Enquiries, which was now online and renamed 192. It gave a list of Jayne Batemans. He scrolled through 24 and found the one with the nearest postal address. It only gave the town, which was Ross-on-Wye, the rest were all over the UK. He clicked it, and the line showed 'other occupants' under another column. Then he had to register to get further information so he did so, but the entry for Jayne's mobile number was blank, and her address was also withheld. Very sensible, he decided, and felt a bit weird as if he was some kind of stalker.

He thought hard for minutes, and couldn't think of what else to look under. These days, personal data is so carefully protected.

He left the laptop and made a cuppa. Whilst sipping it, he came up with another possibility – social media. People liked to share photos, interests, and other info on the most popular sites. Dianne had set him up on Instagram, Facebook, and Twitter ten years ago. Although he rarely entered anything, he sometimes wished people a happy birthday or commented on their news.

He decided on Instagram first. It was no good, some Jayne Batemans came up, but not her, or anyone of the same name in this part of the UK. He tried again and discovered Twitter was now called simply X. After logging in with his usual password, he drew a blank. Last, he tried Facebook, and this time something did come up. Jayne had set a page up when her daughter was an infant in 2007. Under, 'interests', it said Ross-on-Wye Toddler Group. She had been a reserve minder if others fell ill. It had her mobile number on there, luckily, she had never deleted it. Matt hoped she still used the number. He read the entry again; she even had her daughter's name in the Profile section, it was Raven.

'Means to an important end,' he muttered to himself, feeling even more as if he were intruding on her privacy.

He tapped in the number and was pleased to hear a ringtone.

'Hello.' A voice picked up.

'Hi, is that Jayne?'

'It is.' She sounded guarded.

He wasn't used to having to put on any charm. His life until now had been in the car repair shop or with people in the pub. Even Dianne had fitted into the pub drinking life he had and didn't need to be charmed too much when he met her – the booze had done that.

He did his best.

'Hi. I'm really sorry to bother you but I'm trying to contact someone whom I believe you have information about. I found your number on Facebook, the Ross-on-Wye Toddler Group.' As he spoke, he found he was beginning to relax, and the next bit flowed out very naturally. 'I'm a metal detectorist and I believe you were sweeping a field near where I live. The problem is ...'

Jayne interrupted, 'That's wonderful, I'm only a beginner at detecting. You're a proper hobbyist or probably a more experienced one?'

'Well, I have found a very important artefact and I'm trying to track down information about it. That's why I'm contacting you in the hope of...'

'Interesting, what did you say your name was?'

'It's Mathew Bradley. Err... Matt will do.'

'Okay, Matt. How can I help?'

'Well, this is a bit complicated. My friend Rippo was walking his dog, and he saw the guy I need to contact talking to you when you were detecting in a field nearby.'

'Yes, I remember, it was last week. He didn't seem very pleasant; I wasn't going to get back to him.'

'Ah, yes. I heard. Rippo wasn't impressed with his attitude either. I believe the guy gave you his card. I'm hoping you still have it.'

'Not sure. I might be able to find it when I get home. I'm curious, Matt, how can I be of any help beyond giving you the number?

'It's difficult to explain and a bit awkward. I found this beautiful necklace with gold and silver leaves hanging from braided gold. It…'

'Hold on, this is blowing my mind. That does sound valuable. You want help in detecting its location for other items?'

'Umm, not sure yet. I need to explain the rest of the disaster first.'

'Okay, now look, Matt. This is a bit complex and I don't know you; also, I'm at work. I love metal detecting, and this sounds intriguing. Can I phone you back this evening? I'll search for the card too.'

'Err… Yes sure. I'm grateful for your help Jayne.'

'I'll phone later.'

'Thanks.'

The line went dead, and Matt reviewed in his mind how he'd come over. Not too badly, he decided. Maybe he was better at the charm thing than he thought. But would she return the call? He had no choice but to wait for this evening to find out.

He spent the rest of the day back on Edgar's fields. He needed to clear his head, and detecting gave him something to do while he waited. He had no other leads, so Jayne was his only hope. The field nearest the house gave him a few signals; the detector screen indicated the probability of junk despite not being set to 'all-metal'. He found an old battery, a small length of barbed wire, a large nail, and a washer. His usual luck had returned. He gave up and went home at three o'clock before the winter sun was due to set. He sat in a chair in his kitchen to await Jayne's call.

CHAPTER FIFTEEN

Amber had settled down in her favourite armchair with her laptop and a cup of cappuccino from the coffeemaker when her phone rang.

'Hi Dad. You been keeping busy?'

'Sure have. I've made progress, Amber – but not that it gets us any nearer to the stones. I'm about to send you an email with photos attached. To save you looking, I'm going to read you something that's turning into quite an extraordinary account of 18th-century religious persecution.'

She forgot her cappuccino as Dave read aloud the latest pages from the Reverend's diary.

Amber held her breath, absorbing the tale of woe. 'Oh my God,' she gasped after the last word reached her. 'Can you email this to Ben?'

'Of course. I'd like to search for their temple this weekend as well. Let's see if we can draw all the ends together.'

'Don't look too far ahead, Dad. There's something from the latest diary pages we need to discuss.'

'What's that Love?'

'As I remember, the line you read out was exactly worded, *I and Glenys had to run to a prepared and blessed hide to bury there our sacred chalice, ceremonial jewellery, and other treasures. I will tell more about the location later in this account.*

The Reverend didn't mention it again. There must be another page somewhere. Possibly the most important page to Nathan's criminal backer, even more important to him than the location of the stones.'

'Ahh, yes, I was so excited about finding the account, I hadn't yet focused on that. Unlike me, I must admit. Let's get Ben in on this before we go any further. How about a meeting, say, at yours to save Liz any more distress?'

'Sure. Best place.' She agreed and liked the idea of two of the three of her favourite people coming over for the evening. Then a subdued thought rose to the surface. It would be nice if Dave had something urgent come up, and she and Ben could be left to discuss the matter alone together. Maybe with a bottle of wine, and she could prepare a meal, and … she stopped herself there. I'm not throwing myself at anyone again. She reestablished the pledge made at the end of her disastrous marriage to Timothy. It was still a raw but fading experience, and she idly contemplated how these hurtful things did fade as more experiences and good times replaced them.

'Hello, Amber. You've gone quiet.'

'Sorry, Dad. Just lost in my thoughts. Must be tired.'

'Shall we say tomorrow night at yours then? Also, I'll send you and Ben JPEGs of the new pages.'

'Sure, and thanks. I'll text Ben.' After a moments contemplation, she carried on debating, 'I reckon this next page must have been very important, not just to the Reverend and Glenys but to the rest of their surviving group. The treasures were probably blessed by the Gods and used or worn in their ceremonies every time the group met. They might have had individual significance to a particular ceremony or maybe to more than one. They would all cherish these possessions for their significance, especially if the group kept going. It will be interesting to brainstorm a location where they could be hidden.' While they were talking, Amber texted Ben. She pressed 'send' as she chatted with her father.

'Their location could be more impossible guesswork, Amber.'

'True, maybe I'm just thinking it would be nice to find the ceremonial treasures, in honour of Nathan.'

'Of course, Amber. This has all hit us hard.'

'It really has, and surprisingly so. I didn't realise the guy had made such an impact on me.' She paused in thought, then ended the chat. 'See you tomorrow, Dad,' and broke the connection. Amber resumed thinking about the poor, obsessed man she shared a Uni course with all those years ago.

Her phone pinged with a quick reply from Ben. *Sure, Amber, I'm back from the gym at 5:30. Will shower and come straight over. Do you have something new? Anything you can share in advance?*

She messaged back with the gist of what Dave had just read her over the phone.

Wow. See you tomorrow, he messaged, and she left it at that for now.

The next evening, Amber had the kitchen and living room as tidy as possible after the break-in. It felt more like home again, she thought, casting an eye over the puffed-up cushions, cleaned carpets and straightened wall art.

Dave arrived first – bang on time. Has he been waiting around the corner again, Amber wondered as they hugged.

She had coffee brewing and freshly baked blueberry muffins on a plate, ready. They chatted about her mother, and Amber was relieved to hear she had got over the break-in and hospital ordeal and had gone back to organising her social-club meetings and worrying about her adversary, Cowpat, again.

The doorbell rang, and Dave let Ben in.

'Hi-', said Ben as he stood in the kitchen door. 'Coffee smells fantastic. What's your brand?'

'Oh, thanks. Its Original Home, from Kenya. Local shop imports it specially.' She'd made a good decision last week to prioritise a new coffee machine to replace the smashed one.

Within a few minutes, they were all seated and passing around muffins.

'Let's begin,' Dave announced. 'You have the JPEGs of the latest pages, so we're all up to speed. I propose quickly discussing the next search criteria first before talking about the reverend's latest. Specifically, do you think we ought to wait until Nathan's colleague Ken is fit enough to join us?'

'Ken apparently is not well enough to answer messages; he was transferred to a private hospital,' Amber began. 'I think we have to carry on without him. Which, if he reports to the opposition anyway, is possibly the best course of action.'

'Seconded. You agree, Ben?'

'Yes, I do. Let's see it through on our own. Even if Ken is only a friend of Nathan, I'm not convinced he won't go and use night-hawkers to rip the site apart when we find it.'

'A distinct possibility. Why would a bunch of muggers be searching as well? The hotel's a mile away from our nearest search point.' Amber puzzled over the circumstances behind the horrendous event as she spoke. 'Why attack Nathan there?'

'No idea. I mean, it must have been a convenient place for them to lie in wait,' Ben replied. 'It was easy to sneak around the back and look for a fire-escape to get inside, and with Ken coming out they just lucked into an easy assault.'

'I hope the police can get to the bottom of it all.' Dave frowned and made an attempt at changing their mood. 'Saturday it is then. 10 o'clock. Usual place?'

They both nodded in agreement. Amber appreciated that Dave was trying to get some distance from discussing the awful event for too long.

'We're agreed on that - good.' He went straight to the next item. 'By the way, I've just been texted by Jayne at

Springborough. I have permission to search the library next Monday. It'll be my last chance before the New Year.'

'Saturday would be best to go searching again. I hope we find something this time, though.'

'The snowstorms are back Saturday evening, so we can just about fit it in. Thank God for the thaw this week or we'd never be able to spot a thing under snow.'

'Yes, "under" is the operative word here, Dad. I wonder whether there will be much to see above ground now anyway.'

'Winter is a good time of year to search for ground-level items. All the ferns and bracken have died back leaving the ground easier to traverse and examine. Searching now has advantages too.'

'Yes, it's definitely easier. We must have narrowed the search area now as well,' Ben added. 'There must be some evidence locally. Sometimes, even an old road name is linked to the past. I've seen many examples of this where, for instance, there used to be a monastery and now it's a built-up town without physical remains left, but there are road and building names such as Friary Lane or The Monks Tavern, for instance, still indicating the almost lost past.'

'An interesting avenue of research to follow up on,' Dave gave Ben a look of approval. 'Let's move on to the lines included in the last of the Reverend's diary pages. I'll just recap them again. He says, *I and Glenys had to run to a prepared and blessed hide to bury there our sacred chalice, ceremonial jewellery, and other treasures. I will tell more of the location later in this account.* So what can we make of this rather definite reference?'

'That they must have existed,' Amber offered.

'And that it may well have been dug up by the Reverend later,' Ben added.

'Or the items may not have been removed if he thought they were hidden somewhere too risky to return to.' Dave added that argument. 'It was a prepared site, so it would be well hidden. Not somewhere that could easily be found by chance, I'm guessing. It all hinges now on this next page, possibly the last one the Reverend wrote. That large leather-bound volume would have been difficult to carry around if you were always moving from one safe house to another.'

'True,' Amber muttered, feeling a little deflated. 'Would a record of the ceremonial artefacts have been kept by Lawrence Thorpe-Wellington. He was a trusted friend.'

'But possibly one who would have been known about by the authorities, and may have been questioned later by the Watchmen to see whether he was a secret cult member. They would have searched his premises for the cult's treasures or references to them. No, I'm guessing the location would only be known by someone else, one unknown to the lawmen.'

Ben added his thoughts. 'This part of the account mentions a character called Archie Woodright. Would he have helped them hide anything? He was with them through the fight and then their flight and was the only other cult member not arrested.'

'That's a possibility. Maybe he returned later to retrieve the items.'

'Could we find anything in ancestry records about the man?' Amber wondered aloud. 'I mean, if we can trace where he lived, he may have left some account of the event on record.'

'A big ask, if he were a commoner. Detailed records are scarce unless he was well known in his village or town. I doubt whether he had any links to Springborough Manor; it was too far away from the site of their worship. I'm guessing he lived locally to the stones. But I'll give it a try,' Dave stated.

'An interesting avenue of research, Dave. Do you mind if I work on that too? We could compare notes and see if they match. Two different sources stating the same information would verify their accuracy for instance.'

'Be my guest, Ben. The quicker we can find out if there's any information still hidden away about what happened, the better for us to beat our opposition.'

That sounds like my team is working well together. Amber felt the pleasurable thought lift her spirits. She looked forward to the next search on Saturday. Just the three of them without complications – perfect.

They met in the Rising Sun car park for the third time early on Saturday morning. It was another cold and dark start; the sun had risen only an hour before, as the shortest day was only in ten days' time. A breeze was rising before the forecasted snowstorm, which was due to hit this area that evening. Fifteen minutes later, they were parked up beside the footpath signs that pointed in both the directions they had already explored. Dave and Amber took five minutes to wrap themselves in thick arctic scarves with waterproofs over fleeces, fleece-lined walking trousers, and woolly hats finished off with bulging rucksacks. Ben seemed not to feel the cold with a thin jumper, jacket, waterproof, jeans, and his usual canvas hat. They took to the east footpath again and then struck north toward Great Kensley Inclosure and its nearby lake. The surrounding woodland was mainly open, with scrub trees and occasional stands of thick conifers. It looked like the area had been felled a few years ago and badly replanted with mostly plastic sleeve shielded trees dead and bent at angles. Not good for any intact archaeology she realised, anything interesting would have long ago been spotted or destroyed.

Soon they were into woodland that was older with large alder, sycamore, and hawthorn. Amber felt reassured that Dave had his OS map folded in such a way as to reveal the area they were walking. Her father was something of an expert map reader, having completed orienteering courses and even getting her and her mother out of a thick fog on Exmoor once, using only compass bearings to get them within metres of a footpath sign on the edge of woodland. Ben had his hands thrust deep into his pockets. Amber guessed he, like her, would rather keep warm than use his phone with the internet and GPS on it to follow their route. An hour passed, and nothing stood out that was worth investigating. Along the way, they discussed the possible points where they would have to leave the path to explore dense woodland.

The sun left a watery half-light in the woodland as they crunched through thin layers of glassy ice. By midday, they had explored three areas away from the track, one of which had looked so promising they detoured for 15 minutes to get to the rising ground leading to a hillock. They drew a blank each time.

The three took a quick lunch break on another fallen tree trunk – it was too cold to stop for long. Amber had packed a flask of soup and bread rolls. She'd brought along an extra plastic cup for Ben and extra food, knowing he wouldn't think of it. He looked really grateful and thanked her. Whilst they ate, two men looking to be in their thirties passed by. They looked rugged and fit and wore a military, slightly menacing bearing. Neither spoke, although they gave Dave and Ben icy stares.

Then flakes of snow started to fall.

'What do we do, carry on or turn back?' Dave asked with a note of alarm as more flakes settled on their waterproofs. The snow was arriving earlier than forecasted.

'Carry on, it won't lie for now,' Ben said, and Amber readily agreed. She tried to walk alongside Ben as much as she could, as this seemed to warm her. They examined a rise beyond some marshy ground, then walked across to another hillock that looked like a large manmade mining waste dump. It looked so promising as they reached it. She wondered if she could even see the slight rise around it of an embankment through the now swirling snow. They even found a flooded dip bordering one side of the rise in the ground.

'Is it the remains of a ditch?' she asked.

'I think not,' said Dave as he finished walking most part of a circle around the hillock.

'All the right signs from the Reverend's directions,' Amber muttered and hoped this was the place. She walked around with a sudden spring to her steps. But it wasn't the site – on closer examination. Everything around and on top of the hill was undisturbed natural features, with no recumbent large trilithons or smaller stones concealed under brown and decaying winter foliage. Although the hillock was roughly circular, the ditch shape meandered off to the west and proved natural.

'Unfortunately, I agree with Dave,' said Ben a few minutes later, with disappointment in his words.

Their mood degenerated to near despair as they circled back to the path and then couldn't find it.

By four o'clock, the snow was turning into a blizzard. They had to resort to Dave's compass bearing skills to navigate their way back. Amber couldn't feel her toes, and she noticed Ben's nose was bright red. She was sure he was trying to stop his teeth from chattering by the look of his clenched jaw. Dave was shivering, and she began to worry about hypothermia. She held her dad's arm, fearing it was all too much for him.

They slid and staggered for another 20 minutes. Her toes within the thick socks and walking boots were so numb she could no longer feel them. Dave slipped over, and they helped him up.

The blizzard intensified, and she felt as if they were struggling through a frigid barrier. Her feet were frozen, and Dave looked awful. Ben supported him. Her legs were like pillars of ice and were barely able to take another step. Her hands and nose were so cold now that she thought she may have frostbite.

They had only minutes before either she or Dave fell and could not get up.

CHAPTER SIXTEEN

Matt had almost given up at 9:30pm when the phone rang. He'd been carrying it around the house all evening in case he missed her call. He grabbed the phone and saw it was Jayne.

'Matt. Hi.'

'Hiya, Jayne. Thanks for calling me back. Much appreciated.'

'No probs. Sorry, it's a bit late, but I'm still waiting for Raven to get home, I think I may have handed the card to her. I definitely haven't got it I'm afraid. She went to see some friends about six o'clock, and at that time, I hadn't remembered that I gave the card to her. Didn't want it myself, I don't think the guy had any people skills.'

'Oh, okay, that's fine. Would you like me to phone back tomorrow?' He really hoped she wouldn't say yes. There was something he really liked about Jayne and wondered whether it was just their shared hobby. Or maybe the evenings were just a bit lonelier for him than the days. The revelation seemed to work its way up from his subconscious.

'Maybe. I'm just intrigued by the sound of this necklace, though. There was something about it that you were alarmed about. You used the word disaster, I believe.'

'Yes, my incredible find has turned into a nightmare. Straight after I reported it to the local Finds Liaison Officer, it was stolen from my shed…'

'Hold on. Your shed – that doesn't sound very secure.'

Matt laughed despite his continuing upset, 'No I guess it doesn't, but I built a secret hideaway into the floor, and stupidly I went out there at night to admire my little treasure. I must have been spotted by someone lurking in the field beyond my garden.'

'Oh dear. You sound like you've become quite attached to it, despite it not being yours.'

'Yes, it really feels like I own it,' without thinking, he put on a miser's theatrical voice, and said, 'it's mine, she be all mine.'

He heard her giggle down the phone. The sound was somehow relaxing and exciting. He would really like to meet up and go detecting with this lady. Even over the phone, she was bringing something lost out of him - an ability to laugh at himself, even in this stressful situation. 'I must get it back, Jayne. It was the most beautiful thing. Never thought I'd love an inanimate object, but I do.'

'I understand, Matt, you're grieving in a way. I'm going to help you. I do wonder whether it might actually belong to someone, though.' He heard a clatter and a key-in-lock sound, and she paused talking. 'I've just heard the front door open. It'll be Raven. Let me have a word with her and see if she still has the card. I'll phone back shortly.'

The phone disconnected, leaving Matt catching up with the conversation. It had gone well, but he was still no nearer to working out anything else about his sneak-thief intruder. He smiled to himself and actually felt his mood changing. There was still a lot to discuss with her. He hadn't had a chance to tell her about the old document he'd read on Edgar's laptop, concerning the treasure.

He put the telly on and made himself a coffee. The caffeine kept him alert; he didn't want to fall asleep and miss her call. He waited and tried to concentrate on articles about metal detecting that Google brought up for him.

He snatched up his phone as its ringtone pierced his thoughts.

'Hi,' said Jayne again. 'We've got the card. Retrieved it from her rubbish bin in her bedroom. She'd ripped it in half, but you can still read most of it.'

'That's good, Jayne. I've got a pen handy.' She read him the name, Georgio Renard.

'Thanks for that.' He tried hard to think of what to say next. She saved him the concern.

'The phone number is illegible, don't know what Raven did with the card, it might be nail varnish on it, I reckon.'

'I have a few more things to say about this guy, and I want to know more about what happened when you met him.' Matt spoke quickly to cover his disappointment at not getting a phone number.

'Okay. Let's finish swopping info on the guy, and then we can talk about our hobby.'

'There may be a lesson to be learnt here. About finds and how to treat them or something.'

'I didn't like the sound of this guy at the time, and after what you said earlier.' Jayne spoke as if he were a friend she'd known for years. 'When I drove home this evening, I stopped at an old friend's, who knows everyone locally. I asked and she said, phone Albert Narbett. He's someone in the village who walks around a lot where I live, mainly at night because he can't sleep, apparently. He's seen something, she said. A few shady blokes, one of whom could be this guy who confronted me and Raven.'

This was working out far better than he could have hoped. 'Where were these guys seen, and what were they doing?'

'Don't know but I'm going to ring Albert next.'

'Thanks, Jayne, much appreciated.'

'I'm pleased to help you. But I want something in return.'

'Yes, name your price.'

'No, no price. I feel I can trust you. I just want to go over and detect on the find site with you, and I want to bring my daughter, Raven. It'll be good experience for us. We'll keep quiet about its location too - just in case. We're absolute beginners at this, but some things are obvious even to me. I just struck lucky recently, finding a farmer willing to let us detect in his fields. I doubt we'll find anything there to declare to any Finds Liaison person, though.'

He only had to think for a moment. It was exactly what he was going to suggest, despite having been over there to detect the location twice. 'Sounds like a deal. And yes, bring your daughter too. It'll be exciting if we find more. A proper treasure trove to declare.' He had a sudden thought, maybe he could then detect with them on their fields. Sort of a reciprocal agreement.

'Great. Also, it might placate this Finds Liaison guy a bit.'

'True, didn't think of that.'

'I'm going to try and get hold of Albert now. Speak later.' There was a pause, and she said, 'Oh, and have you any other suspects in your drama? I mean, this guy could be innocent.'

'He's most likely not. I think he was good at what he did. Surveillance, I mean. Someone climbed the horse chestnut at the bottom of my garden. It was an ideal place to view my house and shed from. I did suspect someone else, but I've spoken to him and ruled him out.'

'Okay. I'll get back to you,' she said and rang off.

That went really well, he thought.

He waited until 11 o'clock for her to ring, then went to bed. He wasn't really disappointed; Albert may have been out or something, and Jayne had decided she'd talked to a stranger like him for too long anyway. He would keep his phone very near him all day tomorrow.

The next morning, he was up early; it was a bright day with a winter chill in the air. The first decision of the day was easy. He went online to Directory Enquiries again and logged in. He entered Georgio Renard and Ross-on-Wye in and came up with no one by that name. Then he tried other locations, including London, with zero results. Finally, he entered the name in a people search and came up with nothing. It was as if the man didn't exist. He concluded Georgio Renard was an assumed name. His hopes of progress were dashed again, and he felt deflated.

Then, over breakfast, he thought of another approach. If he drove around the area where Jayne and her daughter were detecting, he may see a black Range Rover parked outside one of the houses. Then he'd have Renard's address. It seemed like a good plan, so after a quick breakfast, he drove the 10-minute journey and located the most likely field that Rippo had spotted Jayne in, then carried on. It was only a single-track road leading into the Forest of Dean toward Upper Tyebank. He drove through the small hamlet, then past a rundown hotel called the Phoenix, then toward the larger town of Cinderford. He gave up at that point and drove back on the same road in the hope that the reverse direction would reveal something different. It didn't, and by 11 o'clock, he was home again.

He was stumped and had no more ideas. His treasure was gone; he would have to come to terms with that.

That left the afternoon free. There was only one way to fill it, he decided to go detecting again. Not Edgar's woodland this time, he would save that for Jayne and Raven's visit. He decided on another of Edgar's fields. First, he dropped over to the farmhouse to see if Edgar had found any leads to the necklace. The farmer was not in, but he met Deidre, who said she'd had a call from a man asking about any metal detectorists working nearby.

'What did you tell him?'

'Nothing, I said he'd have to speak to my husband, but he was out in Higher Meadow and wouldn't be back until supper.' The man rang off without a thankyou even. Very abrupt.'

Matt thought it must be Georgio Renard who phoned. He was zeroing in on the farm. But what for? Last night, on Google, Matt had learnt there was such a thing as a nighthawker, and he began to wonder whether Renard was one. It tied in with the theft of his treasure. A nighthawker would have clients lined up off the radar, ready to buy any rich finds. He'd better put Edgar on his guard.

Ten minutes later, he had set up the detector and started along the boundary of a new field, somewhere where he could see the farmyard in case anything interesting occurred there.

He spotted Edgar bringing his tractor in, so he walked over. The farmer had nothing to report, no leads, and no unusual events. Matt briefed him about Renard, then returned to detecting and found what he thought could be a Victorian farthing, and that was it. He was pleased enough with that and returned home at 4 o'clock.

His phone hadn't rung all day, so he guessed Jayne hadn't got hold of Albert yet. He tried to decide whether to ring her and microwaved a ready-meal while he argued with himself. No, it would be classed as pestering. No, ring her, he could arrange a date to detect the location again before the cold weather came in. Yes, it would show his interest and urgent need to get his treasure back. That last reason swayed him, and he pressed to connect to her number.

The phone rang and rang, and his spirits sank; she had disconnected him somehow. Then, as he expected the voice-mail to cut in, she picked up.

'Hi Jayne, its Matt.'

'Oh, hi. Sorry, I'd left my phone upstairs. Made any progress?'

'Not today. I tried Directory Enquiries and a people search. There is no one on record by that name. It's a fictitious identity, I reckon. However, someone enquired with the farmer's wife and asked about detectorists. I think that Reynard may have located the farm where I was detecting. Perhaps we ought to give the woods a combing through before he does. I'm concerned he may be a nighthawker.'

'What's that?'

'Someone who loots finds sites looking for personal gain and sells anything valuable he finds privately without registering anything with the authorities. Totally illegal, of course.'

'I see. Hadn't heard of that term.'

She went quiet for a moment, and Matt hoped she was thinking over the problem.

'How about going over on Saturday? The weather's good, no rain. A low chance of a snow shower, though.'

'Yes, sure. I don't mind winter weather either. We'll be in the woods, there'll be a bit of shelter there. Would you like directions?'

'Have you got the What3Words location?'

'Um, don't know, what's that? Is it an app?'

She laughed, 'Give me directions then. It looks like I can educate you, too.'

Five minutes later, they had arranged to meet at Edgar's farm entrance at the top of the lane. Jane and Raven were bringing all their gear; it was going to be an interesting day.

There was one lead he hoped she may have now. He was about to mention it when Jayne said, 'Albert is a lovely old guy, but a little vague. Had a long chat with him earlier, and he thinks he knows who I mean. He's seen him but isn't sure where he lives. I ran out of time to chat longer, unfortunately. I don't think he knows any more anyway. Sorry, but I guess that's not a lot of use.'

'No probs. Anything you can find out may help me out, though.'

'Sure. I'll keep hunting. See you Saturday. 10 o'clock, okay?'

'That's fine. I'll be there,' he said enthusiastically, and she disconnected.

He thought for a moment and decided to ring Edgar to see if he'd found out anything that may help.

Edgar was in and with Deidre. 'Matt mate, I was about to phone you.'

'Great, you have news?'

'Yes, I have. Deidre knows a lady who is a kind of home help for a few older people locally. She knows lots of gossip, so Deidre mentioned about your search for this strange bloke. This lady walks her little poodle around Braleton, and says someone who may be Renard rents one of the old terraced houses that used to be mill workers' cottages. One row of cottages is down a secluded lane behind the other row. He lives in the end one, she reckons. There's a nearby footpath that goes in the direction of Primrose Hill Farm, about three miles away.'

Matt interrupted, 'I know the farm. I did work on a tractor and a car there once. Luke Griffin, is the farmer, took over from his dad recently.'

'That's right. The lady reckons Renard has carved a path from the back of his garden to this footpath. She thinks it gives the man a shortcut to the path without going along the main road and fifty yards to the footpath stile. He's very reclusive, she says. I'm not surprised; it's in character.'

'Interesting info, Edgar. I'm wondering whether to take the path from up the road and see if she's correct.'

'Yes, why not. Don't know how that'll get you nearer to recovering the necklace though.'

The next day seemed to go so slowly that he felt time was moving at half-speed. That evening, he walked to the pub. Asked both Chris, the landlady, and Noddy if the military guy had been in. No, was the response. The name Georgio Renard meant nothing to them either. Matt wondered whether the man used other false identities; maybe he wasn't ex-special forces at all.

Saturday morning came around at last, and he had the car loaded up by 9 o'clock. While he drove, he decided to let Edgar know he was detecting in the woodland with guest detectorists. He found the farmer attaching a large plough to the back of his tractor outside his large open-fronted barn.

'Hello me old butt.' Edgar greeted him, and they went into the barn out of the biting wind. Inside, the dark, cavernous barn smelled of hay, oil, and chemicals.

After a quick greeting. Matt asked, 'You heard any more about Georgio Renard?'

'Can't say I have.' I'm guessing he's our main culprit now.'

'Yes, he is. I haven't heard anything different from Jayne either. She has tried and drawn a blank so far. Also, she's a detectorist with a daughter, and both are going to join me in the woods this morning. With three detectorists searching, you never know what we might find.'

'True love mate, that's what.'

'Jeez, Edgar, I forgot your old bloody sense of humour. We've only talked on the phone.'

'Ah, blind date then,' Edgar laughed.

'Let's change the subject,' and they returned to Renard and whether they should both go round to his terraced house after dark and check his property out.

'Maybe. But not till tomorrow,' Matt offered. 'I was going to walk that footpath round the back then.'

'Not in broad daylight, he'll spot you and know you're on to him.'

'That's true, let's work out a plan.'

'I'll go check the diary indoors.'

'Hold on. This isn't the time,' Matt said as a dark blue Volkswagen pulled up at the end of the lane. 'Time to go.' He waved and took off at a fast walk. He'd better not drop me in it if he meets Jayne later, he thought.

As he neared the car, both doors opened and two energetic women jumped out. One went to the rear and opened the hatchback. The other bent into the rear seat and retrieved a parka-style coat. He reached the car as she closed the door, smiled, then waved.

'I'm Jayne.'

'Hi Jayne. Glad you can join me today.'

'Wouldn't have missed it for anything, Matt.' She held out her hand and he shook it.

'Nice to meet you,' he said.

'This is Raven,' she gestured and the teenager gave him a shy smile as she pulled a detector bag from the car. He noticed Jayne was early forties, clear complexion, brown eyes, short blonde hair, and no makeup. She doesn't need any, he thought. Jayne turned, and he noticed her blonde hair was actually long and held in a pony tail. 'I'll get my gear,' he stated and walked to his car, parked nearby. In passing, he noticed Raven looked exactly like a younger version of her mother. He was back minutes later.

Both women had dressed for winter. They now had brand new green wellies on. He frowned; their feet would freeze.

Jayne must have noticed his frown.

'Thermal-lined wellies for comfort, and two pairs of socks.'

'And me,' Raven said.

'I'm sorry,' he said. 'It's good you have such forethought.' He glanced at his walking boots, also with thick socks.

'It's okay.' Jayne said, then lifted her detector, 'This any good?'

Luckily, he knew the exact detector. 'Ah, yes, I would have bought that exact model, had I not got a deal on mine. Modern electronics. Light but robust. Yes, good choice.' He looked at Raven's machine. 'I saw that one on Amazon. One of the best beginner's models. Good reviews – lots of them.'

The ladies seemed pleased.

'Let's go,' Jayne said and pointed to the gate. 'That way?'

'Yes, the treeline is just around the sharp bend in the track. About 10-minute' walk.'

'Follow me,' said Raven, and set off at a blistering pace, closely followed by her mother.

They were both very fit, Matt decided as he puffed along behind. They were in the trees in five minutes and stopped just inside the treeline to switch on, test the detectors, and the women put on headphones. He decided to brief them over his wonderful find's location and took them to the spot of disturbed ground.

'It was here. They must have been running or riding toward Symonds Yat when the female, I'm guessing it was a lady wearing the necklace, fell.'

'You can almost visualise the scene,' Jayne whispered as she glanced around wide-eyed. 'Wait, let me think. Which part of the wood have you properly searched?'

He swept a hand toward the Symonds Yat direction. 'That way mainly, I followed the course they were travelling.'

'What about if they were travelling in a hurry away from Symonds Yat?' Jayne asked. Then qualified it with, 'they could have been travelling that way, perhaps away from chasing lawmen coming from the Yat.' As she spoke, she gestured in the opposite direction.

'Could have been someone who owned the necklace running from thieves or muggers,' pointed out Raven.

'Yes, indeed. Both scenarios are plausible.' He nodded in agreement; he'd lucked in with a couple of bright sparks.

He hadn't thought of Raven's scenario and had to admit these ladies were likely to bring a whole new perspective to his search and the loss of his treasure. 'Great visualisations, ladies. So let's concentrate in that direction from the site of the find.' He pointed to the thicker woodland running uphill.

'This is exciting,' Jayne smiled as she waved her detector. Raven's machine still needed calibrating, so she fiddled for a minute, then said, 'I'm ready,' and began scanning as she swept her detector for a few fast strides.

'Hold on. Can we organise this search.' he said without rancour, but to stop the enthusiasm becoming uncontrolled. 'Let's walk side-by-side if we can. That way we comb the ground without missing areas.'

'Okay,' agreed Jayne. 'But we'll have to miss out where there's some large shrubs, like the wild rhododendrons and laurel bushes over there.'

'Yes, of course. But you can try pushing the detector in a way. It's also hard to dig down into the roots. I know, I tried it and only found a nail for my effort.'

Once organised, they started off working in a line. It went well, and soon he thought there was little ground between them left unexplored.

He had a promising signal with a good strength on his display. About three trowel symbols down, it stated. His detector was set to ignore iron and aluminium, so he was hopeful. He dug and, using his pinpointer, unearthed a brass bolt.

They continued for an hour and found a large rusty nail, a tangle of electrical wire, and a thick metal loop with the join welded over. Matt decided to add the loop to his finds pouch and check it out online later. Then Raven discovered an old, rough-edged coin. They gathered together and poured water on it. A quick clean up and it showed a name, Jack Tartine, along the rim on one side and more faint lettering on the reverse with a head wearing a crown. Matt, with his newly acquired knowledge, thought it may be a token rather than a coin.

They stopped to chat and drink hot coffee from Jayne's thermos flask. She'd bought an extra plastic cup for him. He found out Jayne and Raven had lived in Ross-on-Wye all their lives, and Raven had a biology degree but was working in a restaurant at the moment. He told them of his aborted profession and his recovery from a prolapsed disc with the consultant's warnings. Jayne was very sympathetic, and Raven smiled shyly.

They carried on, again in a line, and slowly combed the ground. This time, they found two nails and a large, corroded nut. By mutual consent, they stopped again and sat on a fallen tree for lunch. Matt realised they hadn't progressed that far through the woodland.

After the break, they decided to carry on for another hour and then pack up. The cold winter air was beginning to chill them, and the frosty ground wasn't thawing either.

Five minutes later, Jayne had a good signal and maybe an interesting possibility, going by the high-pitched tone. She stabbed a trowel into the ground, clearing composted leaves in seconds. He and Raven bent to watch. She dug a few inches of rich soil, then started bringing up compacted soil.

The removed soil piled up in an ever-larger mound, then something glinted in the hole despite the murkiness in the woodland.

'It's gold,' Jayne gasped. And dug a huge clump of cold soil out with enthusiasm. It showed the ragged end of coiled gold.

He hardly dared to believe his eyes. She brushed off the loose compost and broke the soil away with her gloved fingers. Raven poured bottled water over the find. A chain with a delicate hook on one end and a small rosette shaped like a rose appeared, radiating yellow as if brand new.

He recognised it and gasped. 'I know this.' It was all he could think of saying as his necklace leapt into mind and he mentally connected this length of interlacing gold to it. This braid was the missing piece that had been torn away in the owner's fall. 'It's the other end of my treasure, my necklace.' He felt close to tears.

'Amazing Matt. I'm so glad I found it for you,' Jayne looked up at him. He could see her eyes were watering too.

'No. No, it's your find. We've both found the necklace now.'

Jayne just looked at him, then the gold chain, open-eyed and speechless.

'I can't believe it, Mum,' Raven said and hugged her.

'I'll put this somewhere safe. Both my hands are frozen now,' Jayne said and wiped the moisture and soil residue onto a delicate handkerchief. Then, after wrapping the find, she unzipped her parka and carefully put it away in an internal pocket. 'Send me a picture of the necklace, Matt. I want to see the complete thing.'

'Of course. As soon as I get back.'

'Shall we pack up now?' Raven asked. 'We're never going to find anything else as good today.'

'Quick sweep of the area, then. Just in case there's something else that was dropped in her fall,' Matt said, and they combed for another three minutes without another signal. They refilled the hole and packed the detectors in their carry bags. Jayne kept saying, 'I can't believe it,' and looked from Raven to Matt and back.

'Well done, Mum,' Raven said with obvious pride.

'You know what else this means,' Matt said as he stopped packing his pinpointer. 'After you've informed the Finds Liaison Officer, I can then tell him its proof I didn't sell the original necklace.'

'How's that, Matt?'

'Well, I'd have offered to buy it from you if I were corrupt. And then I could sell the complete thing together for even more money. Or if I'd already sold the original to someone, he would have paid even more to have the missing length of gold and its matching rosette. I can phone the Finds Officer, and it should allay his suspicions.'

'Wonderful,' Jayne said, beaming.

'Of course,' Raven laughed with pleasure.

It took only a few minutes to reach the crossing point from the woods to the field. They spent the time in stilted conversation. Matt thought Jayne was overwhelmed with her find and was mentally celebrating. They strode along the track, and Matt felt buoyed up as if he were as light as a leaf blown in the wind. It was not just the uplifting find, but it seemed to him that the three of them had bonded with their first search. 'You know a certain comedy-drama series has a scene where Lance found his first gold and they performed a gold dance. Don't know if that's a real detectorists tradition.'

Raven obliged all the way to the field entrance. He laughed along with her mother.

They approached the gate to the lane, and Matt suddenly deflated. He could see the black roofs of two large four-by-fours above the hedge. He opened the gate and peered around.

'Trouble,' he hissed to Jayne and Raven and strode ahead.

He stopped dead as Jayne was about to close the field gate behind her.

'What have you found today?' said a demanding voice.

Matt saw Georgio Renard standing in front of his Range Rover. Another man was with him, looking just as menacing. He stood stock still and wondered what the men intended. Jayne stood very close, and Raven linked her arm with her mother's and drew close to her.

'This is where you found that necklace, isn't it?' said Renard in a menacing tone. 'I'll repeat just once more. What have you found today?'

CHAPTER SEVENTEEN

The swirling wall of snow seemed never-ending. Soon, Amber could barely see Ben, although they were only feet apart. Then she thought it was her vision at fault and wondered if it was possible for her eyes to ice over in these conditions. Her eyelashes felt heavy, and she rubbed ice away with her gloved hand. As they stumbled along, she tried for a mobile phone signal, but there wasn't one. Her father waved his phone above his head; Ben ran to a nearby rise in the ground. Despite them all being on different networks, there was no signal.

'No hope of calling a taxi then,' Dave mumbled.

No one answered as they carried on walking. Then, when panic and frostbite were only a few breaths away, they found the B road a few feet in front of them, obscured until the last moment by the driving snow.

It was easier to walk on the tarmac surface. The ground underfoot was solid with no hidden pot-holes under the coating of snow. Ben began walking in tyre tracks which had either compacted the snow or, in places, turned it to slush. It was firmer under-foot, so she and Dave did the same.

'The road's turning sharply to the right, the Phoenix hotel should only be around the next bend,' Ben gasped.

The wind through the trees lessened, and the wall of snow seemed broken up by the dense woodland that bordered the road. It was a slight improvement, and anything seemed worth grasping to encourage herself to keep going.

Amber felt too frozen and miserable to think too much about having to return to the scene of the fatal assault on Nathan, so she just held Dave up and they trudged through three inches of snow behind Ben. A thought slipped through her misery – would they have to stay the night at that place? It was the last refuge she wanted to be in. But she knew it was the only hotel for miles around. Yes, it's stay there only, or we'll freeze to death, she answered herself with resignation. It would have been a fatal mistake to have tried to return to the car. A van skidded past, spraying them with a wave of slush. A second vehicle avoided them at the last moment as the blizzard worsened. She decided to flag down the next vehicle to approach them.

Three minutes later, warm yellow lights emerged from the driving snow. The lights multiplied and formed into the hotel, its roadside sign, and front forecourt. Looking like snowmen, they reached the entrance porch, which now had almost a foot of snow blown against it. Dave staggered, and she struggled to hold him upright. Ben kicked his way through the snow as a man appeared from inside with a shovel. He helped them in. It was the elderly manager from their last visit with a comb-over covering his bald head.

'Surprised you risked coming back after what happened,' he said.

'No choice, we're not happy either,' Ben muttered through shivers and chattering teeth. 'We're stranded until this has lifted,' he pointed outside to the swirling snow, which was now a foot deep and leaving deep drifts over everything.

'Yes, you had no choice,' agreed the manager, sounding resigned to his unwelcome guests. 'Let me help you off with those.' He moved to Amber and relieved her of her rucksack and waterproof, which he hung on a nearby coat stand.

'I think we'd all like rooms for the night,' Dave said and plodded to the reception.

'I'll share a room with you, Dad.' Then to the receptionist, 'Have you a room with two single beds?' There was no way she was going to have a single room, even if it had a double-locked door and with a heavy chair wedged against it.

The hotel had one spare double room facing the rear of the hotel, Christmas bookings having taken most rooms, apparently. Ben also got a small bedroom overlooking the car park at the rear. Dave phoned Liz to let her know of their predicament.

Later, after they'd taken warming showers and met in the dining room, they chose the table nearest to the large fireplace with its blazing log fire. It had been a close shave; Amber's fear of frostbite and exposure symptoms had evaporated in the warmth of the building. Her numb feet and fingers had subsided to a warm radiance. Even her father had regained his usual composure and healthy complexion.

As the three of them waited for their meal order to arrive, they discussed the day's frustrating search.

'I think that's it. Search over,' said Dave, rubbing his face and beard in despondency. 'There are no signs of anything either in the landscape or on any ridge or hillock.'

'I think the watchmen dismantled the circle and levelled the embankment.' Amber was feeling just as demoralised. 'They were so bigoted that the thought of another religion drawing the local folk away was too much for their intransigent Christian attitudes.'

'Don't give up. There are still areas further afield to explore, round here and three miles south-east of this hotel.' Ben sounded less despondent.

'Maybe,' said Amber, thinking of the chilling cold earlier and the long winter still to come. 'But the directions clearly indicated the area we've thoroughly searched, so I don't think going further afield will be fruitful.'

'We came fairly close to this hotel's grounds on one detour to a hilltop,' Dave mused. 'So we've covered this immediate area.'

They fell into despondent contemplation until after they'd eaten. The hot food invigorated them enough to restart the conversation. The debate turned to discussing Dave's latest diary find at Springborough Manor.

'I wonder if Archie Woodright or any surviving members of the sect returned to unearth the ceremonial items?' Dave said after they had recapped the text from a photo on Ben's phone.

'They were ritual pieces of importance to them, too valuable to leave behind.' Ben suggested.

'I doubt the ceremonial treasures will still be where they were originally buried,' Amber added. 'The members of the clan that did not attend that last ritual would surely have known the location where the items were concealed. Later, when the furore had been forgotten and loyalty to their clan had diminished, one would surely have sneaked back and dug up the items to make themself rich.'

'Or the horror of what had become of their friends may have permanently scared off other members in fear for their lives. The local sheriffs would surely have patrolled this area, looking for returning cult members doing exactly that.'

'Possibly,' said Ben, 'But you're assuming any of them were let out of prison or even still alive after a gruelling sentence or able to get a message to other still free brethren. There may not have been any more of them that didn't attend that fateful night, either. Also, maybe after the horror of the assault, the Reverend or Glenys returned to rebury the items elsewhere as security for their future.'

'If the Reverend returned to recover them, they could have lived comfortably on the proceeds of the sale of the items if they were sold in London, away from the local turbulence.'

'Well, it's all conjecture. I'm for giving up the search for now. My efforts will concentrate on the diary and the other missing pages. Hopefully, a page will describe the final whereabouts of the ceremonial artefacts, even if they were sold off to fund the future of the sect. There may still be a clue to come ...'

Amber began to only half listen to the debate. She was looking at the barman, and an idea slowly formed.

It was the same barman on duty as on their last visit. He nodded as he recognised her.

'Another drink, guys? I'm buying.' She took the empty glasses to the bar.

'Been walking again? You must love these parts.'

'We do, the woodland is so ... captivating in the winter,' she ad-libbed. 'This hotel is the best stopping point in the forest.' He laughed, and she added, 'especially when you're near to hypothermia.' He'd heard about their earlier condition.

'If I were you, I'd wait until the Spring to walk these parts again.'

'We're thinking of doing exactly that.'

As he poured the first pint, she asked him why the hotel was named after a mythical creature that dies and is reborn from fiery ashes.

'It's a complex story. Thirty years ago, the new landlord here uncovered something which was at the time considered scandalous. It seems a little intolerant now, but a coven of white witches met to dance in the woodland somewhere near this hotel. Being a devout Christian, the landlord confronted them in the car park area when they returned in the middle of the night – he didn't approve of pagan gatherings so he banned them from booking to stay here. Days later, this place was burnt down – arson was proved, but the perpetrators were never found.'

'Interesting,' Amber cooed. 'So has there always been a history of pagan or occult gatherings going on around here?'

'Local whispers only. There were lots of tales when I was a teenager in the eighties, but they've all died down now. I believe going back further, there was quite a pagan community under the radar in these parts.'

Amber nodded with interest. 'So I take it the Christian landlord rebuilt this place? What was his name?'

'Joshua Gallagher, I believe. No, he died within weeks. A heart attack brought on by subtle hexing, or so they say. You know, fox skulls left on his car bonnet, rings of round stones left on his doorstep. A reminder that the coven was watching him.'

'So who bought this place and rebuilt it?'

'Don't know, some mysterious local who kept in the background. A few years after the rebuild, he sold it. Now it's owned by some investment company rumoured to be run by the same guy.'

'Creepy,' mumbled Amber and went to take away the tray of drinks. Then she turned and said, 'These witches, do they still hold any ceremonies locally?'

'Doubt it. The best person to ask is old Dotty Banbridge. She's 85 but still knows everything that goes on in these parts. Lives not far away, been in the same old cottage all her life.'

'Where does she live?' Amber thought it best to justify her inquiry. 'I'm writing a walking book on the area. She could give some valuable background info. Old place names, hauntings, past pagan gatherings, things long forgotten, etc.'

'I understand,' the barman said. 'I've got her phone number; she used to be a great help to my gran when she was alive. Ring her and I'm sure she'll be prepared to show off all her local folklore knowledge and answer questions.' He took his smartphone from a nearby shelf and scrolled through it. Then he wrote on an old stained bar-mat and handed it to her.

Minutes later, back at their table, Amber whispered the barman's account excitedly, 'This could be the breakthrough we need. There used to be a pagan cult in the area. An old lady, Dotty, may remember unusual goings-on from years ago. We could be able to pinpoint our location with her help.'

'It's worth checking out,' Dave's despondency seemed to lift as he spoke. 'This talk of covens reminds me; this coming Wednesday, the 22nd, is the winter solstice. I bet if the coven still exists, it'll meet then. Old traditions die hard. Maybe they will hold a gathering on the site of the old stones.'

'Good one, Cobber. I never thought of that,' exclaimed Ben in his fake Australian accent.

'Me neither,' Amber gasped. 'Maybe Dottie knows someone linked to the witch's next ceremony.

'We could park up somewhere when it's dark and see where shadowy figures converge. Then follow them,' Dave suggested.

'That's exactly what the good reverend did, and look what happened to him,' Ben responded.

'It's not right that we try to gatecrash any private worship. I'm vetoing that idea,' Amber said with conviction.

'Okay, it was just a suggestion.' Dave said. 'I thought maybe we could find out where they hold their ceremonies, that's all. Then on Tuesday or Thursday, I could go and field-walk their meeting place.'

'No, I don't think that's a very ethical way to move forward. I would feel like a stalker,' Amber couldn't help being firm.

With a nod, Dave acknowledged he accepted her argument. 'Ring Dottie now, Amber. We could pop round to see her tomorrow before driving home.' It was nice to hear her father was still optimistic.

'The forecast is supposed to show temperatures only rising to minus one tomorrow. I suspect we're stranded here,' Ben said as he showed them the forecast on his phone. 'Ring her anyway. Let's see if we can walk along the road to her place tomorrow, it must be near enough. It'll be invigorating exercise for sure.'

'I'm walking nowhere in these conditions,' she stated while dialling the number the barman had given her.

'Hello,' said a hesitant voice on the other end of the line. The lady's one word sounded guarded and nervous.

Her phone must have displayed an "unknown caller" message.

'Hello Dotty, my name is Amber Easterton. Sorry to bother you, but I'm a historian researching a project in this area. I'm told you have a fantastic knowledge of events from yesteryear related to these parts.'

The voice brightened. 'Oh, yes, they say I do. Well, I do still remember a lot. My father told me all sorts of things, and I still remember some that his grandfather told him, so I suppose I do. I was six years old and I remember a trip to the seaside with my mother's WI group. Is that what you want to know about?'

'Well, sort of, amongst other things. Perhaps unusual events locally in the Forest of Dean would be of interest as well. It would be wonderful if I could pop over tomorrow. I'm staying at the Phoenix Hotel at the moment.'

'Ah yes, the infamous Phoenix. I remember the poor man who owned it and how upset he was at events nearby.'

'I look forward to hearing about them, Dotty.'

'I still remember his name from all those years ago, old Joshua... he was so ... saintly – but also so naughty...'

'Oh ... really!' Amber didn't like to think about how naughty the man had been. She wasn't sure quite what she'd let herself in for tomorrow now. The interview was going to need a lot of steering. 'If a snowplough clears the road, can I and my father pop round, say, 11 o'clock?' She wondered whether, being Sunday, any B-road clearance would be carried out at all.

'Yes, I like visitors, and I'm not going to church in this weather. What did you say your name was again?'

'She sounds lively if a little dotty, living up to her name,' said Ben. 'I'll leave you two to interview her. I'm going to try to get home.'

'That's fine. But I'm in no rush to get back to my car.' Dave declared. 'We'll need taxis back to the Rising Sun; I'm not walking the forest paths to my car in this weather.'

'That's true,' Ben backtracked. 'I'll wait here for you to get back, then share a taxi. Perhaps I'll walk over the road into the open forest for a stroll. If the snow's not too deep.'

The thought of being out trudging along in the snow and ice filled Amber with dread. She had never felt so cold earlier and was sure they had all been close to hypothermia. Now, having warmed up and eaten a hot meal, she felt really sleepy. 'I'm going up to my room for an early night and some zeds. After what we walked through earlier, a warm duvet is so appealing.'

'Okay, Amber, I'll finish this pint, then I'm looking forward to some shut-eye too,' said Dave.

'I'll stick around here for another drink.' Ben stretched in his chair to bring his feet nearer to the fireplace. 'A brandy in front of this log fire seems perfectly in keeping.'

Amber trudged upstairs to the room she was sharing with her father and was about to put the light on when she decided to have a look at the snow-covered trees she'd glimpsed through the open curtains. The old single-glazed window was a little frosty around the edges, but left a clear patch in the middle to view the woodland. It was a genuine white Christmas scene. The blizzard had reduced to the occasional large flake floating past the window, but outside, the wintry weather had stripped nature back to old-time basics. Bare branches carved jagged silhouettes against the muted grey sky and the snow had laid a crisp white blanket upon the surface of the car park. Eight snow-covered vehicles sat buried, looking like white hillocks. A single car, a black Audi, had arrived since the snow had lain. She traced four sets of footprints from it. Two snowy footprints had gone toward the hotel; the other two sets went toward the trees. She noticed they led to the snow-covered shape of a metal gate, which interrupted a six-foot-tall wire fence. The prints were half-filled with fresh snow and disappeared beyond the gate and into the woodland. She hoped the owners of the prints had dressed for the conditions and wondered if perhaps they were poachers or people who loved to walk in these rare arctic conditions. As she looked further away, the moon appeared from behind the leaden clouds and lit up the woodland. In the distance, the dense branches of yews masked large and mature oaks and ash, which protruded above the oak's top branches. The huge yews looked as if they were spreading dominant branches over smaller sycamore. The smaller trees formed a circular stand around the edges of the yews as if nature had planted them to take up every foot of ground. She sighed, It was so beautiful, but her bed and its warm duvet beckoned more. She closed the curtains and crawled into the warmth without even hearing her father come in to occupy the other bed.

The next morning, she rose at 8 o'clock. Dave had already got up, gone out, and had left her to sleep. She showered, dressed, and wandered to the window, and pulled the curtains. The Audi had left sometime in the night, its tyres had left deep scars in the snow. The footprints into the woodland had also been covered by fresh snow. She yawned and wondered whether she had imagined them.

The manager was wandering around in the foyer as she left the main stairs to head for the dining room.

'Has everything been satisfactory, Madam?' he said with hands clasped before his chest.

'Yes, the room was warm and the bed comfortable, thank you.'

'I trust you won't be wandering around in the woodlands today. It's not safe.'

'No, not in this weather,' the man was beginning to make her uneasy. 'When do you think the snow-ploughs will clear the road?'

'The snow will be gone by midday. We can see the dark clouds are thinning to the west. Brighter weather always comes in from that direction.'

'How can you be sure?'

'We know these things round here.'

She gave him a questioning look and walked away to the dining room. The royal "we" sounded odd, along with his whole demeanour. She felt unwelcome.

Dave was sitting at a table, now laid out for breakfast. A buffet counter to the left was full of cereal, milk, sugar, small packs of jam, marmalade, and rolls. Amber related the strange conversation to her father.

'Forget it. He is right, though. The temperature is already high enough out there to ensure it'll be rain today.'

She looked beyond him and saw a window framed by the trees, which were now dripping and shedding lumps of melting snow. 'Where's Ben?'

'Don't know. Sleeping in, I guess.'

They finished breakfast, then obtained a taxi phone number from the receptionist. Dave gave the taxi firm his whereabouts and Dotty's address, and they waited in the lounge for it to arrive at 10:30.

As the taxi pulled up outside, Amber remembered Ben. 'No sign of him. Hope he's okay in his room.'

'He'll be down soon.'

'I'll text and let him know we're away to Dotty's place.' She had the phone out and was tapping as she spoke.

His reply came back whilst the taxi was negotiating the still slippery road.

Okay. Enjoy.

The old lady's home turned out to be less than a mile away and down a small lane lined with mature ash trees. It was an old thatched cottage built from local stone with windows that were at odd angles to each other and divided by a grey oak timber frame. A large red brick chimney dominated each end of the house and rose high above the recently rethatched roof. She wondered whether the interior would be as quaint as the picture-box exterior.

A white-haired but upright-looking pensioner cracked the door open. An arthritic but sure hand flicked the door security latch, then let them in.

'Hello Dotty, it's so nice to meet you.' Amber shook the lady's hand gently. 'This is my father, he's also a historian.'

'Great to meet you, Dotty,' he replied with his best smile.

'And you too, me old butt,' she used the local colloquialism with the ease of someone who'd always used the term. 'I'm a historian like you two, but only an amateur. I've always had an interest in researching and recording all that has happened in these parts – so you've come to the right person.'

The old lady stood to one side and waved them through to the living room. A narrow hallway had beamed ceilings that were low and crooked, the exposed timber continued in the living room with floral curtains and gold-framed oil paintings of long-dead people. A soot-stained inglenook fireplace added to the ancient ambience that filled the cottage. Dottie was using a walking stick and had trouble getting about; Amber thought she must have been about 90 years old. The room was full of floral print throws on the armchairs and rose flowers woven into three rugs placed over dark varnished floorboards.

Antique vases were displayed in two highly polished cabinets, and an old television sat on a mahogany TV unit.

'I told a friend of our meeting, and he will be joining us shortly. Meanwhile, I've boiled a kettle. Tea or coffee?'

They settled down with hot drinks and pleasantries. After a few minutes, Amber broached the subject that most concerned her and Dave, and began the information gathering. 'I'm told there's an active pagan group nearby. I'm interested in how long similar groups have worshipped in this area of the forest and also whether their ceremonies have always been at the same place?'

'Well, that subject is, or was, controversial with the clergy in these parts in years gone by. For some reason, they kept a tight control of their congregations and went out of their way to rave about paganism being the devil's work. They seemed really obsessed with the subject and usually referred to them as witches' covens and devil worshippers. I can allow you to read a couple of photocopies of articles I found in local papers dating back to late Victorian times, but to our modern ears, it's all pretty bigoted. Live and let live, I say. I remember my father, Cedric said ...'

Dave tried to focus on specifics, 'Have you read about a 18th-century pagan priestess called Linda Rourtier?'

'Oh yes, she was a folklore character around here — although little known these days. Linda led a very dedicated and rich pagan religion back in the early 1700s. She changed her name to Glenys of the Trees and went into hiding after religious bigots tried to frame her with accusations of witchcraft. She was extremely beautiful and had a daughter out of wedlock called Willow. I'm surprised no one has heard of her, even locally. But then I do like to discover obscure characters that lived around here.'

'She sounds fascinating,' Amber didn't want to sound too keen in case the old lady told others of their interest. But she was elated at the confirmation of their research. She glanced at Dave and saw the same triumph reflected in his eyes. 'Where did Glenys hold the cult's ceremonies?' she asked calmly and felt herself tense – it was the million-dollar question and she really hoped that Dotty would know where.

'Ah, yes, it was... it'll come to me in a minute. Legend has it they used a circle of stones called the Priestess Stones, also sometimes known as the Lost Stones. This circle was really ancient and, at the time, hidden in the depths of the forest. It seems to have disappeared these days, and no one knows about them, unless you have an interest in local goings-on like me. I'll think of where it was said to be in a minute. This old grey-matter doesn't work as quickly as it used to.' Dotty stroked her left ear, deep in thought and obviously trying to come up with an exact location. 'Her daughter Willow... I remember more about her. Many years ago, I had a sight of a private diary from an old library in a local mansion, and in it was a page about the legend of a pagan priestess and her daughter. After her parents had passed away, the beautiful daughter, a maiden by the name of Willow, spent many years in the forest standing with the trees. The story said she refused all approaches from either the clergy who invited her to embrace their Christian God or young men who wished to take her as their wife. She was occasionally glimpsed in the depths of the forest in full ceremonial robes, imploring her gods to return her parents. A sad story. I don't know what happened to Willow, but it's the kind of folklore I love. That's why I research the Dean Forest region; it's full of stories about eccentric characters. Take Jack the Forester. He grew such vigorous vegetables. His runner bean plants grew so tall that he climbed them. I wonder if this was the origin of the Jack and the Beanstalk fable...'

'Yes, it certainly sounds like it. Can you remember any more about Glenys's circle, Dottie?'

The doorbell chimed.

'I'll get that. It'll be Dorian.'

Dotty pottered through the dark oak door. After a whispered conversation, she brought a grey-haired man in his late 60s into the living room. The man strode confidently to an armchair and sat, appraising Amber and Dave. Amber returned the gaze; there was something about the man that put her on edge. He still looked fit and wore jeans and a thick jumper. His slicked-back grey hair and neat moustache made him look like a 1950s spiv.

'Good morning. My name's Dorian Granchester Smyth. I believe you are Mr David Dorsett and your daughter, Amber.'

'Yes, good to meet you,' said Dave. 'You're a friend of Dotty?'

'Her name is Dorothy. My time is valuable, so down to important matters. I am informed that you and four friends have been walking in the area in recent weeks. Could I ask what you are looking for?'

'We like the area,' said Dave.

Amber thought her father was being justifiably guarded in what he revealed. She took an instinctive dislike to Granchester Smyth. 'I'm compiling a book of local walks. We're researching those that cover the most varied terrain.'

'You walked and took various excursions off the footpath to the far east of here, near Saintlow Inclosure. Then the next week you searched more this way and arrived at Buckholt Inclosure. You circled back to the B road, then to the Phoenix Hotel. Two of your friends then met an unfortunate accident there.' As the man spoke, his words became icy cold, and his eyes narrowed to match the words. 'You should not be blundering around in these parts, especially at this time of year. Then yesterday you searched north of here and arrived in a random fashion back at the Phoenix hotel again, where you stayed the night.'

'You're well informed,' said Dave, matching the man's demeanour. 'Why have you been checking up on us?'

Amber stared and wished she were somewhere else. They must have been followed every step of the way each time they searched. She felt her breath quicken. Why should they be under surveillance? – It was a free country, they could go where they liked. Angry words leapt from her mouth before she could stop them. 'We're entitled to use public footpaths wherever we find them. And there is a legal right to roam in the Forest here. Even sheep have a right to go wherever they want in the Forest of Dean, so people are entitled to as well.'

'Except where it's trespassing.'

'We saw no such notices. They should be displayed on either side of footpaths, saying Private Land, and I saw none. Therefore, it was common land.' As she spoke, Amber remembered the four men who had looked like army personnel out on a training exercise. They'd been in the hotel bar the night before Nathan and Ken were attacked. 'The OS maps of the area show no private land either,' she added.

'The maps are out of date. I will write to the Ordnance Survey organisation and ask for the local maps to be updated. Besides that, there are other matters best left in the past,' continued Granchester Smyth. 'Churches around this way are well attended because people remember. Others do not attend a Christian church and are not simply atheistic; these criminals attack livestock and mutilate and brand them with occult symbols. We don't want to acknowledge the resurgence of a devilish cult publicly – but these people exist and have been known to threaten visitors. So best to stay away from wild woodland.'

'We can walk where we want, but thank you for the warning.'

'There is an increasing presence of wild boars as well. They will attack if you get too close.'

The man was obviously trying to scare them away and was bordering on threatening them. Amber remembered that Ben had not been at breakfast that morning, and she gasped aloud. Had he met with an "unfortunate accident" as well as Nathan?

'What has animal poaching or mutilation got to do with us?' Dave responded in irritation.

'I think it's time we left, Dad. I'm not prepared to sit here and be threatened.'

Dave got up without another word and said to Dotty, 'Thanks, Dotty, you've been of great assistance. I'll be in touch if that is alright with you?'

The old lady merely nodded. She looked a little alarmed at the way the conversation had developed. 'It wasn't far from here, you know. I think it was ...'

'Good day to you, Mr Dorsett and Mrs Easterton.' Granchester Smyth didn't want them to know the location of the stones. Even the man's formal goodbye sounded menacing to Amber. He motioned Dotty to stay seated and strode to the living room door, opening it wide in an obvious gesture for them to leave. Dave stormed out, and the man followed. Amber paused, bent over, and pretended to tie a shoe lace. She resented the man's attitude and felt an unusual obstinate reluctance to do as bidden. She rose from the armchair, turned to Dottie, crouched down, and asked quietly, 'You mentioned a private diary from an old library in a local mansion, Dottie. Could you tell me the name of the mansion?'

Dottie picked up on the need to whisper. 'Of course, my dear, err, I'll remember it for when you come back again. When I was a teenager, an old lady confided in me about dancing around the stones. She said where they were, I know she did. I'll remember it soon as well. Then, when I next see you, we can talk further about the dancing. She taught me one of the dances, you know, I'll teach you...'

Disappointed, but sympathetic to the old lady's bad memory, Amber nodded, whispered, 'okay,' rose, and took a couple of steps to the door.

'Wait. I remember, the mansion, it was Bedringham House, I think owned by...'

'Time to go,' interrupted Granchester Smyth from the hallway.

'Thank you, Dottie,' she managed before the man ushered her to the front door, then opened it wide with a swift gesture.

'And remember that metal detectoring and removing ancient artefacts is against the local law here,' he barked.

Dave took a step back out of the drive where he had been waiting for Amber. 'Secretly removing ancient artefacts is illegal ANYWHERE in the UK and the rest of the world,' he snapped back.

They left without further discussion or glancing at the man again.

Outside, the snow was fast melting as they strode past an old early millennium Mercedes in metallic silver, which looked in pristine condition. Walking on the track to the metalled road again, Dave phoned for a taxi to take them back to the hotel to gather their rucksacks, waterproofs, and Ben.

Amber's thoughts ran in a flurry through her mind. The ghastly man and his threats, the fresh lead concerning a new player, Archie Woodright, in the long-forgotten drama. Lottie and her memories, and the hint that she had more to say about the stones. Her thoughts settled and focused on Ben.

He was in trouble, she was sure.

The mere thought of Ben alone brought on a feeling of terror. Had he been beaten and left in the snow? Or was he in his room, lying on the bed with the duvet covered in blood? They needed to get back, really, really quickly.

I hope you enjoyed reading my novel, The Priestess Stones, as much as I enjoyed researching and writing it. If so, a positive review or rating on Amazon, Goodreads, and other sites would be greatly appreciated. It would mean a lot to me.

Reviews really help other readers decide to buy, and they go toward rewarding writers for their hundreds of hours of work.

About the Author

Clive Ousley's latest novel is an archaeological and historical detective story called The Priestess Stones. He is currently finishing the sequel called Four Oak Shrine. He has written a series of three apocalyptic sci fi novels – Jadde, The Fragile Sanctuary, The Dark Tide and World of Skulls. He also has two Interstellar reincarnation novels, The 13 Reincarnations of Luke Arthur and Ring of Souls.

In years gone by he exhibited paintings in major exhibitions at The Mall Galleries in London, The Royal Birmingham and a Sotheby's sponsored exhibition. He became an illustrator and completed work for The Natural History Museum and Westminster Abbey. He has worked in the printing industry, two horticultural research institutes and has run a car-parts warehouse.

He currently lives in Pembrokeshire and enjoys walking the coastal paths with his wife and dogs.